Letters from Malta

A secret kept for 50 years

MARY RENSTEN

Published by Corazon Books
(Wyndham Media Ltd)
27, Old Gloucester Street, London WC1N 3AX
www.greatstorieswithheart.com

First published as *Too Strong a Light* in 2009

ISBN:1909752193
ISBN-13:978-1909752191

For Rose and Jeannie

Acknowledgements

For their first-hand memories of Malta during World War II I wish to thank all the ex-servicemen and women who responded to my letter in SAGA Magazine, particularly those who served at Ta' Qali, together with the people in Mtarfa and Rabat, Mosta and Valletta, some of whom had lived through the Siege, who so kindly answered my never-ending questions and gave me valuable background information for my book.

I wish also to thank the following for their most helpful letters, phone calls, research and interviews: John Inguanez at Radio Malta; members of the George Cross Island Association and the Royal British Legion (Malta Branch); the Royal Artillery Historical Trust, Woolwich; the Imperial War Museum, London; the Malta High Commission; the Malta Tourist Office, London; NCH Action for Children; Graham Dalling; Jocelyn Hay OBE and Robert Jackson, author of Malta Victory.

In 1995 I visited the HQ of Radio Malta, at the kind invitation of the then Head of Programmes, John Inguanez. I have based my descriptions of the Radio Malta building on this visit; however all personnel, programmes and events regarding Radio Malta which are mentioned in this novel are entirely fictitious and solely a product of my own imagination.

Mary Rensten is an award-winning
journalist and a playwright.

She is a Vice-President of the
Society of Women Writers and Journalists.

CHAPTER ONE

It had not been much to go on: three old letters; two intact, one torn up and mended with sticky tape … and it had all happened a long time ago. Did it really matter, now? Perhaps not to anyone else, not even my mother. But to me, it did. Enough to bring me out here to Malta in the autumn of 1995. Enough to make me determined not to leave until all my questions had answers. They might not like it – Anthony and Carmela, Rosaria and Joe Crowther's granddaughter – but I had to find out what had happened on this island in the spring of 1942: I had to know how my father died.

I had found the letters in March, the day after my Aunt Kitty Gaunt's funeral; sickly all her life she had nevertheless managed to live to the age of eighty. Although my mother was unwell – she had bronchitis and flu – she insisted on going. The day was cold, with a biting north-east wind and sleety showers. Going back into her house in Dunsinane Close afterwards, having had two glasses of sherry in the *Rose and Magpie* to warm her up and 'send Kitty off properly' she tripped over the doorstep. To prevent herself from falling she reached out with her right arm and fell on it. Rather than wait for the doctor I took her to hospital. Because of the congestion in her lungs they decided to keep her in. She was, after all, eighty-four years old.

I drove back to Dunsinane Close and packed a few things – nightdress, toilet bag, slippers, reading glasses – just to tide her over. Her home help, Mrs. Newsom, promised to come in and keep the house in order; it was my mother's main worry, that people might come in and see the house untidy, or worse, dusty.

On the second day she asked for a different nightie. I'd packed the warm brushed nylon one I had found under her pillow; I couldn't believe such things were still being worn in the Nineties. I shouldn't have been surprised, the house was the only one in the street without double glazing – my mother wouldn't have it; it was unhealthy, she said, blocking out all the air – and she always slept with a window open, even on the coldest nights. But of course in the overheated atmosphere of a hospital ward nylon was too warm. I was to fetch her a summer nightie, two summer nighties actually; a blue and white flowered cotton one and a pink one.

'Cotton?'

'No.' Hesitantly, not looking at me directly. 'Silk. Well … not real silk. Artificial, you know.'

'Satin?'

'Well, yes. Sort of.'

'Fine. No problem, I'll get them for you. Tell me where they are.'

'No, Jane.'

'But how can I …?'

'Mrs. Newsom will get them, she knows where they are.'

I found Mrs. Newsom on her hands and knees cleaning my mother's already spotless kitchen floor. 'She's never going to wear those, is she? I thought the sky would fall in before she put those on her back.' She stood up – she was a tall, thin, bony woman, a bit like Kitty had been in her later years – and squeezed out her floor cloth at the sink.

'Why, what's wrong with them?'

'Oh, there's nothing wrong with them, oh no, nothing wrong. They're new, well, not new in the sense of, you know, just bought, but she's never worn them; they're still in their wrappings.'

'Perhaps she's been keeping them for … for just such an emergency.' It was nothing to do with Mrs. Newsom. 'Just tell me where they are and I'll get them.' I must have sounded a bit aggrieved.

'I'm not criticising her, you know; I'm just warning you.' She reached for the kettle. 'D'you want some coffee?'

'That would be lovely. Thank you.' I sat down at the kitchen table and let Mrs. Newsom wait on me.

'Still writing, are you, Mrs. Thornfield?'

'Yes,' I said.

'She might not show it, but your mother's very proud of you, you know. She always tells me when you've got a new book out.'

My mother wasn't very keen on my Jane Gaunt crime novels, but she enjoyed the Ellen Field romances, provided they didn't get too steamy.

I took a sip of my coffee, then, consciously warming the tone of my voice, I said, 'So what is it you're warning me about? What dread secrets is my mother hiding in her wardrobe?'

Mrs. Newsom laughed. 'Your mother's a hoarder. I have two sorts of ladies I go to; the keepers and the chuckers, I call them. Your mother's a keeper. She buys things, keeps them in their wrappings, puts them away. Oh, d'you take sugar?'

'No, thank you. A spot more milk though, please.'

'It's not just clothes. There's towels, pillow-cases, sheets, tea-towels, never been used, never will be. You name it, she's got it up there. You could start a shop.'

My mouth must have been hanging open.

'Didn't you know?'

'I had no idea.'

'No, well I'm not surprised. They don't talk about it.'

'Are you saying it's a sort of compulsion?'

'Well no, not really. I think it's something to do with the war, when you couldn't get things. I've tried to persuade her to use some of the towels; you can almost see through the ones in the bathroom. But will she? No, not till they fall apart in the wash. Anyway, you go and have a look. Oh, and it's the chest of drawers they're in, not the wardrobe. Second drawer down, left-hand side, the nighties. You won't disturb anything, will you? She knows exactly, and I mean exactly, where everything is.'

'Perhaps I'd better wear gloves. I don't want to leave fingerprints!'

'Not a bad idea. Anyway, I must get off. Can I leave you to lock up?'

'Yes, of course. Thank you, Mrs. Newsom. And thanks for the coffee.'

She let herself out, I rinsed my cup and went upstairs.

This had never been my home; I don't think I had slept here more than a night or two in the thirty odd years since my mother and Kitty had moved here from the flat above their father's hardware shop in Mulberry Road. Going up the stairs that day in March I felt like an interloper.

About to enter my mother's bedroom, I turned away and opened the door of what had been Kitty's room. My mother had asked me to fetch her one of Kitty's bed-

jackets from the dressing-table drawer. I chose a pale
blue lacy one with white ribbons. I put it down on the
banister and went into my mother's room.

'Sorry, Mum,' I said aloud, 'I know you don't want
me in here.' I drew the curtains back; for some reason
they were closed, probably so the sun wouldn't fade the
pink carpet. Immediately inside the door, dominating the
room, was a high mahogany bed with a white
counterpane; my mother didn't like divans, you couldn't
sweep under them, she said. The chest of drawers, also
mahogany, with an upright chair beside it, was against
the opposite wall. Second drawer down, Mrs. Newsom
had said.

It wasn't easy to pull the drawer open, it was so full. I
managed it at last, but not without tearing the poly-wrap
cover of a lambswool cardigan – pale mauve, a colour
my mother loved. 'The Queen Mother and I, we like the
same colours,' she was fond of saying. Mrs. Newsom
was right. Nothing, absolutely nothing in the drawer had
ever been used. The price tags were still on them, some
of them pre-decimal. It was tempting to take everything
out and have a good sort through, but Mrs. Newsom's
words echoed in my mind: 'Your mother knows exactly
where everything is.' Left-hand side of the drawer, she'd
said. Yes, here they were. I found the cotton one easily
enough, but I couldn't see the silk one. I had no option
but to take out, very carefully, the piles of packages, and
place them on the bed. When would she ever wear all
these things? Never, probably; in which case I would
inherit them. Autumn shades were more in my line.
There was no sign of the pink silk nightdress. Pink ... it
depended upon how you interpreted the word. There was
a salmony colour ... that must be the one. I set the two
required garments aside and began to put the others into
the drawer. It had been easier to take things out than it
was to put them back. The problem was the lining paper;

putting the clothes in, I had scrunched it up and pushed it towards the back of the drawer. I took everything out, including the paper.

In the back right-hand corner was a brown foolscap envelope. Something had been written on it and then crossed out, so completely that nothing of it could be read. Oh well, it was nothing to do with me. I put the lining back carefully and began to replace the clothes. The thought came to me: if my mother had died I would open that envelope.

I was reminded of the time when my husband Neville's mother died – it was 1970 and I was expecting Alex – and we had to clear her flat in Leeds. Under the lining in a chest of drawers we had found her birth certificate; she was two years older than she claimed to be. We could only think that she wanted everyone to believe she had been born in this century and not in 1898. Well, good luck to her, if it made her feel younger.

I returned my mother's things to their allotted places, shut the drawer, picked up the nighties, and the bedjacket from the banister, and went downstairs. It was nearly lunchtime; I decided to make myself a snack and then go to the hospital. Cheese on toast would do me fine; there was cheese in the fridge and in the bread bin there was half a loaf that needed using. My mother would be pleased; she hated waste. I sat in the kitchen to eat it, with Radio Four for company. It was a quiz programme I usually enjoyed, but today I couldn't concentrate on it; my mind kept straying to that envelope in the drawer upstairs. It was unlike my mother to hide something away; no, why should I say that, she'd kept her hoard of new clothing a secret; from me, anyway. It certainly wouldn't be her birth certificate. We all knew how old she was; she was proud to be eighty-four. And it wouldn't be letters; on principle she never kept them. Bills yes, and careful accounts of all her outgoings, a habit begun in the days when she kept her father's books in the shop. No letters, though. I'd seen her read through a letter, tear it up straight away and put it in a waste paper basket, or years ago, in the kitchen boiler. 'I've read it,' she'd say, 'why should I want to read it again? You don't listen to a phone call twice, do you?' She wouldn't have an answerphone.

So … if the envelope didn't contain letters, then what was in it? Not the deeds to the house; I had those. Well, if it was nothing important it wouldn't matter if I looked.

Inside the envelope were three sheets of lined notepaper, each one folded separately. They were obviously letters.

I could have put them back, unread. But I didn't, my curiosity was aroused. I just knew, somehow, that whatever these letters were, I wasn't supposed to see them, no one was; and yet they'd been preserved.

At this point the heroine in one of my Ellen Field novels would have had 'a pounding heart and trembling hands, as she unfolded the first of the two letters in the unknown hand'. Which is precisely how I felt.

The paper was pale blue, cheap and thin, and the writing had a childlike quality about it. The date was August 1939 and it had been sent from Malta.

Dear Allie,

Thanks for your letter, what a surprise it was to hear from you. I am glad that you are well but sorry Kitty is no better. The sunshine out here would do her a power of good. It is very hot today, not hot like Southend of course, but there are all kinds of heat. Depends where you are and what you are doing! Yes, it would have been nice if we could have stayed longer.

… then on the other side of the sheet …

With many kisses xxxxxx which you can put where you like them best!

Yours affectionately,

Pete.

P.S. I don't think it's a good idea for you to come out here. You would be in married quarters with Tom and I wouldn't be able to see you.

I sat down heavily on the bed, disregarding the piles of garments I had arranged so carefully. My mother had had a secret lover … and she had been with him to Southend. Knowing my mother it seemed unbelievable. Who was he, this Pete? A pal of Tom's, on leave from Malta? Surely not. The letter was written in August, so this would have been … when? Earlier that summer, that famously glorious summer before the war.

The second letter had been torn into four pieces and then meticulously taped together again. As I unfolded it the old tape crackled under my fingers. It seemed the only sound in the cold, silent, house. I spread the sheet on the bed. Same address. Date: November, 1939. As I read it I began to shake and my lips went so dry I had to keep licking them.

Dear Alice,

I think you have made a mistake. Are you sure it's not Tom's? I don't see how I can help. With the war and that I cannot come to England. Please look after yourself.

Yours truly,

Peter.

P.S. I don't think you should write again. I will get news of you from Tom.

I read it again. And again. And again. It could only mean one thing: I was this man's child. This unknown man, this Pete, Peter … was my father. Tom Harper was not my father. It comes as a shock when you are fifty-five years old to discover that the man you thought was your father … isn't. Not that it matters, in a way. I haven't had a father since I was nineteen; I don't miss having one, not now. All the same it would be nice to know … who he was, what traits, good or bad, I may have inherited from him, and why, oh why, my mother kept this secret from me. Not until she died, and I had found the letters, was I to learn the truth.

And my father, whom I must now learn to think of only as Tom – no, damn it, he was my father, he brought me up – did he know? Was that why he was so moody sometimes, looking at me as if he hated me one minute, then almost smothering me with love the next.

I turned to the third letter, also from Malta. It was dated April 1942.

My dear Alice,

I got your last letter but it took a long time. It is very hot here just now, lots of the lads are finding it too hot. Jim has gone and Bill Connors, and young Peter Anderson (remember him?) he's gone too. They are all buried at Imtarfa. It is a nice place, with trees. I shall miss Jim, he was a good pal to me. And Bill. How is the Ariel? I hope Ted Strong remembers to give it a turnover now and then. If you could check it stays well sheeted I shall be most grateful.

Keep writing, even if you think it may not get here.

Then two lines that were crossed out.

Your loving husband,

Tom.

For a long time – well, it seemed a long time, perhaps it wasn't; I had lost any sense of *real* time – I sat with the letters in my hand, not reading them, just trying to piece together the information they contained.

What had happened in the summer of 1939 that brought a young soldier – a gunner I imagine, if he came with Tom – and Tom himself, to England? Did servicemen abroad get home leave at that time? Obviously they did, but not without some good reason. My knowledge of army regulations was almost non-existent; that didn't worry me, I could find out. Doing research was something I revelled in, although I'm not sure that revelling was the right word this time.

Was someone ill? Did Tom have compassionate leave? Was it Alice? No, obviously not, or if it was she made a remarkably quick recovery. Kitty? Tom wouldn't have come home for Kitty, not at any price.

My family were Methodists and the only social life my mother had as a young woman was centred around the local Methodist Church. It was there she met Tom Harper. He had come from Kings Lynn to work in the railway depot next to Enfield Town station. He was a charge-hand fitter, living in 'digs' not far from the shop. After their wedding Alice and Tom lived at Mulberry Road, taking over the main bedroom. And there they stayed, until, I presume, Tom decided he'd had enough – it must have been a dull, stultifying existence for someone used to the open skies of East Anglia – and joined the Royal Artillery. As a married man in the services he would have decent living accommodation to offer his wife. Perhaps they would be able to start a family – he had probably never felt comfortable making love to Alice with Kitty in the room next door.

He had reckoned without the bond between the sisters: Tom could go off and join the army if he wanted to, but as far as Alice was concerned, her duty was to

Kitty. Tom's next move had been to apply for an overseas posting; get both of them right out of the country and start a completely new life. Alice might not go with him to Yorkshire, but if he went abroad ... well, she would have to come; it was only right, she was his wife. In 1938 he got himself posted to Malta. Alice refused to go.

Something important must have brought Tom back to England, then sent him away from Enfield long enough for my mother and Tom's pal to ... Of course! My other grandmother, Violet Harper. He must have gone to Kings Lynn, to see her. That was the year she died; perhaps he had come for her funeral. No, if it had been the funeral, surely Alice would have gone with him?

And then there's Southend. How did they get there? I presume Tom had gone off to Norfolk on his bike, his precious Ariel 'Red Hunter'. And what was Kitty doing all this time? There were so many questions to which I wanted the answers, the most important one being: did Tom know I wasn't his child?

Well, there was one simple way to find out: ask my mother. Go to the hospital, give her the nighties and Kitty's bedjacket. Had Kitty known? Oh, why hadn't I listened to Kitty's ramblings. I hadn't listened for two reasons: firstly, she chattered so much it became like muzak; and secondly, – and now, in the light of those letters this seemed significant – whenever she started to talk about the war my mother shut her up. I can hear her now: 'Jane doesn't want to hear about that; we had a hard time and it's best forgotten.' Which was odd, because she herself never tired of telling me what a struggle they'd had, 'with your dad away and your grandfather not able to lift things and Kitty not well' and how hard it was to get supplies for the shop and the air raids and the rationing and making your clothes last... Her recollections were endless, but Kitty mustn't talk about what she remembered.

Tom's letter puzzled me. Why had he told Alice that Peter had died? Did Tom know about Alice and Peter, and was he punishing her, by telling her he was dead?

There was no point in trying to read into it more than was there. I put the letters back where I'd found them and went downstairs again.

It was by now the middle of the afternoon; my mother would be wondering why I was taking so long. I closed the front door behind me, got into my car and drove to the hospital … the hospital in which I had been born, had my appendix out at the age of ten, visited my grandfather … and Tom. Tom had died here.

I gave my mother the nighties and the bed-jacket.

'If it's so hot in here,' I said, 'why'd you need a bed-jacket?'

'For when I'm sitting up. I'm not sitting up in just a nightie, Jane.' Of course not; silly of me to ask. A cheeky, impertinent thought popped into my head: had Tom ever seen my mother naked? I doubted it. And Pete … had he?

'Mother …' I began, but I couldn't go on.

'What?'

'I … I just wondered … is there anything else you need … from the house? I could easily nip back and fetch it for you.'

'No. No, I don't want anything.' She knew her tone was sharp. Relenting she said, 'If you like you could get me a book from the shop.'

'Yes, of course. What do you want?' Book, in my mother's vocabulary, sometimes did mean a book. At other times it meant a magazine.

'Oh, *Woman's Weekly*. Or that other one …'

'*Woman's Realm*?'

'That's the one.'

I could do that, no problem. I could bring her all the

magazines in the world, I could buy her armfuls of flowers, I could write good wishes in the most elaborate and expensive cards … but I couldn't ask her a simple question.

In the hospital shop I bought both magazines, a *Daily Mail* and a box of Berry Fruits.

'I've got a paper,' she said, irritably.

'Don't worry, I'll find someone who wants it; it won't be wasted.' I picked it up, quickly.

'It was kind of you to bring the magazines.' Oh, Mother, you don't change, do you. All my life it's been the same: a harsh word followed by a soft one, sometimes the other way around. Now I would get in first.

'If you don't want the sweets give them to one of the nurses.'

'Oh no, I'll have those. Thank you.'

A pause. Were there things she wanted to say to me? It didn't appear so. The pause became a silence between us. I had to break it.

'Would you like any visitors? Is there anyone I should …?'

'Not really.' She reached out her hand and touched mine. I hope the surprise didn't show too much in my eyes.

'You know, dear, when you get to my age there aren't many people left. All the ones I'd want to see have gone.'

I was about to say: You'd want to see Alex if he was here … Instead, I took a leap into the dark.

'If someone could suddenly be here, right now, just appear, in the ward, who, of all the people you've ever known, would you most want to see?'

She didn't look at me as if I was talking gibberish, which surprised me. I'd touched a nerve, I think.

'No one,' she said, slowly. 'Well, perhaps one.' Oh,

well done, Jane; you're there. No silly questions now; just wait.

'No. No, I think not.' Where was she for those few moments? In the arms of her lover? Oh come on, this is your mother, not an Ellen Field maiden. 'The trouble with that, what you suggested ... is that if they've gone a long time ago, they'd still be young, and I'm old; we'd not know one another.'

'Well yes, that's true.' I felt so near I couldn't let it go. 'But if you *could*?'

Her eyes filled with tears. 'Kitty's the one I really miss. Now she's gone there's nobody I can talk to about ... about all the years we had together.'

'You can talk to me.' She still held my hand, which she squeezed and then withdrew.

'I can't, Jane. You wouldn't understand.'

'I would.'

'No, you wouldn't. It was another world.'

'I'm not a child, Mother. If there's something you need to tell me ...' Wrong word, need. The mood was broken, shattered.

'There's nothing I need to tell you. There's nothing you need to know.'

I patted her hand. 'Well now, you rest; I'll be in tomorrow.' I bent over and kissed her cheek. Although the skin on her hands was papery and loose, on her face it was still soft. No soap, that was the secret, she said. She would share that kind of secret, one that didn't matter. There was no reason for me to return to my mother's house today; no reason, just my need to look again at those letters, to see if there was something in them I had missed, some clue to ... to what I didn't know.

I went straight upstairs, took the envelope from its hiding place and sat down on the bed. About to take the letters out, I had a better idea: I would take them home, photocopy them and return them the next day. That way I could pore over them at my leisure, without fear of interruption. I know it was silly, but reading them there I felt myself in imminent danger of discovery. I put the envelope into my handbag and shut the drawer. I looked at the wardrobe, the dressing-table under the window, the bedside cabinet. Was there anything else that I should see, hidden in this room? A photograph perhaps?

Kitty had always kept the family photographs going right back to Victorian studio portraits of my great-grandparents. Maybe in her room …? If not a photograph, there might be a drawing of the man I now knew to be my father. Kitty used to do little sketches of people; she was quite good, too; and she wrote letters, to pen-friends mainly, people all over the world that she knew she'd never see. She told me once, and I was impressed by the fact that she wasn't at all ashamed to be lying, that she made up stories about herself, told them she lived in a grand house and had lots of dogs. What did it matter, she said, it was only fun; they probably did the same. It was liking reading a story, except that this was a story written for just one person.

Standing in Kitty's room thinking about her strange secret life I remembered something else about her: she had kept a diary. Not a small, pocket diary. I had bought her one of those once, for Christmas. I couldn't have been more than about ten, and she said: 'That's no good to me; that's for people who go out, to tell them where they're going; I want mine for what's in here,' and she touched her head with a finger. Would she have preserved her diaries? Or thrown them away when she came here in 'sixty-two? Had she kept a diary in 1939, that's what I really wanted to know.

I had no idea where to begin looking, or in fact, what I was looking for. Notebooks? Pads? Something bigger than a pocket diary, that I knew. There was nothing here;

a few books on a shelf, a pile of magazines, but no diaries. Of course not; one didn't keep a diary on show. Had she kept them with the photographs? I knew where they were: in the wardrobe; she had once asked me to get them for her.

I pulled open the door and felt among the hanging dresses. The photograph albums were there, but a cursory flick through showed me no pictures from the Thirties or the war years. Beneath them was a long, shallow, old-fashioned dress box. I drew it out and put it on the bed. I had no qualms about looking through any of Kitty's things; I felt she had wanted me to know the secret that my mother had kept from me. I lifted the lid: nothing but old newspapers, crumbling at the edges: the Coronation and the ascent of Everest 1953, Princess Elizabeth's wedding in 1947; cuttings from the Enfield Gazette about a murder in the 1960s.

I knew her diaries wouldn't be downstairs; Kitty spent most of her life in her bedroom. When they moved from Mulberry Road a lot of stuff had been put in the loft; the wartime diaries could be there. I let down the hinged loft cover, pulled down the folding stairs and climbed up. I switched on the light and looked about me: there were boxes and suitcases, pieces of carpet and linoleum, a camp bed, a card table, an old washbowl and matching jug with pink roses, a dressmaker's dummy, bunches of dried flowers, their colours still bright, preserved with glycerine. The cases were empty and the boxes were full of remnants of material and bits of ribbon and braid. Another aspect of my mother's hoarding. Well, that was that.

The diaries had to be in Kitty's room. I went back in there and opened one of the drawers in the dressing table. Nothing. I looked at the books on the shelf, seemingly a set of condensed novels from The Reader's Digest, bound in mock leather. Of course. How could I have been so stupid. Call myself a crime writer! If I'd looked more closely I would have seen there were no titles on the spines. I pulled one down from the shelf and opened it. It wasn't even a book; it was a box, fashioned to look like a book, rather like a video box. Inside were notebooks, about eight to a box, the sort I remember using for French vocabulary. On each notebook there was a date. The box I had taken down was from the Seventies; there were nine boxes in all. I began opening them at random; in the third box were Kitty's dairies from 1933 to 1940. I started to turn the pages in the one for 1939, then stopped ... I suddenly felt I couldn't cope with any more 'secrets' until I was in my own home, and preferably with a drink in my hand.

CHAPTER TWO

I drove home to Hertford with the car more or less on auto-pilot, my thoughts still in the past. I had lived there, on my own, for three years now, and I knew the route from Enfield well: up the A10 to the Hertford turn-off, round the one-way system, down into the narrow, winding streets of the town, across the canal and into Stags' Run, to my artisan's cottage, now 'elegantly refurbished' – according to the estate agent when I bought it. It is actually very nice and it's all I need. Two bedrooms, a bathroom, a sitting-room, kitchen-dining room, a tiny garden, and … what really sold it to me, a field next door, so that, although my living quarters are confining, I have the countryside literally on my doorstep.

My cottage was welcoming, warm and sweet-scented; I had only yesterday renewed the pot-pourri in the green lustre bowl on the hall table. The door to the kitchen-dining room stood open and the last of the afternoon light was filtering through the window at the back. I walked into the kitchen, opened my sideboard and took out a bottle of sherry, nothing special, a supermarket amontillado. I poured myself a full glass and drank it, almost at one go, something I wouldn't normally do. On a normal day.

With my coat still on I sat down at the dining table – round, pine, not my choice, it had been left by the previous owner and it seemed to fit so I kept it – and took the envelope from my handbag and the diary box from a carrier bag I'd taken from my mother's kitchen. I laid them side by side and looked at them for what seemed a long time. Then I stood up, poured myself a second glass of sherry, took off my coat and sat down again.

Eager as I had been before to look into my new-found history, now I was almost loathe to open the box, or re-read the letters. I knew all I needed to know: Tom Harper was not, and never had been, my father; my father was a young man about whom I knew nothing except that he had loved my mother ... well, made love to, anyway. Had she loved him back? I hope so. Whoever he was I did so want my mother to have loved him, lusted after him even, felt about him as she had never felt about Tom. No, I can't say that, I don't know how she felt about Tom; she never spoke about that side of their life together. They were never very affectionate to one another in public, nor when I was around, but that doesn't mean they couldn't be passionate in the privacy of their bedroom.

I got up from the table, opened my back door and stepped outside into the now-dark garden. As I moved away from the door the light sensor was activated and the small courtyard was flooded with artificial light. A sensible precaution for a woman living alone, but right now I didn't want to be standing there, lit as if on a stage. I went inside and shut the door; after a few moments the outside light went off.

I turned the key in the door, and then, something I rarely did, closed the curtains. Another sherry and I would be ready. No, not another sherry – some food, that's what I needed. I made myself a couple of scrambled eggs and cheese on toast and a pot of tea, real tea, not tea-bags this time. I put the meal on a tray, a tray I'd bought in Florence with Neville in the early Eighties just before we split up; a plastic, heat-resistant touristy tray with a scene from a fresco in the Medici Chapel on it. I used it all the time but hardly ever looked at it. Today I did and I wanted Neville … needed him, to be here, with me.

But he wasn't, and he wouldn't be, ever again.

I had sent him away, told him I didn't want him in my life any more, that I wanted to live as I pleased, not sharing, not having to consider him as well as myself, most of all not having to have him around the house when I wanted to work; because he never understood that 'writing' didn't mean you were sitting at a computer every single minute, that you could be 'writing' when you were in the bath, or just walking around the garden, that you didn't switch off the life of your characters when you switched off your computer, that they were there with you, all the time, until the book was finished, and even then they sometimes hung around, like shades.

I didn't need anyone to tell me that I had been unfair, that it wasn't Neville's fault that he had been made redundant. It was a brave move of his setting up his own company, selling advertising space for magazines, putting those who wanted to advertise in touch with those with space to sell. It was a pity it didn't work out.

It had been fine to begin with, the first couple of months; it was nice to have him at home. We had both been in the magazine business and knew it inside out – it was how we had met – so it was natural he should want to use me as a sounding board for his ideas. I should have laid down some ground rules at the beginning, when he first mooted the idea of working from home, but I didn't. Who ever does? So that when I began to say, more or less: get out of my hair, give me space, don't talk to me, I'm working – I wasn't polite or kind – he was hurt and retreated to the room he had made his office. Then came the sarcasm and the 'notes': Do you think, if I made an appointment, I could possibly have a word with you between 2.15 and 2.30 this afternoon? Which, of course, ended in a row.

For a few weeks afterwards we would be thoughtful for one another, working in our separate offices for set hours only, leaving time each day for us to be together, cooking, eating, doing the garden, watching television. Fine, until I got deep into a new Ellen Field and couldn't stop.

All right, wouldn't stop, writing in the way I had done when Neville was working away from home, living for the whole day in my fictional world, getting myself a coffee, lunch, walking round the house, but with my brain still locked into the story I was writing until half past five each day when I switched off everything: the answerphone, the computer, the characters in my head, had a drink and began to think about the evening meal. If I could do it then, Neville argued, why couldn't I do it at lunchtime, say, or in the middle of the morning, just for ten minutes, to be with him, to see how *he* was getting on? Because I didn't work that way, was the answer. Because I liked my routine, I'd got used to it, so why should I change it just because his routine had changed. And of course it had, very much; instead of having a battery of people around him to whom he could delegate work, discuss ideas, have lunch with, chat, chat up? – probably, and why not, it was harmless – suddenly he was on his own, and it was natural that he thought his wife, whom he had met because he chatted her up in an office at *DAMES* magazine in the Swinging Sixties when she was an assistant editor and he was a sales rep, would want to share in his new business-from-home.

For a few brief moments I was back in those heady days when the Beatles were young lads and everyone was wearing Mary Quant clothes. I was sitting in my office, chewing a pencil – funny how you remember these silly things – when this incredibly good-looking, dark-haired, tall young man walked in, stretched out his hand in greeting and said – his transatlantic approach at odds with his Yorkshire vowels: 'Hi. I'm Neville Thornfield, you must be Jane Harper.' It struck me as being so funny that I just burst out laughing. He recoiled slightly, his brashness gone, and said, hesitantly: 'Oh … I'm sorry, I must have got the wrong office.' To which I replied, 'No, you're in the right place and I *am* Jane Harper. Hello.' 'So why did you laugh?' he asked. 'Your name'. 'My name?' 'Yes, it sounds straight out of a Brontë novel.' 'It is,' he said, 'that's where I'm from.' The least I could do was buy him lunch.

For a long, long time we were very happy. Everything was right with us: the sex was good, never mind-blowing stuff, but always natural and spontaneous; we were good friends too, enjoying the same things.

Now, sitting in my kitchen, about to read Kitty's diaries for 1939, I wanted him here. To share in something momentous, because that is how it felt … momentous.

I had his phone number; he'd gone back to his roots in Yorkshire. He could be here in hours, and I knew, too, that he would come. We still saw one another from time to time, usually at media events, and we spoke on the phone, mainly about Alex whom we both loved deeply, and of whom we were very, very proud: he had won an Exhibition to St. Catherine's, Cambridge. Dear Alex; he was eighteen when we finally separated – we hung on till he left school – and he didn't blame either of us.

I didn't phone Neville. Or Beth. Beth Lindale had been my friend since my very first job in publishing. I was straight out of university and still very wet behind the ears and Beth, three years older, had shown me the ropes. I didn't see her often now – she'd gone to live in Scotland – but it was one of those friendships that you can pick up at any time and know that it will be intact. 'Hi, Beth,' I could hear myself saying, 'Guess what, you know how you used to call me, affectionately, a bastard … well, I am, sort of.'

Kitty had small, old-fashioned sort of writing, full of loops and curls, and she had filled every inch of the narrow-lined paper. I put aside her diary for 1933, the first one in the box, and those for 1934 and 1935. About to do the same with the diary for 1936, I remembered that that was the year Alice and Tom had got married and that Kitty had been one of their bridesmaids. There was a drawing of Kitty's frock and headdress followed by an account of the wedding at the Methodist church and the reception in the church hall. They had gone to Bognor Regis for their honeymoon – something I didn't know – and come home to find confetti in their bed, put there by Kitty, who comments: *I wonder if Alice will get a baby! Perhaps she already has!!*

And so, at last, to 1939.

There was nothing significant in the first half of the year, but then, on July 11th she wrote, *Tom is coming home from Malta because Grandma is very ill. Please God, don't let her die, unless that is what she wants because she is in pain.*

And on July 12th: *A friend of Tom's from Malta is coming to stay. He is coming home because his sister has died.*

Entry for July 13th. *Tom's friend, Peter, arrived. He is very nice! He has blue eyes and lovely blond wavy hair. I wouldn't mind k...ing him!! We went for a walk. He wanted me to go with him to a p.h. (!!) but I wouldn't. If I had he might have k...ed me.* Oh Kitty, how unworldly you were. Nineteen, longing to be kissed and afraid – naturally enough with your Methodist upbringing – to go into a public house. I presumed that was what p.h. must mean.

I read again her brief description of Peter: blue eyes, blond hair. Tom's hair was dark, so was Kitty's; mine was fair, but there was no significance in that: my mother's hair had been fair, so had her father's.

Back to the diary. *July 14th. Tom has gone to see Grandma. Alice and Peter have gone to Southend.* By train? Or on Tom's bike? His precious Ariel? Surely not. He could have gone to King's Lynn by train, probably had a free rail pass. The entry continued: *It's not fair, he wanted me to go, not her. Tom brought him here for ME. I hope they have a rotten, horrid time. If I hadn't gone for that walk and got tired I could have gone.* Had Peter asked Alice to go with him, then taken Kitty out the day before on purpose to tire her out? Surely not. *I hope it rains and they get wet. It would serve them right.* Did it rain? I could find out. I doubt if they would have cared what the weather was; they'd still have gone. Another thought: would they have had enough petrol? Was it in short supply? Something else to check.

July 15th. Tom is back from seeing Grandma. He says she may not live very long but he is glad he has seen her. If I was ill, very ill and dying, perhaps P. would come to see me.

July 16th. Tom and P. have left. P. k...ed me goodbye. I said I would write to him. He didn't kiss Alice. Ha ha! T. and A. said goodbye to each other last night. I could hear them!!

The remainder of July revealed nothing that I felt I needed to know. Exactly why Peter was there, at the house, I wasn't sure and I couldn't see that I had any way of finding out, other than asking my mother and that, clearly, was not an option at the moment. What did seem feasible was that Tom had brought Peter home for Kitty. What was he hoping for? That Kitty and Peter would fall in love and she would then want to go to Malta, and therefore Alice would have no alternative but to come with her?

I had no way of knowing exactly what had taken place during that week in July, but nevertheless I needed to construct a scenario for myself. After all, this was my life, my beginning. If I could do it for some imaginary female in an Ellen Field novel I could damn well do it for myself!

He was beautiful, he was the most beautiful man she had ever seen: wavy hair, shining blue eyes and a glowing skin bronzed by the Malta sun. 'I'm Pete,' he said. He was standing on the doorstep, kitbag over his shoulder, the grin she would come to love spreading across his boyish face. 'You must be Alice.'

Well, something like that. And as he looks at her she experiences a sensation she has never felt before, an almost shaming sensation that she is certain he is aware of. I know I am running away with myself here, but something of the sort must have happened to make my strait-laced mother go off the rails. I think her feeling for Peter, a suddenly-awakened, urgent sexual need, would have sent all other considerations – moral, social, practical – out of the window.

I've been there myself. Brief though the affair was – it was when was I a student – it was glorious, heady stuff. Everything else becomes unimportant: you are possessed and obsessed.

That, I think, is what happened to my mother.

So ... there it was: I was a wartime love-baby,

conceived in Southend. Under the pier? On the sands? At sometime in the future I could let my imagination loose on that, but not now.

Once my mother was out of hospital and I had made sure she could cope on her own – 'I don't want nurses or any other busybodies coming in, no thank you' – I had to get on with my life: I had some research to do in France for a novel which should be on my editor's desk by the beginning of August and in September I was speaking at the Hertfordshire LitFest.

Driving to the hospital the following day I passed a group of teenage girls – laughing, eating chocolate bars, drinking from cans, probably skiving off school. How would one of them cope in my situation? With aplomb, no doubt. Well, on the surface anyway. Being illegitimate today was no great problem and having two dads was becoming the norm. I would simply say to my mother ... 'Hey, Mum, what's this about you and this soldier? Is he really my Dad? Wicked!' Wicked, yes, but not in the way today's children used the word. To my mother it meant sinful. Is that what she felt she had been? It was another question I couldn't ask.

There was one thing I could ask her, though, and having to fetch her a pair of bed-socks from Kitty's room had given me a lead in.

'Mother ...'

'Yes?'

'You know that photograph on Kitty's dressing-table, the one of me in fancy dress?'

'Well, what about it?'

'How old was I?'

'Oh, I don't know. About ... eight I should think. Why?'

'Oh, nothing special, I was just looking at it today ...'

'You've not been touching her things, have you?'

'No!'

'I'll see to them.'

'I know you will. I haven't touched anything (since when did a hurtful truth help anyone?) it's just that the picture was there, and because it was me I looked at it. You know how you always look at yourself in a photograph. Well …'

'I don't.'

'Mother, you are a paragon! Lesser people like myself do. Anyway … in this photo there's a bike, a motorbike …'

'Yes. Well?'

I wished my heart would slow down. If I was like this asking a totally innocent question what was I going to be like when, if, I ever got to the really difficult ones.

'I just wondered if … if that was Dad's … bike.'

From inside my voice sounded squeaky and nervous, but there was no change in my mother's expression nor her tone of voice, so I assumed I must sound normal.

'Yes, of course it was.' A sudden softening of tone. 'He loved that bike.'

'Did you ever go on it?'

'What, on the pillion, you mean?'

'Yes.'

'Not if I could help it.' Her face had closed up again. 'I was glad when he sold it.'

'I wish I could remember going on it; I know he took me on it, but I can't remember what it felt like. I can't remember whether I was frightened or whether I liked it. I expect I liked it, holding on to him, and with the wind blowing in my hair …'

She gave me one of her come-down-to-earth-this-is-real-life-not-one-of-your-stories looks.

'You wore a woolly hat, and anyway, he never took you far.'

'Do you think I could have that picture?'

'Yes, if you want. I don't want it.'

'Not even for the bike?' I shouldn't have said that.

Her answer surprised me. 'A bike's nothing, Jane. It's just … just a means to an end.' She sounded sad. 'Yes, you have it. It's right you should.' Why is it right? Because that was the bike that might have taken you to Southend fifty-six years ago?

'Thank you, darling,' I said, and bent over and kissed her.

'It'll remind you of Kitty.' Of course … Kitty had made my costume, out of crepe paper, and it had been Kitty's idea – a winning idea, too – that I should go dressed as a banana. That was why the photograph was on her dressing-table. It was her triumph, not mine.

CHAPTER THREE

Spring came, my mother recovered and went home, and in May I went to France. I had still said nothing to Beth or Neville about my 'new' father. Talking to them would only open everything up again and for now I needed to put it to the back of my mind.

Going to France did me good; I became absorbed in my research. My 1880s heroine, Emiline, had fallen head-over-heels in love on the packet boat from Dover to Calais. The object of her affections was Lucien, a young Frenchman returning home, but Emiline was with her father, the stern Sir Giles Covering, who had little time for foreigners and would not welcome one as a son-in-law. Once in France Emiline eludes her father and sets off on her own to follow Lucien to the address he has succeeded in giving her. Finding out how a well-brought up English girl would manage on her own, how she would travel – she had some money – where she would stay, what, if anything the French authorities would do, etc. was fascinating. I gathered all the information I needed, went home and got on with my book. Through June and July Emiline and Lucien demanded all my attention: Peter Anderson would have to wait.

In August I had a dentist's appointment, and as I waited, I leafed through a magazine. It was offering a six-day holiday in Malta, and because this was 1995, fifty years after the end of the Second World War, the itinerary would include 'visits to places made famous during the war – the Lascaris War Rooms, the nerve centre of Mediterranean operations; the famous harbour at Valletta; Ta' Qali, now a craft centre, which had been an airfield from which Spitfires and Hurricanes had taken off to fight the foe; the military cemeteries, the final resting place of so many of our gallant servicemen who had laid down their lives for their country and the brave people of Malta; the George Cross given to the island by King George VI in 1943 ...' I stopped reading. When was this trip? May. Three months ago.

I couldn't have gone even if I had known about it in time. But it had given me an idea: I would go to Malta and find the grave of Peter Anderson. I would see the place where he, and Tom, had worked and lived and fought, and he had died. I would come home and tell my mother ... and then, then she would talk to me. She would want to talk, she would be pleased that I had seen the place where her love was at rest; she would answer all my questions.

My euphoria didn't last long. By the time the injection for my filling had worn off I was back in the real world, but the resolution to visit my father's grave was still strong. All right, so it wouldn't tell me anything about the man, but I could place some flowers there, maybe say a prayer, perhaps feel a sense of belonging. I understood now why some apparently happily-adopted children felt compelled to search out their biological parents. It was like finding the missing piece of a jigsaw;

it might be a let-down when you found it, but at least the puzzle was complete.

Where was Imtarfa? The atlas was no help. The only places marked were Valletta and Mdina, and Victoria on the sister island of Gozo.

I phoned the Malta Tourist Office. Yes, there was an Imtarfa military cemetery, open to the public, and moreover they had a leaflet about war graves which they would send me. Two days later the package arrived: maps, list of hotels, information about golfing, diving, food and drink, car hire, pre-historic temples and feast days. Together with all this was a two-page, typed list of the cemeteries containing Commonwealth War Graves and Memorials. Imtarfa was on the first page: 'Just below Mdina, about one kilometre to the north east, is Imtarfa Cemetery. It lies on the road that runs from the village of Rabat to the village of Mosta. The cemetery is signposted in the vicinity.'

It was a start. Where was the nearest hotel? Mdina? Rabat? Mosta? The island was only sixteen miles long; I could stay anywhere, and hire a car. The idea of taking a working holiday began to form in my mind: I would go for a fortnight, ostensibly to do research for a crime thriller. Or a romantic novel. Yes, I would write a romance, a modern romance this time, set in Malta. I began to warm to the idea: sun-kissed beaches, starry nights, young lovers thwarted by an ancient curse then brought together by ... Enough. I would find something there, some storyline ... and I would have a holiday, too, a rest ... which I needed. I was, of course, giving myself reasons, which were really just excuses, for going there, for going to Imtarfa. Besides, that expedition ... no, it is not an expedition, it is a pilgrimage. Or is it an exorcism? Well, whatever it is, it won't take me more than a morning, at the most.

I booked myself in for fourteen nights at the Hotel

Melita in Mellieha Bay, on the north-west coast. I would be leaving Luton on November 10th.

I had no plans, nor any desire, to mingle with my fellow holiday-makers. I had sat with a nice-enough middle-aged woman on the plane; she'd been to Malta before and had plenty of tips for me. She invited me to join her, and the friends she was meeting, for a drink in the bar before dinner. She probably thought I was rude, or ungrateful, when I declined; and she would be right: I was. I didn't want to get myself into a situation where I felt forced to become part of a group; let me get tomorrow over, and then perhaps, in a day or so, I would seek her out and reciprocate her invitation. I had also had what sounded like a come-on from – I have to say it – a very attractive man in his late fifties, Ken Pickard. Later, maybe, I would be nice to him, too.

My room, on the third floor, overlooked Mellieha Bay. Hang-gliders flitted to and fro over the sparkling water, and across the bay, rising sharply from the shore, was the village of Mellieha. In the sloping gardens of the hotel papery mauve bougainvillea, red hibiscus and lantana, shading from yellow and orange to deep purple, were in bloom, and beside my balcony hundreds of tiny sparrows twittered in a tall cypress growing against the wall. The air was warm and sweet, and gentle waves lapped the tiny beach far below.

I took a deep breath and let it out slowly. I felt surprisingly relaxed ... and why not? Yes, I was apprehensive, but I could still enjoy myself. I would have a good dinner, a good night's sleep; then tomorrow, after breakfast, I would take possession of my hire car ... and drive to the cemetery.

CHAPTER FOUR

Armed with my map and the instructions from the Malta Tourist Office, I set off. I knew how to get to the cemetery; I had pored over the map at home long enough. Turn left out of the hotel drive, down past Mellieha Beach, up into the village of Mellieha, take the coast road to St. Paul's Bay, at the next roundabout go right for Mosta, and just before I got into the town turn right for Mdina; then, approaching Mdina, look out for the signpost for Imtarfa Cemetery. Easy.

I had not allowed for the fact that this was Malta, not England, that the roads had no numbers, that signposts were sometimes ambiguous, that although they drove on the left, officially, most of the drivers I encountered seemed to have their own set of rules, which was really only one rule: me first. I had to keep my eyes on the road to such an extent that I couldn't appreciate anything around me. Never mind, I could look at the scenery another time, perhaps from the safety of a seat in one of the ancient-looking, but newly-painted orange buses that frequently overtook me, often on a bend.

I turned into the road where the military cemetery was supposed to be. It was little more than a lane and a rusty sign said it was the way to Ta' Qali Craft Centre; it didn't mention the cemetery. Most tourists would want to see living crafts, not the graves of the dead. Besides, the cemetery was right here, on the corner, its high, stone boundary wall running alongside another, wider road. I pulled up outside the wrought iron gates and switched off the engine. There was no one about, either in the road, or as far I could see, in the cemetery. Although it was November the day was hot and there was no breeze.

For a few moments I sat there, taking in deep breaths. Part of me wanted to switch on the engine, turn the car around and go straight back to the hotel, to England even. What a damn stupid thing to be doing: sitting outside a cemetery in which I may or may not find the grave of the man I believe to have been my father. The other part of me said: having come this far you may as well go in.

I got out, locked the car and pushed open the gate. A long stone path led to a war memorial, topped by a cross and framed by the dark green of cypresses, which stood at the far end; to my right was a sort of lodge, which was locked. Probably gardening tools and possibly records of the burials were kept there. On the right hand side of the path there were stone slabs with three or four names on each; on the left there were individual memorials, some topped with a cross on a plinth, all of them in the warm, pinky-cream limestone of Malta.

As I had no idea where to begin looking, I just walked, slowly, down the main path, glancing first to one side then the other, trying to see if there was a pattern to the burials. In death, were officers and other ranks segregated? Not here by the look of it: a squadron leader was buried next to a corporal; no officers, though, appeared to be buried under the multiple slabs. I wandered down a side pathway and found myself looking down on the graves of soldiers and sailors who had died in the Great War; elsewhere there were airmen who had served here in the Fifties and further on graves of the children of servicemen. I walked back up the main pathway, the multiple slabs on my left.

I stood, looking down at one of them. It marked the burying place of four men killed in action in April 1942: a private in the King's Own Royal Regiment, a private and a corporal in the Durham Light Infantry and a Bombardier in the Royal Artillery. There was a simple cross at the head of the slab and beside each name, etched in the stone, was the man's regimental badge. Next to it was a slab covering the graves of three gunners and a member of the Royal West Kents; again they had all died in 1942, when the air raids on Malta were at their peak. Somewhere close by Peter Anderson would have been buried. I moved on to the next slab: his name wasn't there; it wasn't on the next one, nor the one after that. I was now back at the lodge. Perhaps he had an individual memorial: unlikely. I retraced my steps, looking carefully at each slab, re-reading the names. He wasn't here; Tom's letter was a joke. What an idiot I was to be taken in by it. But why, if it was a joke – and what a horrible joke it was – had my mother kept the letter. No, he must be here. This was Imtarfa Cemetery – it said so on the pillar by the gate – and this is where he had been laid to rest. A shady place with trees, Tom had written.

I began walking slowly up the path again, searching as I walked. Suddenly I knew what I had done: I had totally ignored a whole row of slabs lying behind those next to the path.

I found the one I wanted almost immediately: Gunner P. Anderson … and then his number; and on the next line, Royal Artillery. Below that the date on which he had died: 22nd March 1942 aged 23. Gunner P. Anderson – I read it aloud – twenty-three years old. Twenty-three. A mere boy, younger than my own son. I could feel the pain of stifled tears in my chest and then in my eyes. I knelt down, threw my arms across the slab … and wept. Not for a father, but for a young man, for a young life ended so far from home, for a lad who had loved my mother. I put my fingers to my lips, placed a kiss upon them, and pressed my fingers onto the cold stone. Sobs racked me and I rocked back and forth, still on my knees.

I had not been prepared for this. I had expected to be interested, pleased even, to have seen the grave … but not moved, not like this. I got up slowly, stood for a moment looking down, then running my hand across my eyes to wipe away the tears, I walked back to the car.

So … what now? After the brief emotional storm I had a feeling of anti-climax. Maybe I could find out how he died; there must be records somewhere on the island, at the War Museum possibly, or back in England on a dusty shelf in the archives of the Royal Artillery; here, on this spot, there was nothing more.

If only I had told Neville, or Beth, then one of them could have come with me; we would have seen the grave together, I would have had a shoulder to cry on, and then we could have gone off somewhere and enjoyed ourselves. As it was I was in a self-imposed purdah. I felt depressed and lonely. Perhaps it was the place, the fact that there was no living soul around – at least I managed a smile at that – and I had no idea what to do with myself for the rest of the day. My lady from the plane, and Ken Pickard with her, were off on a day trip to Valletta and I didn't feel like making more new friends just yet.

While I was here, near Ta' Qali and Mdina, I might as

well do a bit of sight-seeing. I drove down the lane towards Ta' Qali. So late in the tourist season the Craft Centre was all but deserted – I spoke to one young man – and many of the Nissan huts, selling silver filigree, lace and pottery and plastic Knights of St. John, were closed. I wandered about aimlessly. The only connection with the war years was a sign pointing to 'Spitfire Workshop'.

The airfield, along with those at Luqa and Kalafrana and Hal Far, had been a centre of activity during those years, when first the Italians and then the Germans bombed Malta without mercy and the fighter pilots and the ground crews and the gunners, all of them on starvation rations, fought back until the enemy gave up and turned its attention elsewhere. It was a time of heroics and pain, of gallant deeds and patient suffering as the raids went on and on, night after night, day after day, with more bombs being dropped on Malta in two months of 1942 than were dropped on London in a year. It was a time of fear and fatigue and disease, and jubilation when a convoy, bringing its precious cargo of food and ammunition and fuel, did get through. Now there was nothing here apart from the huts to serve as a reminder of those days. The aircraft pens had gone and the runway, which had been like the long handle of a warming pan, had become a road leading to the National Stadium. For me, searching into the past, there was nothing: this is not the Ta' Qali that Peter Anderson would have seen.

But not everything had changed so drastically. Mdina, the old capital of Malta, would be much as he had seen it, and the barracks where he and Tom had lived were still standing, so the young man at Ta' Qali had said. There were some things I could see, some places I could visit. My spirits rose. I turned the car around and headed back, past the cemetery, to the roundabout; a signpost pointed to Mtarfa. The road was bumpy and full of potholes; it didn't look as if it was much used nowadays. It wound up and up, between rubble walls which divided the road from the fields on either side. Over the tops of the walls and through gateways and gaps I could see maize growing, and prickly pears, and huge pumpkins drying on the flat roofs and walls of the occasional farm building. Finally I was at Mtarfa: modern and some older houses on my left, on my right the barracks – huge, stern-looking, rectangular buildings of reddish stone, dominating the landscape, as if they were saying: we are British, we are part of the Empire. And like so much of that Empire, these once-proud barracks had had their day. The young man at Ta' Qali had told me that they were to be turned into holiday flats and that the Military Hospital next door was now a school.

I parked the car under a tree by the school wall, got out and walked to the entrance. So this had been the hospital. Had Tom or my father been here, to have a wound dressed perhaps, to be given some medicine, to have an operation even? There was so much I didn't know, and there seemed no way I could find out. I could walk around the grounds of the old barracks, but what would that tell me of the life they had led fifty years ago?

I drove back to the roundabout and took the road to Rabat and Mdina. I had already seen the cupola and twin bell-towers of Mdina's Baroque cathedral standing high above the other buildings as I drove to the cemetery.

For the rest of the day I would be a tourist: I would walk through the old city, or maybe even ride around it in a horse-drawn *karozzin*; I would have some lunch; I would enjoy myself. And as I walked and looked, I might, you never know, find the perfect setting for the romantic story I had, ostensibly, come to research.

The road, now full of traffic, climbed steeply toward

Rabat. At the top of the hill I made a sharp turn right. The road was very wide here and traffic – cars, buses, luxury coaches, lorries, many of them with horns blaring – was hurtling in both directions. Driving as slowly as I dared, looking for somewhere to park – both sides of the roads were crowded with cars – I passed a red pillar box and a red phone box and began to wonder if I had left England. I took the first turning left; ahead of me were more parked cars, and at last a space, abutting a piece of waste land.

Thankfully I parked the car, locked it and looked around. On my left, with their double doors giving straight on to the road, was a row of old houses, many of them with small religious bas-relief decoration on the stuccoed walls. Opposite the houses were public gardens and through the trees I could see the walls of the fabled silent city of Mdina.

I walked through the gardens and came out on to a pathway leading to the main gate into the citadel. Despite the never-ending flow of tourist groups babbling away in a dozen languages, the whirring and clicking of camcorders and cameras and the clip-clop of the horses' hooves, there was an extraordinary feeling of peace about the place. The thick stone walls and the tall buildings protected the narrow streets from the fierceness of the sun; I felt quite chilly and in need of a hot coffee. I turned into a doorway, past a board advertising lunches and snacks; at the far end of a passageway I could see chairs and tables, wrought iron and vines … and sunshine. Soon I was warm again. I sat drinking my coffee and looking at the guide book, trying to decide what I should see next. Perhaps I should just walk around and look at the impressive façades of the ancient palaces, once the homes of Malta's aristocracy. Or I could walk to the end of Villegaignon Street and enjoy the 'fabulous view from Bastion Square, with the patchwork quilt of fields and terraces that is Malta laid out before you'. Not just fields and terraces. If I looked down from the square I would be able to see the cemetery as well. My thoughts went back to the stone slab and its inscription. As long as I was on my own this was going to happen; when I wasn't driving or parking or looking at a guide book I would come back to my main reason for being here: my father. It was naive of me to think that having visited his grave I could now toss the subject aside: I couldn't.

I drank my coffee, paid the bill and went back to the car. My enthusiasm for Mdina had waned. I wanted to get back to the hotel, have some lunch and then think hard about what, if anything, I was going to do next. I knew that I wouldn't be able to put my mind to any serious, or even frivolous, research for a book until I had satisfied myself that there *was* no more to be learnt about my father on this island.

I switched on the engine and noticed that the petrol gauge was registering well under a quarter – the car hire firm had started me off with five litres only. Having no idea of the car's m.p.g. I would need to fill up soon or risking running dry. I knew I'd seen a garage somewhere near. I drove out of the side road; the garage was almost opposite, on the other side of the main road. Cutting across the never-ceasing stream of vehicles was not easy; nobody was willing to give way, but eventually the driver of another hire car took pity on me stranded perilously in the middle of the flow, and let me through. I pulled up under the garage's canopy and waited. A young man served me; I had fifteen litres put in and remembered to ask for a receipt. This was a research trip, after all, and I needed documentation for my accountant and the Inland Revenue. I took my change and the receipt and stuffed them into my purse.

'Thank you,' I said, and smiled at the young man. He

gave me a warm smile back. 'Is it always this busy here?' I asked.

'Always, and getting more so.'

'Good for business,' I said, and he agreed.

There were bunches of red and pink carnations in a metal pail beside the door of the kiosk.

'I'd like a bunch of those,' I said. He wrapped them and handed them to me through the window.

'Would you like a receipt for them?' he asked, his eyes twinkling; he had lovely eyes, dark brown and deep. He would be a good prototype for the Maltese hero in my romantic novel.

'No, thank you,' I said. 'My travelling is for business, but the flowers are for … for a friend.'

I put the carnations on the passenger seat beside me, waved to the young man – he was already attending to another customer and didn't see me – and drove off.

The receipt, which I hadn't bothered to examine beyond checking that the amount was correct, was a small square, torn off a block-pad; most tourists wouldn't need receipts and the young man had looked a bit surprised when I requested it, complete with the date, please. It was to prove the most important clue I could possibly have found.

CHAPTER FIVE

I pushed open the cemetery gate and walked slowly towards my father's grave. I held the carnations by my side, their heads hanging downwards as if in salute to the dead. This was to be the quiet act of homage, of commemoration, that in my mind's eye I had seen myself enacting, not the impassioned outburst of my first visit. Not that there was anything wrong with that; there was no one right way to express grief. My mother, I knew, would have been horrified and embarrassed by my earlier exhibition, so perhaps this act was for her, performed in the way she would have considered seemly. I couldn't resist a smile: here was I, her daughter, about to lay, in a seemly fashion, flowers on the grave of the man with whom, probably for the only time in her life, she had exhibited unseemly behaviour.

On my first visit I had been so intent on finding the grave I hadn't noticed that the cemetery was … well, a bit unkempt, untidy, unlike other military cemeteries I'd seen, all manicured grass and gleaming headstones. Somehow, though, the pile of gravel waiting to be laid, last year's pine cones strewn on the side paths, the worn and dusty stones and the general feeling of age made this resting place a friendlier spot, more like an old English churchyard than a military burial ground.

Before I placed the flowers on Peter Anderson's grave I would dust the inscription and try to remove some of the lichen that had grown on the slab.

Quickly I flicked my handkerchief over the incised words, then dampening the hankie with my saliva, I began to rub over the letters one by one. First P, then A.N.D.E.R.S.E ... E? That should be an O. Why had I not noticed that before? Because, Jane, you see what you expect to see.

Andersen, not Anderson: this is not my father's grave. It had to be: a gunner in the Royal Artillery, died in 1942, initial P. It was the stonemason's error, nothing more. It had to be Anderson; Andersen was a Danish name, as in Hans Christian. Maybe ... he could be a Dane! Why not, there were Danes and Poles and Dutch in the British armed forces during the war. This could make me a completely different person with a whole new pedigree. I laughed out loud. 'Jane, you're getting fanciful again; stop it!' The name was Anderson; that's how Tom had spelt it in the letter; it was how Kitty had spelt it in her diary.

I placed the carnations on the slab, just above the name. I felt I should say something. Words were my work, but now they failed me. If I truly, rather than vaguely, believed in God, I would have said a prayer. Those lines by Dylan Thomas about raging against the dying of the light came to mind. It was too late for that; this light had died too long ago for rage now. Better to say nothing at all, just a whispered: 'I'll come again before I leave.'

It was excessively hot in the car, which I had left locked and parked in full sun. With both front windows wound right down I drove back at Malta speed to Mellieha Bay. I had a late lunch in the cafeteria, a rest in my room, determinedly reading a paperback I'd bought at the airport – a page-turning, brain-numbing, pseudo-political bonkbuster which eventually sent me to sleep. I woke with that feeling of stupor that sometimes follows an afternoon sleep. A swim in the indoor pool soon refreshed me.

By now it was early evening. I had a shower, dressed and went down to the dining-room. I hoped that I would have to share a table: I felt in need of company.

I had not reckoned on queueing for a place. At last my turn came – I spoke to no one in the queue; they were all chattering ten to the dozen about the wonderful day out they'd had, the sights they'd seen and wasn't that bus driver a hoot and how good and kind the courier had been to the old lady who had fallen over – and when the head waiter asked, 'How many?' I lamely replied, 'One' and followed him to the far corner of the room, to a small table next to a family of six – four small children and their parents. It serves you right, I thought. If you hadn't been so snooty and stuck-up yesterday you could be part of one of the jolly tables for four you passed on the way here, instead of being tucked away out of sight. Young children and single women; nobody wants their company for dinner.

I hadn't even brought a book with me. This was a new experience for me, eating alone in a hotel and being miserable. I had lunches in pubs or canteens when I was doing research, or a snack when I was out shopping, but this was different. I had to face it: I was lonely. And my clothes, which I had thought would cheer me up, only added to the gloom. Mutton dressed as lamb, my mother would have said: short, tight skirt that rode up when I sat down, satin blouse, big earrings, hair piled high. Like a barmaid on a bad day.

I ate my meal as quickly as I could and left the room; I couldn't say whether the food was excellent or barely edible. Out in the foyer I took a deep breath. What now? Sit in the lounge and feel even more miserable? Go to bed? Certainly get out of these awful clothes.

'Hello there. My, you do look smart.' It was the man from the plane, the last thing I wanted just now.

'I look awful,' I said.

'I think you look ...'

'Tarty, that's what I look.'

I had embarrassed him.

'No, you don't. You look ...'

'I don't dress like this normally, let me tell you that. I don't know why I did it. Excuse me, I'm going upstairs to change.'

'Oh.' He looked disappointed. 'I was going to suggest that we went for a walk.'

'Well ... yes. Thank you.'

'Shall we say ... by the bookshop, in ten minutes?'

'Ten minutes. Fine.'

He stretched out a hand. 'Ken. Ken Pickard.'

'Yes, I know.'

'Of course. I told you on the plane. It's Jane, isn't it?'

'Yes.' I took his hand. The grasp was firm and warm, a bit like Nev's. But Neville's not here tonight, and this man is. I'm going to enjoy myself ... in a very restrained way, of course ... and see if, with his help, I can maybe rescue something from this ill-conceived venture.

I went up to my room, changed into jeans and T-shirt and flat shoes, let my hair down, brushed it hard and tied it back with a band, threw a cardigan over my shoulders and returned to the lobby. Ken was waiting by the bookshop door.

'Don't say it,' I said.

'I was only going to say ...' A little smile played about his lips. '... you still look nice.'

'Thank you. Where shall we go?'

'I thought, through the gardens and along the cliff path, if it's not too dark.'

It wasn't; there was just enough light for us to pick out the path. We walked as far as an old pillbox and sat down.

Ken was a retired teacher. He was fifty-nine; he'd had the chance to retire early and had taken it. 'So that I can enjoy life,' he said. 'It wasn't the classroom I had had enough of, it was the paperwork: tests and forms and assessments and league tables. When was I actually supposed to teach the kids with that lot to see to?' He was also divorced, and happy to be so. 'It was nothing dramatic,' he said. 'No other man, nothing like that. Or woman. We'd married young, too young, and just grown apart. We see each other now and then. I still like her, she's a very lovely, talented woman; I just don't want to be with her day in and day out. Nor she with me.'

I told him about Neville and Alex and my mother, and what I did for a living – he'd never heard of me and hadn't read any of my books, which was a great relief – and that I was here to do some research for a new novel. I made no mention of my real reason for being in Malta. At first glance Ken had such a look of the comedian Russ Abbot that I had almost done a double-take when he'd spoken to me on the plane. He was tall and willowy and had the same lop-sided grin and friendly eyes, but there the similarity ended; Ken was bald. There were a few hairs left, creating a half-halo round the back of his head, and as if in defiance of the retreat elsewhere, he had cultivated long, thick, grey side-burns.

It was his manner, his graciousness to use an old-fashioned word, that was so appealing. I felt safe with him, unthreatened.

'Isn't it glorious to be outdoors in the evening in November,' I said.

'It is,' he replied, and we both laughed. 'Shall we have a drink before we turn in?'

'That would be nice,' I said, and grinned.

'I like you, Jane. I think you and I are just what we both need this week. Come on.'

Was I about to embark upon a holiday romance? Heaven forbid, but I had to admit to a slight frisson – only slight, mind, nothing to get silly about – when he took my arm. I couldn't think that he was feeling anything; he was behaving more like a big brother than a prospective lover. We had our drink, in the hotel lounge – I had a white wine, he had a whisky – and arranged to meet before dinner the next evening; afterwards, if we could find a quiet corner we might have a game of Scrabble and then perhaps another walk. It sounded very pleasant.

'I shall look forward to that,' I said, and meant it. I could not have faced another dinner on my own. I felt grateful to Ken for rescuing me. Or was I rescuing him? He had given me no explanation for his solitary visit to Malta; perhaps he too had a hidden agenda.

Out on my balcony I stood looking at the lights across the bay, the stationary lights of the buildings, the moving lights of the cars winding up the hill to Mellieha, and listening to the gentle plish-plash of the water against the shingle. Then, calmly and quietly I did what I always tried to do whenever I was away from home, thought myself back through the day just ending, fixing things in my mind before the next day's events overtook them. Today there had been Ken, an enjoyable walk, a dreadful dinner; Mdina, Ta' Qali, Mtarfa. And the cemetery. The cemetery, the grave ... and the flowers. Flowers, bought at a garage in Rabat. Garage – petrol – receipt. I was not keeping a written diary – when I began to research my book I would make copious notes on a pad and on tape – but I must keep track of my daily spending.

I went inside and sat down on the bed. I took the receipt out of my purse and a pen and a small notebook from my handbag. November 11th, I wrote. Petrol. 5 Maltese lire. I would reckon it in sterling at the end of the fortnight. Ta' Pawlu, I read. That must be the name of the garage. It was in bold lettering. Ta, someone had told me, meant 'place'. So this garage, presumably, was Pawlu's place. Underneath, in smaller letters, and enclosed in brackets, it said: Andersen's. I read the name ... without reading it, if you know what I mean; it was just a name on a receipt. Then ... it was like being hit, a shock wave coursed through me, my fingers went cold, my heart began to pound. Andersen. I couldn't begin to think what it meant, or if it meant anything at all. There could be lots of Andersens. Maybe it was a Maltese name as well as a Danish one, maybe there were lots of Andersens, dead ones and live ones, all over Malta. And anyway, what possible link could there be between my father, whose name had surely been Anderson, and Andersen in brackets on a petrol receipt?

Forget it, Jane, close the book, get into bed and go to sleep. Tomorrow you are going to look at Mosta, at the famous cathedral where the bomb dropped in April 1942, dropped and rolled and didn't explode. The miracle of Mosta it is called. You will go and see it and take pictures, or buy postcards and send one to your mother. And one to Neville.

CHAPTER SIX

Eventually I slept … and awoke late. There was no sign of Ken in the dining-room, for which I was thankful. Charming as he was I didn't want to talk to him just then. I stopped by the table of the lady from the plane. She was well in now with a group of three other women, all of them around her own age. It wouldn't hurt me to be nice to her.

'Good morning,' I said.

'Oh. Good morning.' So you're speaking to me now are you?

'I'm sorry if I was a bit pre-occupied yesterday. It takes me a some time to switch off from my work.'

'Oh, what do you do?'

'I'm in … advertising.' What is writing but a sort of advertising?

'Oh, I see.' A grabbing, mercenary sort of job, not her cup of tea at all. 'Well, I hope you have a nice day today.'

'Thank you. And you.' I smiled and walked away. I had made my peace, no more was required. If I turned round now, I would see her leaning forward, explaining; condemning probably. Well, I deserved it.

It was a beautiful sunny morning, not too hot, just bright and breezy and inviting. I drove past Mellieha's small sandy beach, then up through Mellieha village, past signs for Jimmy's car hire, Henry's car hire and Billy's car hire, all much cheaper than the international firm I was using. On the hillsides outcrops of stone rose up among the sparse grass and the sandy, red soil, and on both sides of the road were flat-roofed stone houses. If I ignored the traffic and the television aerials it was like an illustration from the Bible I had had as a child. After Mellieha the coast road ran through Xemxija Bay – I couldn't attempt to pronounce it. Most people seemed to call it Smelly Bay, and I wasn't surprised; the scent – although that is really too polite a word – was … well, bad drains would sum it up. Not even the blue and yellow fishing boats, the *luzzu*, bobbing up and down on the water could entice me to linger. I drove speedily past and on towards St. Paul's Bay. Being in no hurry I took the coast road and drove through the town. The bay was beautiful, but I was glad I was staying in Mellieha; there was too much of St. Paul's, too many cafes and discos, too many hotels; in a word, too touristy for my taste. Alex would like it, just as he would like the kind of car – a low-slung, metallic red sports model – that overtook me and nearly had me up on the pavement.

I headed away from the coast, back to the main road, following the signs to Mosta. I began to recognise the route from yesterday. At the next roundabout, almost on the outskirts of the town, a road led off right to Rabat and Mdina.

Today, though, I needed to go straight on. I had seen Mdina, not a lot of it, but enough. So what if my father had been there as a young man, he might well have been to Mosta, too, visited the cathedral even, heard about the miracle ... No, that was in April, and by April he was ...

I turned off, sharply, to the right, deserving the hooting and raised fists and angry looks from the drivers whose path I had cut across. If I went on like this I, too, would be lying a under a tree somewhere before the week was out.

It was a long shot, a very long shot, but there might, just might be – this is what I was telling myself as I drove, steadily now, keeping well over to the left, on the road to Rabat – some connection between the Andersen of the garage and the Andersen, or Anderson, in the cemetery. I couldn't see what the connection could be, but having come all this way to Malta, it would be silly not to enquire.

I drew up at the garage; the young man I had spoken to yesterday was nowhere in sight. Another young man was putting petrol into the tank of a hired car. I smiled at the driver, recognising him vaguely from the hotel. When he had driven away I moved my car forward and switched off the engine.

'Petrol?'

'No, thank you. I filled up yesterday.'

'Oh. So, how can I help you?'

'It's this receipt.' I took it out of my purse.

'It is not right?'

'Yes, it is right. It's just ... well, it's the name.' I pointed to Andersen's but he must have thought I meant Ta' Pawlu.

'Ta' Pawlu? It's the name of the garage. Pawlu is the owner.'

'No, it wasn't ...' I stumbled over the words. '... Ta' Pawlu, it was the name below. Andersen's.'

'Andersen's.' He peered at the word. 'Oh, that is what it used to be.'

'Oh.' Before I could ask who Andersen was, the man went on. 'Pawlu, he is Pawlu Andersen. It was his father's garage and when Pawlu took it over he gave it his own name.'

'So Pawlu is Pawlu Andersen.' He must have thought me very dim.

'Yes, that is what I tell you.'

'And his father's name is?'

'Anthony.'

'I see.' Not that I did. 'When will Pawlu be back?'

'This afternoon, I think. He has only gone to Mosta. If you want to come back?'

'Yes. Thank you. I'll do that.'

I walked through the gardens, the Howard Gardens they were called, and spent a long time looking at a beautifully sculpted, poignant war memorial in warm brown stone: crumbling buildings, stricken aircraft, emaciated bodies; people taken to the very edge of human endurance, yet triumphant. The Second World War was the last in a long line of wars that the people of this island had fought over the centuries. If Hitler had read his history books he would have known the Maltese could never be conquered; they had only accepted the British because they rescued them from Napoleon.

For some reason Mdina was less crowded today; there were hardly any tourist groups. I walked the length of the main street and out into Bastion Square. I stood by the wall of the old fortress and gazed out over Malta, at the patchwork of fields, the twisting roads, the clusters of buildings wherever there was a village or a town … and beyond it all, the sea. Not quite in the foreground, just a little way beyond it, I picked out a stone wall and a ring of cypress trees. A man standing beside me was viewing everything through binoculars and telling his wife what he could see. She didn't seem very interested.

'It's all changed,' he said.

'Well, it would have,' she said. 'It's forty years ago. Things do change.'

'Fifty.'

Fifty years ago. The 1940s. I looked at the man. Yes, he was the right age, about seventy-five, possibly eighty.

'Excuse me. Were you here during the Siege?'

'Aye, I was that,' he said. 'Right through it. Came out here in 1940; just in time you might say.'

'He's lucky to be alive,' his wife said.

'Aye, she's right. I lost a lot of my pals here. Left them all behind, too, those you could find enough of to bury. See that, down there ...' He pointed towards the cemetery. 'That's where they are, some of them. There's others in the bigger one at St. Andrews. D'you want to have a look?' He handed me the binoculars.

'Thank you.'

'See that road, that wide one, it's just to the right of that.' I trained the binoculars on the cemetery wall. There was nothing my eyes could see that I couldn't supply from memory. I handed them back.

'You didn't happen to know someone called Anderson ... or it could have been Andersen ... did you?'

'In the war, you mean?'

'Yes.'

'No-o. No, I don't think so. What were he in? You know, what regiment?'

'He was in the Royal Artillery.'

'Oh aye. Anderson, you say? No, doesn't ring a bell. I were in the Manchester's. Eighth Battalion, Manchester Regiment. Grand lot of lads.'

'I'm sure they were.'

'Aye, we had some right old times together. There was one, the time when we ...'

'Eh, the lass doesn't want to hear about all your ...'

'No, please go on, it's very interesting.'

'No, the wife's right, I do go on. This Anderson ... somebody you knew, was it?'

'Yes, he was my … He was a friend of my father. Tom. Tom Harper.'

'Harper. I knew a Harker. Sorry I can't help you, lass. But I'll tell you who can. You go to Valletta … you can go on the bus, it's a nice trip … and you go … well, there's two places you could go. You can go to the War Museum, that's at Fort St. Elmo; it's on the harbour. Or … you could go to the British Legion, they'll find him for you.'

I thanked him, and his wife, and turned away. No war museum could help me to find what I was looking for. I wasn't sure that anybody could. Not anybody here. Not even Pawlu Andersen, unless … unless my father's name *was* Andersen, and Pawlu was a relation. Perhaps, just perhaps, Peter had asked to be posted here because this is where he had some family. A brother, maybe, or a cousin. I would have some lunch and then go back to the garage.

I ate at a restaurant, high on the wall, overlooking the plain. It was shady and cool and the food was good; I had sandwiches and some excellent coffee. I could easily have succumbed to the array of pastries, but I knew I should be sorry if I did. I had only just learned – how long it had taken me! – to stop eating *before* I felt full.

At the garage there was no sign of anybody, no customers, no attendant, and the door of the kiosk was shut. There was a café just across the small road adjoining the garage; perhaps I could wait there, in the window, with a lingering cup of coffee, until someone appeared at the garage. I was about to enter the café when there was a roar of a hotted-up engine, almost at my heels it felt. I turned round sharply. A truly beautiful young man – tall, dark haired, creamy-skinned – leapt athletically from an open sports car.

'Sorry,' he said. He took a bunch of keys from a pocket and walked towards the kiosk.

'Excuse me,' I called. He turned round.

'Yes?'

'Are you Pawlu?'

'Yeah, I'm Pawlu.'

'Pawlu Andersen?'

'Yes.' His tone said, 'What is this?'

'I'm sorry. Let me start again. My name is Jane Thornfield. My father served in Malta during the Second World War ... and I think he may have known someone called Anderson ... I'm not sure it was spelt the same way, though ... and I wondered if he might have been a relative of yours.'

'I'm sorry, I don't quite get what you ...?'

'My father, Tom Harper, was in the Royal Artillery. He was based at Ta' Qali, and he had a friend called Peter Anderson ... which could have been Andersen ... they're both dead of course ... but I just wondered if anyone might have known Tom, or if ... your name being Andersen ... there might be some ... I don't know ... some connection.' I was floundering badly.

'Oh ...' A long sound of comprehension. 'Right. Got you.' I waited; he grinned again. 'It's my grandfather you're talking about.'

'Pardon?'

'My grandfather is the connection, he was in the war.'

'Your grandfather?'

By now there two customers waiting. 'Look, d'you mind, I must open up.' He inserted a key in the lock. 'I'll be with you in a minute.' He attended to his customers – one wanted petrol, the other, in a hire care, was asking for directions – and I stood by the door, trying to make sense of the conversation we had just had. His grandfather? He would be Tom's age, and Peter Andersen's age, if they had lived, that is. A brother! In his seventies, at least. Peter Anderson had a brother in Malta, and this boy ... Pawlu ... was his grandson. This was more than I had dared hope for. So … what relation was he to me? His father would be my … cousin, and he would be my … second cousin. And Alex would be …

'Please, do come in.' His voice broke into my reverie. And brought me down to earth, too. There must be no falling on his neck, claiming kinship, not just yet. For now Tom Harper was still my father.

'Thank you.' I stood just inside the doorway; there was nowhere to sit down.

'So … your father knew my grandfather, yes?'

'Well, no. Not your grandfather, well, not as far as I know.' He looked puzzled.

'But you said …'

'No, my father knew *Peter* Andersen.'

'That is what I said. Peter Andersen was the name of my grandfather.'

'Peter Andersen was your grandfather?'

'Yes!' By now he was looking at me as if I was either very dim or a refugee from a mental institution. 'What is the problem? Like your father, my grandfather was also in the Royal Artillery. You can go and see his grave if you want; it is down there in the cemetery.' My whole body felt cold and my face must have gone very pale.

'Are you all right? Shall I get you some water, or something?'

'No, I'm all right … thank you. It was just rather a shock. I didn't realise …' And I didn't understand either, but what had got through to me was that if the man lying in Imtarfa cemetery was this boy's grandfather then I wasn't the only child that Peter Andersen had fathered. Pawlu was staring at me, waiting.

'What?'

'That he was … dead.' Of course he was dead, I knew he was, but what else could I say?

'He died in the war. He was killed in an air raid.'

'An air raid?'

'Yeah. Well, I think so. I think that's what my grandmother said. Oh ... you were hoping to meet him. Oh, I am sorry. This must be a shock for you. Please, let me get you a drink of water.' The last thing he wanted was a mad Englishwoman passing out on him.

I smiled, as cheerily as I could. 'It's all right, I'm not going to faint. Thank you for talking to me. I mustn't keep you, you've got people waiting.' There was a queue of three cars and a lorry behind them; the lorry driver, already pounding his horn, yelled out of his cab window. I didn't understand the Maltese words, but the meaning was obvious.

Pawlu yelled back at him. To me he said, 'If you would like to meet my grandmother I will take you there. She likes to talk about the war, and about my grandfather. Ten minutes,' – he raised both his hands, the fingers spread – 'and I will be with you.'

'No.' Now my hand was raised, the fingers also spread, but in protest. 'Not today. Please. Look ... I'll ... um ... I'll come back tomorrow ... in the morning.'

'Yes, if you like.' He had offered hospitality and friendship and I was rejecting it; he looked puzzled and hurt. I tried to make amends.

'I'd love to meet your grandmother; it's just that I have to be somewhere else very soon and it wouldn't be fair to her just to say hello and then have to leave straight away.'

It had worked. He smiled, 'You are right; she would not like that. I will tell her that you are coming. Tomorrow morning, at eleven o'clock, yes?' I nodded. 'At eleven o'clock you come here and I will take you to her house.'

'Thank you. You are very kind.'

We said our goodbyes and I left.

It was quite true, I had to be somewhere else. Anywhere but there in that tiny, suddenly claustrophobic, kiosk. Momentous events in my life have never chosen their settings to match.

In the car, with all the windows wound fully down to disperse some of the stifling heat, I recalled Neville's proposal. No roses or wine or music in a moonlit garden, certainly no bending of the knee. We were in a lift in John Lewis in Oxford Street, a lift so crowded that I just hoped that what was digging insistently into my back was a man's parcel and not part of his anatomy: there was no way I could turn round. We had gone there to choose a wedding gift for Neville's cousin and I suppose it had put the idea of marriage into his head. I didn't hear him the first time. 'What did you say?' I said. 'I said, should *we* get married?' 'Oh ... well, yes, if you like.' And that was it. We emerged from the lift on the ground floor, turned to one another ... and laughed. To be fair to Neville he did then say, 'I'll do it all again if you want, with the moon in June and all that jazz.' 'I'd like that,' I said, but we never did.

Thinking about that had helped me through a difficult few minutes. Was this a momentous event? No, not really. This was just the follow-up to the shattering moment when I read those hidden letters. What I had learned today I couldn't really absorb until I could sit down somewhere quietly and think it through. I drove out of Rabat, towards the south coast of the island. A signpost said Dingli, but not how far away it was. It couldn't be far; nowhere in Malta was far. I drove until I was overlooking Dingli Cliffs. I parked the car and switched off the engine. There was no one about; I could hear a distant motor of some kind and there were seabirds, wheeling overhead. The sun was beating down but inside the car it was now cool.

Time to take out the facts and look at them. How did what I had learned affect me? What, in fact, had I learned? Not a lot, just that Peter Andersen – I must try to think of him as Andersen – had married ... a Maltese girl I presumed ... sometime between his visit to England and his death three years later. Well, there was nothing surprising in that. British servicemen did marry Maltese women – one of the girls in the office at *DAMES* had had a Maltese mother and a British army father. So my father had taken a wife and they had had a child, Pawlu's father, whose name was? Anthony, the young man had said. I couldn't think now why I should have been so amazed, and why on earth I had concocted that camouflage about a brother, when the truth was so much simpler. Don't kid yourself, Jane, you know why. A brother for Peter, his son a cousin, is distant enough for you not to be affected. But this way, his son is your brother, Pawlu is your nephew. My nephew. My brother. Oh God ... What do I do now? Tell his ... his widow that I am her husband's bastard. Oh, don't be an idiot! For the time being I am still Tom Harper's daughter, holidaying in Malta and now, through a chance visit to a garage, about to meet someone who might, just possibly, have known Tom during the war. Anything else I would play by ear.

A bizarre thought struck me and I laughed aloud. Did I have other half-brothers, or sisters, in other parts of the world? Hardly likely, as Peter had died at twenty-three. But then there was Tom. Tom, on his own here in Malta, later in Egypt and Italy, so sexually frustrated that his Methodist upbringing – my mother had hinted as much – would have been set aside without too many pricks of conscience. What a lovely title for a story: Pricks of Conscience. I must use it sometime.

I didn't even know her name, Peter's widow. There was so much I wanted to know: how they met, when they married, what he was like. Was he clever, funny, charming, moody, musical, athletic? Was he a rogue or a saint ... no, he wasn't that. Did he love her, were they happy, does she still grieve for him? What did he look like? Would there be photographs? Please God, let there be photographs, even just one.

However I played it, tomorrow was going to be difficult.

CHAPTER SEVEN

I didn't know what to do with myself for the rest of the day. I wasn't tired, I didn't want to sleep. I couldn't read, I didn't want to swim and out on the cliff it would be too hot for walking. I would stroll in the garden, look at the flowers and the shrubs, maybe talk to somebody. That would be nice, to talk about something that didn't matter. Perhaps that lady and her friends would be sitting in the shade somewhere.

They weren't. It was siesta time and, apart from the gardeners in their straw hats and green overalls, no one was about. I talked to one of the gardeners, Michael, he said his name was. He told me how a guest the week before had found a pigeon with a broken wing on his balcony. It had stayed there all night, sheltering from a sudden storm and the next day Michael had taken it to his brother in Mellieha village. Did his brother keep pigeons? No, but his brother's wife made a very good pigeon pie.

'On this island we don't waste anything,' he said. He was not old enough to remember the war, but his father had worked at Ta' Qali when it had been an aerodrome and his uncle Joseph had been a porter at the military hospital at Mtarfa. They had had a lot of stories to tell, stories of privation and suffering, of traumatised soldiers and airmen, of children with diphtheria and typhoid, of near famine and lack of fuel even for lamps; but there were stories of heroism, too. Great acts, and lesser ones that never reached the outside world. Like the story of Michael's father, Emanuel, who, watching the skies for enemy aircraft, had seen a German plane raining down not bombs, but tiny objects that looked like sweets. And sweets they were, poisoned sweets for the children of Malta. Emanuel alerted the other members of his patrol, then quickly, before the starving children could get their hands on them, picked up as many of the *gifts* as he could find.

'How did he know they were poisoned?' I asked.

'He didn't,' said Michael, 'he just didn't trust anything that the Germans did.' Bravely, Emanuel had tasted one of the sweets; it was sugary and delicious, but laced with a deadly poison that gave him stomach cramps within minutes. 'My father survived; he said his belly was too full of petrol fumes – but that's another story – to be troubled by a little dose of arsenic or whatever it was. A child would have died.'

There was no getting away from the Second World War on Malta. It was all-pervading. If it wasn't the war stories of the Maltese people I was hearing, it was British ex-servicemen reliving their glory days.

'That other story …' Michael began, but I cut him short.

'Could you tell me that another day, I've …' He looked offended. 'I want to hear it, I really do, it's just that I've seen someone I need to speak to.'

'Oh. Okay.'

'I'm here for a fortnight; we'll talk again. I'd like to

know what all the plants are.' He smiled; I hoped he knew that I wasn't merely trying to get away.

Or was I? I had done the self-same thing three times already on this holiday … cut off a contact when I needn't have done. Why was I doing it? Because I was too tense? Probably. I knew the signs only too well. 'Go with the flow', is what Beth would say to me, 'forget the schedule, just hang out, man.' She wasn't a hang-out person at all, she just loved the language. 'It's like poetry,' she'd say, 'poetry that hasn't been written yet.'

I smiled back at Michael. 'I'll see you soon,' I said. And then on an impulse. 'Is your uncle Joseph alive?'

'Yes. He is.'

'I'd love to meet him.'

'Oh.' He looked doubtful.

'My father was in the Royal Artillery and I think he was billeted at Mtarfa.'

'Ah. Then yes, my uncle would like to speak to you; he likes to talk about those days.'

But just now I wanted to live in the present for a while. I wanted to be with Ken Pickard; it was him I had glimpsed a few minutes ago, making his way to the indoor pool.

I waved goodbye to Michael and walked down to the pool.

I opened the swing doors and the warm, chlorinated air hit me. It seemed bizarre to be swimming in such an artificial atmosphere, surrounded by plastic foliage, when there was all that natural beauty outside.

Ken was standing by the pool, a big, brightly coloured Snoopy towel draped around his shoulders.

'I should have called for you,' he said. 'How thoughtless of me.'

'You didn't know I was here.'

'I did. I saw your car drive in.'

'So … why didn't you call out to me?'

'The look on your face said "I vant to be alone". Was I right?'

'Yes.' I suddenly wanted to hug him. 'I did want to be alone.' He really did have lovely eyes. 'I don't any more.'

'See you in the bar at seven then.'

'Yes.' He pulled off the towel and put it down on a seat by the pool. He had a very good figure, taut and trim. He turned back; he knew I'd been looking at him.

'I like the towel,' I said.

We had our drink in the bar, we had dinner together, we played scrabble in the lounge, then walked on the terrace of the hotel. Just before we went in he kissed me, on the mouth, gently. One of my heroines would have said, '... but with a promise of passion to come.' I responded, also gently, but with, I hoped, the same promise. We said goodnight and went our separate ways: his room was in a different wing, reached by a different set of lifts.

Although we had talked ten to the dozen all evening he still hadn't revealed why he was in Malta and I hadn't said a word about my visit to Rabat.

It was as if this was a novel I was writing, a novel with a plot so fragile that if I aired it in any way, to anyone, it would get blown away like a dandelion clock. When I am writing a book I never tell anyone what it is about. On one level I am afraid the idea might be ridiculed, or praised insincerely which would be worse, but on a deeper level creating a novel is, for me, like creating a child. It has to come to full term before I show it to the world.

I had that feeling about this story that I was seeking out, here in Malta ... because having met Pawlu, there had to be a story ... and I didn't want it to miscarry. I couldn't even talk about Tom with ease any more. Tom had been there throughout my childhood and my adolescence, and whatever I did and whatever I found during this fortnight in Malta, I had to remain true to him: I couldn't cast him aside just because I now knew he was not my father. Meeting Peter Andersen's widow had nothing to do with my relationship with Tom.

CHAPTER EIGHT

I dressed with care. I wore a plain black skirt with a white blouse and a cotton jacket and a minimum of jewellery. Apart from the fact that my jacket was yellow I dressed as I used to in the days when I did interviews for *DAMES*, unobtrusively and, I hoped, inoffensively. I was, after all, meeting an elderly woman, a woman who, as far as I knew, had never been further than Malta. It was patronising of me I know, but I envisaged her as small, sallow-skinned, white-haired, and dressed totally in black. As a person I knew nothing about her, except that she had married Peter Andersen and borne him a son. She might, of course, have remarried; I hadn't thought to ask about that, or even what her name was.

The great citadel of Mdina, always ahead of me on the road, was now close and the traffic was heavy. Time to stop musing and concentrate on getting into Rabat and finding a place to park. That was easy. I would park at the garage, at Pawlu's place. Pawlu's car was not there, nor was Pawlu. But the other young man was there, and he knew that I was expected.

'You are early,' he said.

'No, I'm not. Pawlu said eleven o'clock and it's just gone.'

'In Malta that is early.' I hated to be kept waiting. To me, eleven o'clock meant eleven o'clock, not five past. He could see I was annoyed. 'He won't be long.' If on time was early how long was not long? It wasn't the young man's fault. I smiled at him. 'It doesn't really matter. Tell me ...' I would use the time positively, '... Pawlu's grandmother, is she ... Mrs. Andersen?'

'That's right, Mrs. Andersen.' So she didn't marry again.

'Is Pawlu her only grandson?' This young man might not even know the family, but it was conversation, and I might learn something.

'Oh no. He has two brothers and two sisters.'

'Oh, quite a big family.'

'For us that is a small family. I have four brothers and three sisters. Excuse me.' A car had drawn up; someone wanted petrol. I watched as the tank was filled. A second car drew up. I had now been waiting ten minutes and was thinking of going across to the café when Pawlu's car roared up the road and swept into the forecourt.

'Oh, you are here,' he called merrily. 'Where is your car?'

'Just here,' I said.

'Okay, you follow me.'

'Oh, I thought ...'

'It is better this way. I will take you to my grandmother, then I have to leave you. I am sorry, I have to go into Valletta. Don't worry, my father is there, he will look after you. I have told him you are coming.'

I got into my car and followed – it would be more correct to say chased after – Pawlu. It was fortunate his car was red; I could spot it ahead, as he wove fearlessly, and recklessly, in and out of the traffic. I hung on as best

I could … out of Rabat the way I'd come in, down the hill to the roundabout by the cemetery, a sharp left turn – he honked and waved his arm to show me where we were going – and we were on the rough bumpy road that I recognised as the way to Mtarfa. We drove past the barracks, slower now, so I was just behind Pawlu, and we were about to pass the hospital when suddenly, in a flurry of dust, he brought his car to a stop. I nearly hit him, I was so taken by surprise. You idiot, I thought. I wanted to rage at him and very nearly did, but he was out of his car and opening my door with a heart-melting smile before I could say a word.

'You drive well,' he said.

'You mean I kept up with you.'

He laughed. 'Yes. Sorry.'

'I have a son like you. Drives like a maniac.'

He grinned. 'Come. I will take you in.' He took my hand and helped me out of the car. I didn't know whether to be flattered or insulted. I decided to be flattered.

'Thank you.' I wished Alex's manners were as good. Perhaps they were, with strange old ladies he met in Canada.

We were outside a terrace of tall stone houses, their front doors right on the street. Pawlu skipped across, up the one step and pressed the buzzer on the inside of the doorway. I stood below. The double doors, each one with a black doorknob, were a dull olive green – no paint could stay shiny with all that dust around – and the wrought iron fanlight above had segments of coloured glass. To the right of the door was a shuttered window and above the doorway was a balcony, also painted olive green. It was one of those closed-in rectangular balconies with windows that were to be seen all over Malta, especially on old buildings.

Impatiently Pawlu pressed the buzzer again. 'They are

upstairs,' he said. 'I have told them to have a bell up there, but they don't.' They? Did Peter's son live with his mother? I would know soon enough. The doors opened and a tall man with grey hair, who looked about my age, stood on the threshold. There was a brief exchange in Maltese and then Pawlu turned to me. 'Father,' he said, 'this is Mrs. Thornfield. Will you take her up to Grandmother? I have to go.' To me, as he walked backwards towards his car, he said, 'This is my father, he will look after you. I'll be seeing you. Ciao!' He was into his car, and off, spinning it round to go back the way he had come, stirring up the dust as he went.

'Pawlu!' his father shouted, stepping into the road. Pawlu's only response was a wave as he sped past.

The man in front of me shook his head. 'Do you have children?'

'Yes. A son. Just like that.'

'Then you know.'

'Oh yes.'

'He's not a bad boy, just ...'

'Young.'

'Yes. Young. I'd give anything to be that age again.' He looked ruefully into the distance, the way Pawlu had gone. It almost seemed as if he had forgotten me.

'I wouldn't.'

He turned back.

'I am sorry. Mrs ... Thornfield.'

'Jane.'

'Jane. Er ... I'm Anthony. Come inside. I will take you up to my mother.'

'Is she not well?'

'I'm sorry?'

'You said *up*. Is she in bed?'

'No, oh no.' He threw back his head and laughed. His eyes when they rested on me again were shining. This man was my brother. Had our father laughed in that way? Had his eyes shone like that?

He ushered me into the front room of the house. 'She lives upstairs,' he said, 'all the rooms are upstairs. Except this one.'

The front door had opened directly onto a dark high-ceilinged room. At least it appeared dark after the bright light outside. I didn't have much time to take anything in. I was being led up a marbled staircase that rose steeply almost immediately inside the front room, keeping against the left hand wall of the house until it could go no further then turning sharply to the right, following the back wall of the room below. Looking over the wrought-iron balustrade on my right I glimpsed an upright sofa with stiff cushions, a round table with a lace cloth and a large leafy plant, a sideboard of some kind, again with a lace cloth on which there were rows and rows of photographs, nearly all of them in silver frames. It reminded me in its style of the 'best' room in Tom's mother's house in Kings Lynn: for show only. Above it all hung a spreading crystal chandelier, which, as I turned the corner of the staircase, was now on a level with my eyes.

Ahead of me now was a landing, with doors, some open, others shut, on either side. Anthony led me across the landing and into a room so different from the one below I could have been in a different house. Where that was dark, this was light, with a huge picture window with Venetian blinds almost filling one wall. The chairs and sofa were modern and comfy; if the chintz wasn't a Sanderson print it was something very similar. I took in a television set and lots of plants, and striped rugs on a polished floor. The room below reinforced my expectations of the stereotypical old Maltese woman dressed from head to foot in black; this room shattered it.

As did the woman who now rose from the sofa and

held out her hand to greet me. 'Mrs. Thornfield, how delightful of you to visit me.' Whatever I had anticipated, it certainly wasn't this: a beautiful, sophisticated woman in a beige linen skirt, sage green blouse and high-heeled shoes, her dark hair drawn back from a face which was immaculately and subtly made up. I suppose at heart I was expecting to find a homely woman, someone like my own mother. This was the lawful wife, my mother was the Jezebel: it didn't fit.

Somehow I found my voice. 'Mrs. Andersen.' I stretched out my hand and took hers. She had beautifully polished nails. 'It's very kind of you to see me.'

'Not at all. It's my pleasure. Do sit down.' I backed myself into a chair. 'Now what would you like to drink? Some tea? Or perhaps a glass of chilled wine?'

It was a bit early for wine, but she had offered it, so...

'A glass of wine would be lovely. Thank you.'

She looked up at her son, who without a word went off to do her bidding. She was the matriarch, there was no doubt of that. And, if I was not mistaken, a very shrewd lady, too. I would have to be careful.

'So,' she said, settling herself back on the sofa cushions, 'your father knew my husband?'

'Yes. He did.' As dispassionately as I could I relayed the circumstances of their meeting, here in Malta, as far as I could ascertain. I didn't think they'd met before that, I said; then the visit to my parents' home just before the war, when they were both on leave. My grandmother was dying I told her, but I wasn't sure what had brought her husband to England, and my mother couldn't remember.

Don't start lying Jane, it can only cause problems.

'Oh, Peter went to attend his sister's funeral.' So Kitty's diary was right. 'His twin sister, Amy.' A *twin* sister!

'It was very sad. Poor Peter. I don't know how much

you know about him?'

'Nothing really, other than what I've told you. I just know that your husband and my ... father were in the Royal Artillery together, and were friends.'

'Oh, I wouldn't say that they were friends particularly. I can't actually remember anyone called Harper. Still, who's to say? It's all a very long time ago and there were so many young men and ... well, to be quite frank with you, my dear, my memory's not what it used to be. He may well have been a friend. Anthony ...' Anthony had just come in with the wine, white wine in tall clear glasses with green stems. 'Bring those old photo albums, will you, dear. Perhaps we can find a picture of Mrs. Thornfield's father in one of them.'

'The photo albums? Up here?'

'Yes, dear. And the envelopes with them.'

'Of course, if it's what you want,' he said, leaving the room.

'And bring our wedding pictures, too,' she called after him.

My stomach felt knotted; I hoped I wasn't going to be sick. This was all moving too fast. Wedding pictures, a twin sister. I took the wine and gulped it down.

'Are you all right?'

'Yes, of course. Just ... thirsty.' How embarrassing. 'You were telling me about your husband's sister.'

'Yes, Amy. She was only twenty. I'm not quite sure what she died of. I think it was tuberculosis, but her parents never said, and they never told him.'

It could have been the wine, drinking it so fast. All the same ... 'Her parents? But ...'

'I'm sorry. I should have said her foster-parents. Yes, I can see you're confused. Let me begin at the beginning.' Yes please, do that, because right now I'm feeling very confused. And don't miss out anything because I want to know, I need to know, absolutely everything.

Mrs. Andersen sipped her wine, delicately, as if to show me how it should be drunk, then placed the glass on a china coaster on the small polished table in front of her.

'Peter was an orphan; he and his sister were put ... into care is the phrase we use now, I don't know if it was then. Anyway, they were both in a home in Southport, until ... oh, I think they must have been about six, and then Amy was fostered. By a very nice family, somewhere in the north of London I think. Oh, you don't want to hear all this, you want to talk about your father.' She picked up her glass.

'Oh but I do!' Curb the enthusiasm, Jane. 'It's most interesting.'

'You're very kind. And I will tell you, because I like to talk about it. When you reach my age, it's the past that's real. Not today.' A shadow of sadness flickered over her face, then she brightened, forcibly. How old was she? In her seventies, probably. She was remarkably well-preserved; women in hot countries rarely had such good skin at this age.

'Well ... Pietru ... it's what I called him ... Peter was left at the orphanage and Amy was fostered and ... well, they lost touch with one another. It wasn't until he came to Malta, and met my large family that he tried to find her. And when he did, they, he and Amy, wrote to one another constantly. So, when she died ... he went to the funeral. It was very sad that he wasn't able to see her when she was alive.'

'Yes, very.' Well, there wasn't much there. Or was there? 'Your husband's parents had died, I presume, when he was a baby?'

'Yes. Well, his mother ... the children were only two years old when she died. She was from Denmark.'

'Denmark?'

'Yes.' Her look said, 'What's so strange about that?'

'How interesting,' I said. 'And his father?'

'He never knew who his father was. Peter was … illegitimate. It is nothing now, I know, but then it was shameful; he didn't like to speak about it. My father was never told; he might not have allowed me to marry him. It was bad enough that he did not have my religion.'

Illegitimate, and half-Danish, but it said nothing about the man himself. Perhaps if we talked about the war.

'So, during the war, did you live here?'

'Oh no, we lived in Rabat.'

'Near the Howard Gardens.' Anthony entered the room, his arms filled with photo albums. 'I didn't know which ones you wanted, so I brought the lot,' he said. He dumped them down on the sofa; one slid on to the floor. His mother reprimanded him in Maltese.

'Sorry, Mama.' He picked the album up and put it on the table.

'You should have put them all on there.' He began to move the pile from the sofa. His mother put out a hand to restrain him. Again she spoke to him in Maltese and he left the albums where they were. She turned to me. 'My family is very big, so we have many photographs.'

'Indeed. How many are there, in your family?'

'Oh! How many? Well, there is … let me see.' She began to count on her fingers. 'I have one, two, three, four brothers; I did have two sisters, but … they both died. The boys all have families and I have all the photographs!'

'How lovely.' Just show me a picture of your husband, please, that's all I really want to see.

'I will show you.' She rummaged among the pile and drew out a large Manila envelope. 'Somewhere in here is a picture of all of us together. I also have it hanging up downstairs,' she said, proudly. 'It was taken in Valletta, in a studio, just before the war. I remember the day very well. My youngest brother, Emanuel, had just been born and my father said we should have a photograph taken together, all of us. Here it is.' She put it on the table in front of her. 'Come. Look.' She beckoned to me with her fingers and I leant forward. The black and white photo showed a family group carefully arranged according to height, with the exception of the baby on its mother's lap. 'See, there is my father and my mother, and Emanuel, and there is me; I am the oldest. I was eighteen. Then there's Francis, he was fifteen. That's Wenzu, he lives in America; he was thirteen. Then there's Carmelita; she was ten.' So many names: I would never remember them. 'Next there's Teo. It was because of Teo that I met my husband.' She looked up. A show of interest was required, and I could offer it, readily.

'Oh! How ... how was that?'

'Oh, Mama, Mrs. Thornfield won't want to hear about that.'

'No, please, do tell me. I'd love to hear about it.'

Mrs. Andersen's look to her son said, 'You see.' She turned to me. 'I was seventeen and Teo was six. My mother was soon to have Emanuel and she was feeling tired and needed to rest. Teo had not been well and was having a few days off school, so it was my duty as the eldest girl, to look after him, and my baby sister, Gewza; she was two. That is Gewza, next to Teo.' She was a chubby, rather blank-looking – Down's Syndrome? – child. 'She had problems; she died young.'

'Oh, I'm sorry.'

'Thank you.' She paused. 'Anyway, as I was saying ... I was looking after Teo and Gewza and I took them into the public gardens near our house. Teo wanted to play football ... he had his football with him ... but I could not play with him because of Gewza. She was in a pram, and because of her ... her weakness, she could not sit up for very long; she kept slipping down, and I had to keep propping her up, so when a young soldier appeared and asked if Teo would like to play football with him … well, I knew God was watching over me. The soldier was, of course, Peter. Not only did he play football with Teo, he talked to me as well. He was very handsome.' In the face of the now elderly woman I could see the young girl who was charmed by the good-looking soldier. Just as my mother had been. 'That's my husband, next to me.' She laid a finger gently, caressingly almost, on the tall, slim figure in uniform.

'Oh. But …?' But this picture, she had said, was taken before the war. So when Peter Andersen made love to my mother … he was already part of this family. The knot in my stomach tightened.

'My father felt it would be right to include him in the family group, as he was now a son-in-law. Once Peter accepted our faith my father was happy to accept *him*.'

My head was spinning; I knew that I should either faint or be sick if I didn't get out of that room. I stood up, abruptly.

'I'm sorry, I must go. I don't feel very well, I need to get out in the air.' Anthony and his mother got to their feet, fussing round me, offering me a bed to rest on, tablets to take, even a doctor. That was the last thing I wanted.

'It must have been the wine.'

'There is nothing wrong with the wine.' Her eyes had lost their concern. I could see she didn't believe me.

'It was too early in the day.' I grasped her hand. 'I'm so sorry.' I almost fled down the stairs. I was aware of Anthony following me, then overtaking me, opening the front door to let me through.

'I'm so sorry,' I said again. 'I shouldn't have come.'

'Why did you come?'

'I can't … I can't tell you. I'm sorry. Goodbye.'

Somehow I got to the car, started it and drove away. Anthony stood by the door, watching me. I couldn't see his expression for the dust kicked up by the wheels, but I could imagine it. Puzzled, to say the least.

I drove for maybe a mile, not seeing where I was going except to know that it was a narrow road with rubble walls on either side. Suddenly the road widened and there was a place where I could pull in. I switched off the engine and sat, hunched over the steering wheel. The knot in my stomach had gone, but I was still shaking. After a moment I sat up and leaned back against the seat. Around me there was peace, but inside I was in turmoil.

Why had I ever started on this foolish quest? What did it matter who my father was, and if he was a married man when I was conceived, so what? It made no difference to the person I was. You've either got to face facts, Jane, and be prepared for revelations of the kind you've just heard, or forget the whole thing. You've seen the grave, now you've met the wife. That's it. These people, Anthony and his mother, have nothing whatever to do with your life, the life you live now. Go back to the hotel, go to bed with Ken, enjoy yourself.

I had no idea where the road I was on was leading to. I could turn round and go back the way I had come, but that would mean going past that house again. I would go on; I was bound to come to a crossroads sometime. Crossroads. I always seemed to be at a crossroads these days. Maybe I should speak to Anthony, tell him why I left in such a hurry. Oughtn't he to know he had a sister? He might be pleased. Besides, I did want to know more. I wanted to look at that photograph again as well; at other photos, too. To go away from Malta knowing nothing more about my father than the fact that he was a bit of a rogue – which didn't, on reflection, displease me – would be a waste.

I would drive past the house, note the number, then write to Anthony and arrange to meet him. Not there, but somewhere neutral. At the hotel perhaps. I would also write to his mother and apologise for leaving so peremptorily. I might even suggest visiting her again. This time, if she agreed, I would turn up with flowers ... and a stronger stomach.

Having reasoned things out and settled on a plan of action I felt better. It was the way I'd coped with stress all my life and it usually worked. Even if, in the end, I never did the things I planned, the planning helped me over the difficult bit, the initial shock. I would still go to bed with Ken. It would be therapeutic.

CHAPTER NINE

It was, very.

We had had drinks in the bar, dinner, coffee in the lounge.

'More coffee?' he said.

'No. Thank you.'

'So ... what shall we do now?'

'Well, we could ...'

'Yes, let's do that,' he said.

I picked up my handbag, he left a tip for the waiter and we went upstairs.

Now, as we lay side by side on the single bed, I needed to talk.

'Ken ...'

'Mmm?' He turned towards me.

'No.' I moved his hand away. 'I want to talk to you.'

'We can talk and ...'

'No, we can't. You may be able to, but I can't. It won't take long,' I said more softly.

'I'll give you five minutes, not a moment longer.' He folded his arms. 'Right, I'm listening.'

I took a deep breath. 'It's …' Oh, why prevaricate? 'Look …'

He raised his head. 'I'm looking.'

'I don't mean look, I mean listen!'

'Yes, ma'am.' He shut his eyes tight, like a little boy, then peeped out of the left one. 'Will this do?'

'Fool! No, seriously …'

'Folks.'

'What?'

'Nothing; forget it. Go on. Talk.' He kept his eyes open, but he was looking at the ceiling.

Perhaps this wasn't the right time, perhaps I shouldn't say anything anyway.

'I'm listening.'

'I'm not here to write a book.'

'Oh.' He kept his eyes on the ceiling.

'I'm here to research my past.'

'Your past?' He sat up with a jerk. 'Oh my God, what have I got myself into!'

'Don't mock. I don't mean my past in that way.'

'Oh, you disappoint me.' He lay down again.

'Ken, will you listen? This is important.'

'Sorry.'

'I need to find out something about my family. My father was here during the war and he was … he was buried here. I've been to the grave and … well, there's something I need to know about … about that time. I have to … meet people … and talk and …'

'And you don't want me hanging around?'

'Well …' I didn't, so why pretend. 'D'you mind?'

'Of course not.'

'I don't think I can even tell you about it.'

He sat up and began to pull me towards him. 'You don't have to tell me anything. You didn't even have to tell me this much. And now that you have it makes no difference. You go out during the day, do what you have to do, just as if you were doing research for your book … and then, in the evening, I shall demand your undivided attention.'

'I shall be happy to give it.'

He went back to his own room to sleep. I took a shower and sat on the balcony. The only sound was the gentle, muted lapping of the waves. The sparrows were asleep, even the traffic had paused. Across the bay Mellieha village was a dim, dark shape; here all the balcony lights were switched off. I sat on, in the darkness. I was in a strange state of limbo, not happy, not sad, not troubled either, not really thinking about anything, just there, just being. In a way, cleansed, renewed. Tomorrow I would do all the things I had to do. Now … I would sleep.

I didn't see Ken at breakfast. I was glad, not that I would have been embarrassed in any way; it was just easier, less complicated. I wouldn't have wanted to shun him, but at the same time I didn't fancy any fond farewells as I set off in the car. Nor did I want a man checking that my tyres were okay or that I had enough petrol. Ken might not do that, of course, he might not be that sort of man; and then if he wasn't that wouldn't please me either. It was best he wasn't here. To meet him for dinner, walk with him by the sea, go to bed with him again … that was all I wanted.

Before breakfast I had written to Anthony, and also to his mother, a note of apology. I hadn't, in the end, suggested meeting Anthony. In print the idea looked too pushy and I couldn't find the right words to make it sound casual and at the same time important; I wasn't able to write the correct tone of voice. I settled for a polite, and, I hoped, friendly letter which gave him an opening to contact me if he wished. I bought stamps at the hotel shop and posted the letters in the foyer. With luck – I had no idea how efficient the Maltese postal service was – they would be delivered the next day, Wednesday. I might, or I might not, receive a reply, but until Anthony got in touch with me – I was certain his mother would not – I could learn nothing more about my father.

In the meantime ... I needed to keep occupied. I would become a simple tourist and see all I could of the island. I put the maps and the guide books on the passenger seat, adjusted the mirror and started the car. Today I *would* go to Mosta, and then perhaps drive on to Valletta, go round the harbour on a boat, visit a museum or a market.

The car was parked at right angles to the hotel entrance. I reversed out of the parking space, swinging the car round with its boot facing the hotel. In my rear mirror I saw Ken. Damn. Just what I had not wanted. Not that he would have seen me seeing him, although he would have recognised the car. I drove forward ... and stopped. I wound down the window and stuck my head out. He waved and approached the car.

'I'm going to Mosta,' I said. I paused. 'Do you want to come?'

'Ooh, yes please. Any time.'

'Mosta, I said. Are you interested?'

'Good idea.'

'Right. Get in.'

'Yes, ma'am. Whatever you say, ma'am.'

'I'm sorry, that was very ...'

'Peremptory.'

'Yes.'

'Don't worry, I like forceful women. Give me five minutes and I'll be with you.'

We drove to Mosta; I drove, he navigated and that made things much easier because all I had to do was concentrate on the road itself and the other drivers. We didn't talk, there seemed no need. In Mosta we parked the car and visited the cathedral. We admired the art and the architecture and saw the place where the bomb had entered. We marvelled at the miracle and came out into the sunshine. We stood on the steps.

'Are you religious?' Ken asked.

'No, not particularly. Are you?'

'No. But if I'd lived through that, been in there that day, I think I … well, I'd certainly have believed in something.'

'Faulty German armaments,' I said.

'Cynic.'

'Not at all. Divine intervention led the bomb-loader, or whoever, to load a dud bomb.'

'It wasn't a dud.'

'So perhaps there is a God. Oh, I don't know. There were other miracles on this island you know, in the war, not just that one.' I told him about the poisoned sweets.

'That wasn't a miracle, that was just somebody showing common sense. Look, are we going to stand here all day arguing …?'

'We're not arguing, we're talking.'

'… or shall we go and have some lunch?'

'We'll have some lunch.'

We drove north through Naxxar, where many British servicemen and their wives were billeted during the war – would my mother have lived there if she had come to Malta? – and on through Gharghur, then, having got lost several times, we hit the coast road east of White Rocks, where the sea crashes against the rocks, making them white. We found an unpretentious café and had an unpretentious lunch. But the coffee was hot.

'Siesta?' said Ken.

'Maybe.'

'You could sound more enthusiastic.'

'About sleeping in the middle of the afternoon? And don't say "It depends what you mean by sleeping".'

His voice was haughty. 'Do I take it that madam was less than pleased with last night's performance?'

'Idiot! I just … I think I need to be on my own for a bit, that's all.'

'Fine. No problem. Anyway, we wouldn't want a chambermaid barging in, would we?'

'No, we wouldn't.' It was silly, I know, but although I had given of myself freely to Ken the night before, not just given but taken … and delighted in it, too … I didn't want to talk about it. It wasn't that I was embarrassed about anything I had done, but talking about the sex we had had together gave it an importance it didn't deserve. Unlike it had been with Neville. Right from the beginning we'd talked about it afterwards; probably that was one reason it was so good. We both knew what the other liked, because we discussed our needs, openly. Words were too important, too special, for what Ken and I had enjoyed. And I didn't like his 'nudge nudge' attitude either; it made me feel sleazy, and last night hadn't been sleazy. And I wanted to do it again as well – there was no denying the stirrings I felt – so I didn't want it spoilt by a quick grappling to the accompaniment of a hoover and the chambermaids' chatter in the corridor. I smiled at him. 'Save it for tonight.'

'You're on.'

'Actually … I've changed my mind.'

'Oh, but you just said …'

'Not about tonight. Now. I'd like to see Valletta. Let's go round the harbour on a boat. If it gets boring we can sleep. You can put your head on my shoulder if you want.'

'There are words for women like you.'

'I know, but don't say them. Time and place for everything, that's my motto.' I fluttered my eyelids at him. 'I'll make it up to you, don't worry.' It was very silly, this teenage-type banter; it wasn't really me, either.

Replaying it in my head it made me cringe. This wasn't why I had come to Malta, to flirt like a schoolgirl with a middle-aged stranger. Get a hold of yourself, Jane.

The harbour exceeded expectations. Sleep? There was too much to see – the huge fortifications and the myriad collection of ships from all over the world – and too much to wonder at. Amid all the suffering of the war years there had been moments of great exhilaration, as when, for instance, a flotilla of Italian E-boats, the elite of their Navy, were sunk in the early hours of July 26th 1941; and so much relief and joy later, particularly in 1942, when the convoys, against great odds, brought desperately needed food and fuel into the harbour. As I listened to the commentary my heart went out to the people of Malta.

'They were so brave, so brave.'

'My God, you're crying!'

'Sorry.' I sniffed and reached for a tissue. Ken got there first with a folded, white handkerchief.

'Is it … is it to do with your father?'

'No, it's … Well, yes, it is … in a way. It's … I don't know why, but this place moves me in a way that no other place I've ever been to …'

'What, Valletta Harbour?'

'No. *Malta*. It's … small and brave and beautiful and dirty and brash and proud and ancient and tatty and …'

'Enough. I get the picture: you're besotted.'

'I think I must be. But I don't know why.' I looked him straight in the face; no tears now. 'And that troubles me, Ken.'

'Why?'

'Because it means I'm not in control.'

'And up to now you always have been.'

'Yes.'

'But you still can't tell me what it's all about?'

'I could, but … No, not yet.' I lifted my hand to his

cheek. 'I shouldn't have brought you out with me today. I'm not very good company at the moment. There's too much going on in my head. I thought I could be a tourist for a couple of days; I can't. I have to sort something out, one way or the other. Sorry …'

'Can you do it before Friday, do you think?'

'Friday?'

'I'm going home on Friday.'

'I think it'll take longer than that.'

'So, that's the end of that then, isn't it?'

I looked away across the harbour entrance, to where, in the war, a chain had lain under the water, ready to trap any enemy submarines that dared to enter. I could see the parallel only too clearly. This was no way to conduct an affair, even a casual holiday affair, shutting the man out. All right if you've said nothing in the first place, never hinting at things below the surface that were troubling you, but to say you had things on your mind and then not talk about them, that wasn't being fair.

'I'm not here just for your therapy, Jane.'

'I know.' I still wasn't looking at him.

'Look at me.' I turned to him. 'I did think, last night, that, maybe … we could …'

'No.' I shook my head more violently than I intended. 'What I mean is …'

'You've said it: no. All right, I accept that. But don't play with me, I'm too old for that. And so are you.'

I wanted to say: you haven't told me why you are here. Haven't you got some hidden agenda, too?

'I do this, Ken. I spoil things. I never get things quite right. You should have realised that when you saw me that first night … in that ridiculous outfit.'

I looked out again across the harbour. Our guide was showing us the houses where the 'ladies of easy virtue' had 'plied their trade' during the war. 'They were sometimes referred to as comforters,' the man said. As a child I remembered my mother and Kitty knitting comforters, a kind of scarf, for servicemen, and wondering, at four years old, why the name amused them so much.

The other passengers, mainly men and women who had lived through the war years, appreciated the joke.

'Do you want to tell me?'

'Tell you what?' I must have sounded brusque.

'Forget it. I just thought I might be of some help, that's all. You obviously need to talk to someone.'

'I do.'

'Well then.'

'I'm not shutting you out, Ken. I just don't know whether what is happening … what I'm looking into … is something which is going to change my life, or … or something which, in the end, won't really matter at all.' Does it matter who your father is? Does it matter if your mother has deceived you? We live by lies, we need them: telling a lie can be kind, considerate, easier. 'I have a friend whose uncle once joined a group called the M.R.A.' I said.

'I've heard of it, I think.'

'The M is for moral and the R is for re-armament and I presume the A was for association. Anyway, he went to their centre in Switzerland, where he became converted to absolute truth – that's their watchword, the whole truth and nothing but – and when he came home he started putting this into practice. Some of the truths he revealed were hilarious, like confessing to a cousin that he'd peed in the wash-basin rather than go across the landing to the loo … but he also hurt people, close friends, one in particular, by telling her that he'd always been bored in her company and only visited her out of a sense of duty and moreover he never liked the presents she gave him even though he'd always said he did.'

'My God, he must have been popular! And this has

something to do with you?'

'Not directly, no. But yet in a way, it does. You see … I'm trying to decide whether or not I need to know the whole truth …'

The boat had stopped. The guide was showing us the spot where in August 1942, the tanker Ohio, part of the celebrated Pedestal convoy, had finally docked, after limping into harbour supported by two destroyers. 'For us on Malta, it was one of the most significant moments of the war,' he said. 'Another two weeks, without supplies, and we would have had to surrender.' I was glad to see the German tourists on board looking suitably abashed. Quite suddenly I hated them: they had killed my father. It was a thought I'd never had until that moment. What if he had lived? Would he have come for me? Would my parents have divorced?

'That must have been quite something, seeing that tanker arriving. Jane?'

'Yes, it must.' Had Peter's widow stood and cheered, with Anthony in her arms?

'The whole truth, you said. About something in your past, is that what you mean?'

'Yes.' Should I stop now, or go on? 'And this is what is troubling me … and it's why I'm being such a bitch to you …'

He shook his head. 'You're not.'

'Yes I am; I know I am.'

The boat had started off again and the German tourists had relaxed. Good for them, they hadn't lost a father. Or maybe they had? Perhaps that's why they were here.

'And what is troubling me is … I know, the rational part of me knows … that I should stop. But I also know that I won't, that I shall go on ferreting away, like a good journalist, because I sense a good story here and it's my story and I have a right to know it. So, now you know.'

'Except that I don't. I haven't the faintest idea what

you are talking about it.' Here was my chance to tell him. I would like to have confided in Ken – I know he would have been sympathetic – but having said nothing at all to Neville, or Beth, or, most of all, my mother, I couldn't. 'Well, whatever it is, it's undoubtedly of immense importance to you, so the sooner you get on with it the better. Because, my dear ...' He took my face in his hands. '... as you are, you're no use to anybody. And that includes yourself.'

Ken was right. Having tried being just a tourist, and failed, I might as well get on with finding out what I could about my father. If it was good so be it; if it was bad ... well so be it, too. By the time we got back to the hotel I had decided to phone Anthony.

CHAPTER TEN

At the reception desk, I asked for a local telephone directory. Ken stood by my side.

'Shall I leave you?'

'Please.' What a nice man he was. In other circumstances …

'Will I see you at dinner?'

'Yes, of course. If you want to, that is.'

'Well … I don't know that I do.' He sighed. 'But we can't very well avoid one another, can we?' Oh dear, I have hurt him.

'I don't want to avoid you, Ken. I want to have dinner with you.' And I want to make love to you as well. I want to kiss away the hurt and make you care for me again. I need to stop wanting Neville. 'No histrionics, I promise.'

He smiled. He'd made his point and it had obviously gone home. 'See you in the bar at seven, then.'

'Yes. Seven. I'll be there. Oh, thank you.' The young man behind the desk had given me the directory. I turned to speak to Ken, but he had already moved away across the marble floor of the foyer. I turned back to the desk and opened the phone book.

There were three Andersens, Andersen A.J. – Anthony? Andersen P, and Andersen, Mrs. R. No doubt that was his mother's number. Should I phone her, too? No. Not yet anyway. I wanted to talk to her again; no one else would be able to tell me all I wanted to know about Peter Andersen, but I would have to use Anthony as an intermediary. I made a note of Anthony's number, closed the phone book and went up to my room to make the call.

I rehearsed what I wanted to say, in the event that he answered; in the event that a woman – his wife? – answered. I dialled the number; after two rings a man's voice said something in Maltese. Stupidly I hadn't allowed for that; for a moment it put me off. Of course he wouldn't answer in English; although he spoke it perfectly it was after all his second language.

'Anthony? Is that Anthony Andersen?'

'Yes. Who is that?'

'It's Jane Thornfield.'

A fractional pause.

'Oh. H ... hello.'

'Listen ... I've ...' Away went the prepared speech. 'Could we meet, do you think? I need to talk to you.' I suppose it was really better to get straight to the point. Then I realised he wouldn't have got my letter. Once again, I was doing it wrong. 'I'm ever so sorry about yesterday. I have written, both to you and to your mother. Do please apologise to her for me. It was very rude ... and I'm very sorry.'

'Why do you want to see me?'

'I'd rather not say ... on the phone.'

'Can't you give me some idea of ...?'

'No, I can't. Please, Anthony ... I really do need to see you.' I could hear him sighing.

'Well … all right then.' He'd better humour this crazy woman. 'Where do you want to meet?'

'How about that Swiss restaurant in Rabat?'

'I'd rather not.' Too near to home to be seen with a strange woman. 'Why not your hotel?'

Yes, why not. What did it matter if Ken saw him. Anthony agreed to meet me in the foyer at 11.30 the following morning. I put down the receiver … and started to shake. There was no going back now.

Ken and I had dinner together, then coffee in the lounge, where, mercifully, we talked to other people, a couple from Leeds who'd been coming here for fifteen years. He'd been stationed here in the RAF in the Fifties and loved it; unlike his ex-wife who couldn't wait to get back to England. His second wife, Nora, who was with him now, was a different sort, adventurous, liked foreign places 'so long as they're not too foreign, if you know what I mean'. Nora had taken a shine to Malta first off, so now they came here every year, wouldn't miss. Loved the hotel, very comfy, tea in the afternoon and all that. Good food, the breakfast, well, you couldn't beat it. And the bacon. (He was in the meat trade.) Best bacon he'd ever tasted. 'Comes from Comino, you know. That tiny island in between Malta and Gozo. Specially bred those pigs.' And we sat, murmuring appreciatively as he recounted in detail the whole history of pig farming on Malta – which was, in fact, very interesting – while Nora sat and beamed; she did love her Ron.

I had hoped to learn more about Ken; perhaps he would open up more to a third person, but no; he didn't get a chance really, what with Ron and Nora's kids from two marriages, all doing wonderfully all over the world, and Ron's opinion of British farming and his reminiscences of Malta in the Fifties. 'Still got some of the cars, you know. And the buses. Never wear out, they will. Made to last.'

It was gone eleven when we parted. Ken and I said goodnight in the foyer. I had told him I was meeting someone in the morning. 'Someone who can help me with my research, but perhaps we could have dinner together?'

'Yes, of course. No problem. I'll see you in the bar as usual. Goodnight.'

'Goodnight, Ken.' I watched him walking to the lift, hoping he'd turn and smile, or wave. Or beckon? He stood, chatting, in a small group waiting for the lift. Our friends from Leeds were among them. I made my way to the lifts that served my part of the hotel, down the corridor past the games room and the video room; *The Sound of Music* had just finished and the sparse audience, mainly women, was turning out.

'Good evening.' It was the lady from the plane.

'Oh, good evening.'

'Enjoying your holiday?'

'Yes, thank you. And you?'

'Oh yes. We always do.' It was like one big happy family. I walked on, thinking of tomorrow. A woman on her own entertaining a strange man, and a Maltese at that. It would be all over the hotel in no time. Perhaps I should have arranged to meet him somewhere else. Oh, let them think what them want; what does it matter.

By the time I reached my room I was thoroughly depressed. I looked in the mini-bar but there was nothing I fancied. I phoned Reception: could I have a half-bottle of red wine sent up to my room? Of course, madam. I stood on the balcony and looked across the bay. What a romantic setting it was. I knew what an Ellen Field heroine would have done; she would have called her man on the phone, said, 'Hi, I've a bottle of wine coming up, come over and join me' or maybe, 'How about helping me drink it?' No, she wouldn't, you fool, not the nineteenth century women you write about. It's time I had a really sexy, feisty modern heroine, someone onto whom I could unload all my own angst.

The wine came; I drank it and went to bed. I dreamt that Ken and Nora were riding prize pigs along a headland, urging them on with what looked like birch twigs. Then Ron appeared in a white coat, with a stethoscope in his pocket. He looked very angry. When Nora saw him coming she leapt off her pig and began singing to it. Ron pulled Ken off his pig and whacked him with the birch twig. Ken began to bleed and I couldn't stop the blood. It was everywhere, all over the floor, all over the bed – we were in a room somewhere – and it was wet and sticky … and cold.

I woke up and found that I'd gone to sleep with a half-filled glass of wine in my hand; it had spilt over the pillow and over me. I got up and sat on the balcony. My oblivion had been short-lived. Wide-awake, I thought back to the conversation I had had with Anthony's mother. What was it she had said that had troubled me so much that I had fled? There wasn't anything, not really. Then why had I been so disturbed? I had known who she was before we met, so there was no shock there. What was it? Something was niggling at the back of my mind. I replayed the whole visit: the house, the room, the greeting, the wine, the photographs. Yes. The photographs. The photo of all of them together … and Peter there as well. Now, what had she said? Something about the war … They had been married … before the war. When, before the war? A year before; he would have been nineteen; two years before? No. I had been conceived in the summer of 1939. Was he married then? Perhaps Tom didn't know that. The war had begun in September. Oh, I couldn't work it out; I would have to sort it out with Anthony tomorrow. Today: it was four a.m.

I went into the room and lay down. It was some while

before I got back to sleep. They say that just thinking about sex can induce sleep, something to do with endorphins I think. Tomorrow night I would aim for the real thing. The substitute must have helped, because the next thing I knew it was Wednesday and the sun was high in the sky. It was gone ten and I had missed breakfast. And, oh my God! Anthony would be here in just over an hour.

I showered and dressed: full cotton skirt with red, yellow and white flowers, a white T-shirt and a fawn cardigan that picked up the flecks of fawn in the skirt; white sandals, small gold earrings. An ordinary Englishwoman on holiday. Relaxed, friendly, self-assured. I felt anything but.

As I dressed I tried once again – I had tried in the night, but without success – to decide how I would approach the subject of our relationship, Anthony's and mine. Should I plunge straight in and tell him? No, that wouldn't be fair. I ought to prepare him, gently. Talk about Tom, and my mother, and Tom's leave in '39 and how loveless my parents' marriage was, and the letters I had found ... Yes, I would start with the letters. I would show him the photocopies I had brought with me; they were proof of the link between his father and my mother. Could I do that ... let a complete stranger see the letters my mother had kept hidden for over fifty years? No, I couldn't. I would just have to see how it went, judge how receptive Anthony was, and act accordingly. I scribbled a note of apology and explanation for the chambermaid and left it on the wine-soaked pillow-case.

In the foyer bar I had a coffee and a croissant. The hotel seemed deserted apart from an elderly couple reading their newspapers at a nearby table and a small child tinkling on the piano in the lounge. The hotel shop was shut, the tour couriers were out with their charges, there was only one clerk at the desk. It was the quietest, slackest time in the day. In half an hour the less adventurous guests, those walking in the grounds or soaking up the sun by one of the pools, would be coming in for morning coffee – the cups were already laid out on the bar – and the place would be buzzing again.

I finished my late breakfast and walked out on to the terrace. The sun was sparkling on the water of the pool below and I had to shield my eyes. It looked inviting but it was probably quite cold; it was after all November, and the water wasn't heated. Out on the bay two boats with their colourful sails, one blue and white, the other yellow, were dipping and swaying gracefully in the breeze. It would be another forty minutes before Anthony arrived, if he was on time, unlike his son. I couldn't just stand here for forty minutes. I would go for a walk. No, I might meet Ken. Where was Ken anyway? Probably out on a day trip somewhere; I fervently hoped he was. I would go up to my room and get a book, and a note-pad. A note-pad was a good idea, in case I wanted to write down anything of importance. The journalist in me wanted to record our conversation, so that afterwards I would know exactly what had been said. I couldn't do that; this wasn't an interview and I couldn't run a tape clandestinely, the machine I had with me wasn't that sensitive. A book, and a note-pad in my bag: that would have to do. I went up to my room, tidied my hair, had a pee – I was feeling very, very nervous – collected my things and came down to the lounge.

It was ten past eleven. I sat down near the entrance, facing the reception desk, and opened my book, Alison Lurie's *Foreign Affairs* – the perfect traveller's book – and read the same paragraph half a dozen times without one word of it making sense. I shut the book and took out my note-pad: I would make a list of questions I wanted to ask. I had a moment of panic: why hadn't I done this earlier? Oh my God, what should I ask him? I wrote: How old are you? Where was your father killed? Do you have brothers and sisters? I tore off the page and screwed it up. I didn't need to ask that sort of question; those answers would surely come, when he knew who I was. A waiter walked past with a tray of cups and glasses.

'Excuse me.'

'Yes, madam?'

'I'm expecting a visitor. When he comes could you bring us some coffee?' I wasn't going to risk wine again.

'Certainly, madam.'

'And put it on my bill, please. Room 704.' It would break the ice, give us something to do with our hands. I opened my book, re-read the paragraph, looked up … and he was there, asking for me. I closed the book and put it down. 'I'm here,' I called. He turned to face me. His dress was formal: a light grey suit, a white shirt, a subdued tie. He walked towards me. I got up, held out my hand. 'Anthony. Thank you for coming.'

He shook my hand. 'Mrs. Thornfield.' He didn't smile.

'Oh, Jane, please.' Still no smile; this had been a mistake. 'I have ordered coffee.'

'Oh, thank you.' We were still both standing.

'Do sit down,' I said, perching myself on the edge of my chair. He sat, awkwardly, opposite me.

'Your card came this morning. Thank you.'

'Not at all; it was the least I could do.' Oh, for Christ's sake, we can't go on like this! I took a deep breath and released it in a great, heaving shudder. I leant forward and took his hand; Anthony … I … your father and … Before the war when your father went to England on leave … Oh God. There's no easy way to say this: I think I'm your sister.' He withdrew his hand and stood up.

'I don't know what game you think you are playing,

Mrs. Thornfield, but I already have a sister. Now if you will excuse me.'

'No, don't go. I'm sorry, I've done it all wrong.' Again. 'Please, do sit down and hear me out.' Reluctantly he resumed his seat. 'I'm not crazy, honestly, and I'm not trying to con you or anything. I know the impression I must have given you, both today, and at your home. And I'm sorry, I really am.'

In the pause, a long, long pause, the coffee came.

'Thank you.' I said. 'Black or white?'

'Black. Please.' I poured his coffee and placed the cup in front of him. 'Sugar?'

'No, thank you.'

I poured my coffee, added sugar which I don't normally take, stirred it in, put the spoon down in the saucer, lifted the cup, and drank. All in slow motion, was how it felt. The only thing going at any speed was my heart. I just could not think of what to say next. If he got up and walked out on me it was no more than I deserved. I put the cup down. If he wasn't going to speak, then I would have to.

'I've given you an awful shock,' I said.

'Well, yes … you have.'

'So you can imagine what a shock it was for me, when I … when I discovered that the man I thought was my father, wasn't … and that my real father …'

'I presume you have some proof of this?'

'I have letters.'

'From my father to …?'

'Yes.'

'I see.' He rubbed his chin up and down with his right hand, his fingers over his mouth. His eyes ranged around the room, gazing at the walls, the carpet, the doorway, looking anywhere but directly at me. Eventually his fingers came to rest, the middle one on the tip of his nose, and he looked me straight in the eyes. Slowly he put down his hand, folded his arms and sat back in his chair. 'You'd better tell me,' he said.

So I told him, and I showed him Peter's letters and the letter from Tom. He read them and handed them back; I put them away in my bag. They had served their purpose: they had authenticated my story.

'I shall have to think about this.' It wasn't the reaction I had expected.

'What do you mean?'

'Well ... the implications of it.'

'What implications?'

'Surely you must see the effect this would have, if I were to acknowledge you. It would be a terrible shock for my mother.'

'Well of course it would, but ... There's no need for her to know, is there? All I want is to get to know you and your sister. You haven't told me her name ...'

'Carmela.'

'Lovely name. Does she ... have children?'

'Two.' Then, a pause. 'A boy and a girl.' He seemed reluctant to give me any more information.

'Look, I don't want to disrupt your lives, I just want to talk to you and to her and maybe your son and ...'

'No. Not my children. And not my sister either. This is as far as it goes. We keep this between us.'

'Why?' I was genuinely puzzled. And I was hurt. It was as if I had some unsavoury disease.

'Because it shames my family. My father was a hero and my mother worships his memory, and as long as she lives nothing must destroy that.'

'A hero? In the war?'

'Yes, oh yes. He was a very brave man.'

'Tell me.' He looked away. 'Anthony, he was my father, too.' Reluctantly, I felt, he looked at me again. 'I want to know everything about him. I have a right to know. Don't you understand? Based on this new knowledge, I want to reconstruct my life. His genes are in me, they're in my son. I need to know what he was like, who he was, what he did, how he felt.'

'Well, I can't help you much. I was only two when he died. And as for Carmela, she wasn't born until three months after.'

'But you must know things. You said your mother still talks about him. There must be photographs. There are, I saw one. Please, Anthony, this really matters to me.'

'Well ...'

'I promise you, I absolutely promise, I'll swear on whatever you want to swear on ... that I won't say or do anything that will upset your mother, or your sister. Or anybody in your family.'

His hand went up to his chin again. After just twice up and down, he folded his arms. 'All right, I'll do what I can.'

'Oh, you are a love. Thank you.' I reached across the table and grabbed his arm. He looked startled.

'Sorry.' I smiled at him and took away my hand.

'How long are you here?'

'I have another week and a bit. Oh, don't worry, I'm not going to settle in Malta, even though I have fallen in love with it.'

'I meant, if you hadn't long, perhaps we should meet again soon. If I can get hold of any information, photographs ...' He sounded uncertain, as if he didn't know a lot about his father and would have to make enquiries.

'Could I come to your house? You will tell your wife, won't you?'

'No!'

'Oh.'

'I shan't tell anyone. I thought I had made that clear.'

'But ... Look, all this happened more than fifty years

ago, for God's sake. All right, I agree your mother and your children shouldn't know, but surely your wife won't be upset?'

Again he stroked his chin.

'My wife and my mother are not … they are not in sympathy with one another, you might say … and I don't wish to …'

'Okay, forget your wife. Why not your sister, though? She is my sister too.'

His eyes ranged round the room, finally coming back to me.

'Well … Maybe. But no one else. In fact she might be able to help you more than I can. She has a lot of photographs of events during the war; she also has lots of newspaper cuttings. They're to do with her work, she's a producer for Radio Malta. She has just done a programme, a series of programmes actually, to celebrate the fiftieth anniversary of the end of the war. She interviewed people all over the island, old people who had memories of that time. She might be really useful to you.'

'That would be good, and … helpful. Thank you. But it's only your mother really who could tell me what sort of person your father was.'

'I'm sorry, Mrs. Thornfield …'

'Oh please … Jane.'

'I'm sorry … Jane … there's no way I could allow you to …'

'Look … if I promise to say nothing that would disturb her, couldn't I see her just once more? You could tell her I was writing something about Malta during the war years, and I need background material.'

'You could get that from the War Museum.'

'I know! Tell her I'm planning to write a novel set in Malta, a story with a … with a romantic hero, yes that's it … someone who was brave and young and daring, someone who married a Maltese girl and then died for her country. Would she talk to me then? Would she like that?'

He began to laugh.

'Why are you laughing?'

'You sound just like my mother says my father used to be, carried away with enthusiasm; it didn't matter whether an idea was workable or not, it didn't matter what anyone else said about it, if he thought it was a good idea he went ahead with it.'

'You see, you do know things about him. Yes, I am a bit like that. So ... what do you think? Would she?'

'I hate to say this, but ... Yes, I think she would like it. But you must promise ...'

'I will not let you down, I promise. You just don't know how good this has made me feel! Look ... go away now, and when you've sorted something out, give me a call.'

We stood up. He looked at me long and hard, as if searching for something in my face, a resemblance to his father perhaps. 'My sister, you say ...' He bent his head. I thought he was going to kiss me, perhaps he was; he straightened and extended his hand. I took it, what else could I do? 'Goodbye,' he said.

'Bye.' I watched him go. In the doorway of the lounge he turned, half-smiled. I smiled back and lifted my hand. He was gone. I sat down; my legs felt weak.

At last I was getting somewhere. I would talk to Anthony's mother – damn, I should have asked him her Christian name – and fill in, if not all, some of the gaps. When that would be I had no idea. I hoped Anthony would arrange it soon, very soon.

So ... what should I do now, today? I couldn't expect to hear from Anthony until tomorrow at the earliest, yet somehow I didn't want to leave the hotel, just in case he phoned. Ken was out, and anyway I didn't want to talk to him at the moment. Michael, the gardener in the straw hat: I would talk to him; have a swim perhaps, and then … Then I must think very carefully about how I would approach Anthony's mother. If I messed up this visit I knew there would not be another one. A hero, Anthony had said. Perhaps I could write a romantic novel about war-torn Malta and base the hero on Peter Andersen. From three viewpoints: his, his wife's and his lover's … Enough. This was not fiction. The time for fiction would come later, if at all. What I had to do now was sort out the facts, build up a dossier on the real man. Get to know my father. I found Michael hoeing, preparing the flower beds for next spring's sweet-scented stocks.

'I have told my uncle about you,' he said, 'that you wanted to know about the hospital at Mtarfa.'

'Oh. Thank you. Can I see him?'

'I'm sorry, he is not well.'

'Oh, I'm sorry.'

'He said I was to tell you about the coffins, though, in the war.'

'Coffins?' I grimaced. 'I'm not sure I want to hear this.' I had a sudden picture of Peter, badly wounded, lying in his coffin. Michael looked disappointed. 'Go on then, tell me,' I said. The pathway where I was standing was in full sun and the heat bounced back from the stone. 'But can we please move into the shade?'

'Of course.' He looked at his watch. 'It is nearly my lunch time. I will fetch my sandwiches and we will sit at a table under the trees. It is okay if I am with a guest, but on my own I may not sit there. Excuse me.'

He went off to get his sandwiches and I wandered across the lawn to where there were tables and chairs and umbrellas dotted about among the shrubby palms and oleanders. It was a good thing there were umbrellas; the trees gave very little shade. Maybe in a few years when they had grown.

Michael returned, with a carrier bag, from which he drew out a packet of hefty sandwiches. 'I make them myself,' he said, proudly. 'It is a help to my wife.'

'Good,' I said. 'Now tell me about these coffins.'

'You know that on Malta we do not have many trees?'

'Yes, I had noticed.'

He took a bite from one of his sandwiches; the aroma of some kind of garlic sausage wafted over to me. 'Well,' he said, 'in the war, when we couldn't import wood, coffins had to be made of something else. Guess what they used, the soldiers at the hospital?' A stray piece of sausage fell onto the table. It was snatched up by one of the waiting sparrows.

'I have no idea.'

'Biscuit tins! Biscuit tins and petrol drums. From the camp. Beaten out and re-shaped.'

'Oh.' Okay, so war-time coffins were made of tin. Michael was grinning. Was it funny?

'When the burial parties carried them they creaked,' he said.

'Creaked?'

'Yes. It was very frightening ... for the men who were carrying the coffins.'

His story had fallen flat.

'Oh, I see. Yes, it would be.' I managed a faint laugh. Something more seemed to be required of me. 'Dear me, yes. I suppose they wondered if the man in the coffin was really dead.'

He nodded. 'That's right, they did.' So my father might have been buried in a biscuit tin. Well, I suppose that was funny, in a macabre sort of way. And had his coffin creaked as he was laid to rest under the pine trees? I didn't want to know; I was finding the thought disturbing.

'They painted them,' Michael was saying, 'to look like wood.'

'Oh. Very clever.' I wanted to get away from this subject, yet stay with the war. 'Quite a lot of British soldiers married Maltese girls, I believe.'

'Oh yes.'

'How did the Maltese men feel about that?'

'They didn't like it. They felt it was unfair.'

'In what way?'

'Well ... the soldiers had more money and they were able to bring things from the camp to tempt the girls.'

'What sort of things? Not nylons, surely?' I said, thinking of the Yanks in Britain.

Michael laughed, screwed up his sandwich paper and aimed it deftly into a nearby litter bin. 'No no, food. Sugar, sometimes butter. Biscuits, jam, chocolate maybe, although there wasn't much of that. Of course they should not have done it; it was forbidden to take out things from the stores, but food brought by a soldier for a girl's mother would make the mother look kindly upon the young man, and he would be allowed to take her out.'

'In the hope of receiving more food?'

Michael nodded vigorously. Was that what had happened with Peter? Had he wormed his way into the family by bribery? First Teo, then Mama. And when was all this? I still wasn't sure if Peter had been married or engaged. or just 'walking out' when he'd come to England in 1939. No, he couldn't have been married; Tom would never have tried to get him fixed up with Kitty if he'd been married. He could have been engaged though; perhaps Tom hadn't taken an engagement to a Maltese girl seriously. Nor, if he was engaged, had Peter. I needed dates, exact dates: when Peter had met his wife, when he had married her. That photograph, with Peter standing beside his wife: she had said that was taken before the war; she had said 'son-in-law'. They had been married before the war, but when?

Michael was speaking again. 'I'm sorry, I didn't catch what you said.'

'I said, of course that all stopped once the war began.'

'I don't understand.'

'Once the war had started,' Michael said, 'it was very difficult for the soldiers to get anything extra.'

'I'm sorry, Michael, I'm very confused. I thought it was during the war that British soldiers were bringing all these extra goodies to the women.'

'Well, some, but not many.'

'So when you say before the war, you mean 1938?' It was worse than I thought; Peter had definitely been married when he came to England. How could Tom have brought him home and not said.

'No, I mean before June 1940.'

'The war began in 1939. September.'

Michael smiled, shook his head. 'Not in Malta. It began here on the tenth of June.' Obviously I looked puzzled. He went on, 'Italy declared war and there was an air raid, half past six the next morning.'

'Of course. Oh, how stupid of me. That's right. It was only when Italy came in that Malta really got involved.' So Peter hadn't been married in 1939. That photograph was most likely taken after he came back, maybe even the next year. I felt curiously light-headed, relieved: my father was not the totally irresponsible man I had been taking him for. Once the war had started in England, and he could see there was no getting back there, he had courted a Maltese girl. There was no reason why he should take all the blame for my mother's pregnancy. Let's face it, she was the married one, it was up to her to put a stop to things.

'You are looking pleased; have I said something good?'

'Mm? Oh yes.' I was quickly brought back to the present. 'Yes. You have. Thank you.' I could not explain, so I just said, 'It was very funny, about the coffins.'

'I thought you would like that story. I will tell my uncle you like it.'

'Yes, please do. Oh, and I hope he gets better soon.'

After we parted I went for a swim. The indoor pool was deserted. I put my bathrobe – white and fluffy, a freebie from a luxurious press trip last year – on a bench and plunged in. As I swam up and down in the almost-too-hot water I planned what I would ask Anthony's mother. Why was her husband a hero? Had he been a bit of a jack-the-lad, bringing under-the-counter goods to her mother? No, she wouldn't like that phrase. Stick to positive things. Was he kind, considerate, fun to be with? What music did he like? Was he a reader? Was he sporty? Did he like dancing?

'My, you look serious. You're supposed to relax in the water.'

'Ken!' In pale green shirt and beige slacks.

'That's me.' I swam to the side of the pool and hung there, grasping the handrail. 'Do I take it you have finished work for the day?' Had I?

'Yes, I have. I've had a very successful day.'

'And now you're ready to play.'

I tucked my toes under the rail and pushed myself backwards in the water, my breasts rising provocatively above the surface.

'I do believe I am.'

'Good. In that case we don't need to wait until seven.'

'Seven?'

'We're having a drink at seven.'

I hadn't forgotten. 'So … what did you have in mind?'

'Suppose you get out of the water, and we'll talk about it.' I climbed out of the pool, Ken helping me up the last rung.

'Yours?' He held up the bathrobe.

'Yes,' I said, hoarsely. He put the robe around my shoulders and held it, imprisoning me. I turned, within the robe, and kissed him full on the mouth. I couldn't have cared less who was watching. Then I came to my senses. Don't play with me, he had said.

I pulled away. 'I'm sorry, I shouldn't have done that.'

'I'm glad you did.'

I picked up my bag and my clothes and led the way, shamelessly, to my room. To hell with chambermaids. Anyway, what did it matter: we were on holiday, free spirits, answerable to no one but ourselves. My family history could wait; I needed to live in the present for a bit.

'Tomorrow's my last full day,' said Ken, later. 'Seeing we're friends again, shall we do something special with it, go somewhere together?'

'Oh, Ken, I'm ...' I wanted to be around in case I got a call from Anthony.

'It's all right, you don't need to say it. Anyway, I've actually got something fixed up, a trip to the Three Cities, which I do rather want to see, so ... it's fine.' He sounded like a small, hurt child.

'It's just that I may have to see someone, and ...'

'Jane ... it doesn't matter. I shouldn't have asked.' He got off the bed, pulled on his trousers, went to stand on the balcony.

'Ken ...'

He was looking over the bay. 'What?'

'Why are you here?'

He turned, fiercely. 'Because you invited me. Christ, is this how you treat all your men?' He picked up his shirt and made for the door. I leapt off the bed, grabbed hold of him.

'Idiot! I mean why are you in Malta?'

'Oh. Sorry.' Slowly he pulled on his shirt, did up the

buttons. No point in hurrying him; when he was ready he would reply.

Eventually, 'I don't know, is the answer. Sorry if that disappoints you. I was trying to think up some clever reason for being here, something to match yours, something romantic, heroic … but I couldn't. The plain truth is: I suddenly wanted a holiday, Malta looked interesting, and … and there was a cheapie going.'

'How much?'

'Less than half price.' Shamefaced, 'D'you blame me?'

'Not at all. Go on, I'll see you at seven.'

I hoped Anthony would phone that evening, and then, if I wasn't seeing his mother, perhaps I would spend the day with Ken, go on the trip to the famous Three Cities, see the Inquisitor's Palace and the Knights' Church of St. Lawrence and the Cottonera Lines, all part of Malta's ancient history. But no, it was the island's most recent conflict I was concerned with; I couldn't spare the mental energy to think about battles and glories long ago.

I met Ken in the foyer. We had a drink in the bar, dined together and went for a walk. I hadn't wanted any more intimacy: I pleaded tiredness and too large a dinner, but the real reason was Neville. I was missing him and what's more I suddenly felt I was cheating on him. Silly I know, but the feeling was there and it wouldn't go away. And yet, earlier in the day I had been ravenous, and shown it. Too ravenous, that was the trouble. Wanting sex for itself, not for the man I was with. Well, I had done it now, I wouldn't do it again. I wouldn't let myself do it again. Somehow, I think Ken knew; he didn't press me, just walked with me to the lift, said, 'Goodnight, sleep well,' and kissed me on the cheek. Could passion die like this? So quickly? Easily, if that was all it was. Poor man, I had eaten him alive this afternoon.

CHAPTER ELEVEN

The morning, like every morning since I had been here, dawned bright and sparkling, with just enough breeze to ruffle the waves in the bay. I waited first in my room, then when the chambermaid wanted to clean, in the foyer, hovering near the reception desk: I had told the clerk I was expecting a call. Ten o'clock and it still hadn't come. Ken's group had gone, so had the party setting out to walk to the nearby bird sanctuary; the hotel was all but deserted. Oh, this was ridiculous; I couldn't stay in all day, and certainly not on such a beautiful day, on the off-chance of hearing from Anthony. If he called he could leave a message, and I would ring him back.

With no ultimate destination in mind I drove through Mosta – going almost anywhere eastwards means going through Mosta – and then, attracted by the sound of Zebbug and Siggiewi, I turned south, through the two small towns, which didn't have a lot to offer – well, not to me today; I didn't want to look at churches and statues – and on to Qrendi where a battered signpost directed me to the prehistoric site of Hagar Qim, high up on a headland overlooking the south coast.

I parked the car on the grass; there was no formal car park – how wonderfully different from Stonehenge now – and walked across to the site. Other than a couple of backpackers and an Italian family there was no one about. I sat on a boulder, one of many just lying around, and opened my guide book. 'The temple, which was built around 3000 B.C., was excavated at the beginning of the nineteenth century. Hagar Qim has produced seven "fat figure" statuettes, the naturalistic "Venus of Malta" and an unparalleled four-sided altar with a representation of a potted plant on each side. The complex consists of a number of inter-connecting units, each with their own altar.' I closed the book; I didn't care about the history, I just wanted to absorb the peace that I felt sure would permeate such an ancient place of worship. Open to the sky, with wild flowers – yellow and orange, I didn't know their names – growing in the crevices of the rocks and on the sandy floors of the temples, and with the thick stone walls blocking out all other sound, it was indeed a tranquil place. I walked about, touching the stones, laying my hands on one of the altars. Had Peter come here? I doubted it; he wouldn't have had the time. Today Hagar Qim was just a short drive from Rabat, but during the war the only way he could have come here was by bicycle or in a donkey cart. Unless he was here on official business, which was unlikely.

Out on the headland I sat and looked across the water to a tiny island; it was no more than a rock really.

'That's Filfla.' The voice behind me was Australian. I turned round. The girl, one of the back-packers, in frayed, cut-off jeans and T-shirt, was pointing across the water. She wasn't talking to me.

'Yeah, I know,' said her companion, also Australian, also in frayed jeans, hair dark and tightly curled. He sounded bored and aggrieved. He picked up a stone and aimed it towards the island. 'They used it for target practice.'

'I told you that,' said the girl; her hair was long and fair. 'My Gramps used to fire at it.'

'Excuse me, did you say target practice?' I said.

'Sure,' said the girl. She plonked herself down on the grass beside me. 'Soldiers. In the war, you know, the one with Germany.'

'The one you can't get away from anywhere on this bloody island.' Not only bored but angry.

'Yeah, well, it was important, wasn't it?' She looked up at him. 'You wouldn't be here if that war hadn't been fought.'

'I know that!'

'Well then.'

'I just don't want *The War* rammed down my throat twenty four hours a day. Okay?'

I was about to add to the young man's irritation.

'Your grandfather was in the war, you said?' The young man swore and walked away. He stood with his back to us. 'I'm sorry,' I said. 'You go and see to your friend.'

She gave him a fleeting glimpse over her shoulder. 'Oh, don't mind him. He's a pain in the arse. He's Jewish, you see, and well ... I guess it hurts, harking back to those bad times.'

'He's right, though, you can't get away from it here.'

'The thing is, I don't want to, and he does. I feel kind of proud of my grandfather. Coming all the way from Australia to fight for freedom. I think that's really something.'

'Is he still alive?'

'Oh, he's alive. He's old, mind. Eighty-seven. His eyesight's still good and he can still hit a target!'

'And when he was here ... he used to shoot at that?'

I pointed out to sea.

'They all did. It used to be much bigger, so my Gramps says.'

The young man was back. 'Are you coming, or what?' he said.

'Yeah, I'm coming.' The girl stood up and brushed the grass off her shorts. 'Nice to have met you.'

'And you.' I felt she was waiting for me to say something else. 'I found the temple very peaceful. Did you?'

'Yes, I did ... Col?'

'What?'

'Let's go back in the temple.' He shrugged. 'You said it felt good in there.'

'Yeah. Okay.'

'Thanks,' the girl said. I wish I'd asked her name. It was too late now; she had slipped her arm through the boy's and I didn't want to disturb them.

I sat for a while longer on the headland, staring out at Filfla. The young man had been right: that war had penetrated just about every corner of the earth and was still affecting people's behaviour even today. It was why the girl was here;. it was why I was here. If Filfla had been a gunnery target, perhaps Peter, and Tom – I had hardly given Tom a thought in all this, but he had been here, too – perhaps they had fired at it, maybe even fired at it together. I tried to reconstruct those days in my mind. Were they friends? Anthony's mother didn't seem to think so, but perhaps Peter had kept his home life and his army life well apart. Until I learnt more about Peter – what kind of man he was, what his views were, how he spent his spare time – until I knew those things I couldn't tell whether he and Tom had been, not just in the same regiment, but pals. Somehow, I didn't feel they had.

It was almost one o'clock; I realised suddenly that I

was hungry. I picked up a tiny stone and put it in my bag: a souvenir of Hagar Qim. And Filfla.

I drove on down the coast road – spectacular views said the guide book, and they were – to the Blue Grotto. I had a sandwich and a beer and then went, in a blue and red rowing boat, into the grotto itself, where coral tints the limestone pink and orange and mauve and your hand glows turquoise when you trail it in the water. Col and his girl should come here if they wanted peace. Perhaps they were headed this way; I should have thought to give them a lift.

Where to next? The Buskett Gardens, where the Knights trained their falcons, and then perhaps along the Pwales Valley, the only really fertile bit of Malta, where vines and vegetables grew. If I could find the way. My map suggested there might be a cart track, but it seemed to peter out halfway: I wouldn't risk it.

I was barely into top gear when I saw them. So they were going to the grotto. I pulled up beside them.

'Going to the grotto?'

'No,' said Col.

'Yes,' said the girl. 'Well, that is, I want to, he doesn't.'

'It's beautiful,' I said. 'Really worth seeing.'

Col shrugged. 'Seen one grotto, you've seen them all.'

'I'll give you a lift,' I said, hopefully. The girl obviously did want to go there.

'Well, thanks,' she said.

'If we're getting a hitch we might as well go some place else. I mean, we're nearly at the bloody grotto.'

God, if he was my travelling companion, I'd ditch him, fast.

'If there's somewhere else you'd like to go, I can take you.' I smiled at the girl. I wasn't going to smile at Col. If it came to it I'd take her by herself, to the grotto, and wait for her. Col could just bugger off.

'Gee, that's kind. I'll tell you where we would like to go.' Not Valletta, please. 'If it wouldn't be out of your way.'

'I'm staying at Mellieha,' I said. 'That's north-west, towards Gozo.'

'Oh, right. Then I guess it wouldn't be out of your way. Mdina,' she said. 'You know, the old walled city.' No, not Mdina, not Rabat.

'Yes,' I said, breezily. 'Yes, I know Mdina. No problem. Hop in.'

Col climbed into the back, with both the packs; the girl sat in front.

'This is great,' she said, settling herself into the seat. 'Isn't it, Col?' over her shoulder, looking in the mirror.

'Yeah, great.' And as an afterthought. 'Thanks.'

'I'm Ronnie,' said the girl, 'and old grumpy there in the back, he's Colin.'

'I heard that.' Not so much grumpy as peevish.

'Good, because it's true.' The girl twisted round and stuck her tongue out at him.

'I'm Jane,' I said. 'And before you ask, I've left Tarzan at home.' Even Colin sort of laughed. 'Ronnie. Is that Veronica?'

'No, it's Ronaele.'

'Oh, I've not heard that name before.'

From the back, 'Her mother's mad.'

'She is not; she's just a bit eccentric.'

'She's mad. What other mother would give back to front names to her kids?' This had really got him going. 'Her name's Eleanor, the wrong way round.'

'The wrong way?' I said. 'R. O. N. A. Oh, I see …'

'And her brother Kerry, his name's Kered. In other words, Derek.' It was a bit odd; it was the sort of thing I had done for fun when I was about nine years old and beginning to enjoy playing with words.

'My mum wanted to give us unusual names,' Ronnie

said, defensively. 'And she liked words, you see. Still does.'

'Oh, is she a writer?'

'No, she's a calligrapher. She likes the look of words.' A bit more background information, mostly supplied by Ronnie – they were students from Sydney, on vacation, doing the usual thing, seeing as much of Europe as they could for as little money as possible – and we were on the outskirts of Mosta. I could have dumped them here, encouraged them to visit the Cathedral, but I had the feeling Col would object: bloody war again, he'd probably say. And so it was on to Rabat.

I parked the car, as before, near the Howard Gardens, and pointed Ronnie and Col towards the main gate into Mdina. After they had thanked me, asked where I was staying and said could they call me – 'Yes, of course.' What else could I say? – I sat on in the car. This time the place held a significance for me that I hadn't known on my previous visit: not only did Anthony live in one of these houses, but this scruffy patch of land in front of them must have been where my father and Anthony's mother – I still didn't know her first name – had met.

I pictured the meeting: a young woman comes out of one of the houses. She is holding a small child. She puts the child into the pram that is standing by the door. When the child, a little girl with a moon-shaped face, is settled, the young woman calls, into the open doorway of the house, 'Teo! Come along.' A few moments pass, the child begins to cry and the woman rocks the pram. 'Teo!' she calls and a boy, about six years old, emerges from the house, carrying a football. 'It's no use bringing that,' the woman says. 'I can't play with you, I have to look after Gewza.' 'It's not fair,' the boy says, 'no one ever plays with me.' 'I'll play with you,' says a young man, a soldier who has been watching from the shade of the Howard Gardens. The woman smiles her thanks. 'Go on, kick it,' says Peter, and Teo, delighted, boots the ball to Peter. The young woman stands, pushing the pram back and forth. Soon the little girl is asleep. The woman lets go of the pram. 'Want to join in?' asks Peter. The woman shakes her head, but she is smiling. He is so good-looking, tall and blond, and polite too, unlike some of the British soldiers she has encountered. This one wouldn't make rude gestures to her or whistle at her when she went to the bakery. After a while Teo is, unbelievably, tired. The woman tells Teo to thank the soldier. 'I'm the one who should say thank you,' says Peter, looking not at the boy but at the woman. He is not sure whether she is the boy's mother – they marry so young out here – or his sister. She blushes and drops her head. Perhaps he is like the other men after all. 'Do you come here every day?' he asks. 'Most days,' she says. 'In that case, Teo – the boy has told him his name – we'll play again. Ta-ta.'

'Excuse me.' A male voice. 'Are you going or have you just arrived?' I realised I had been standing, for how long I didn't know, with the car keys in my hand. I looked down at them, feeling foolish. 'Oh ... I've just got here. Sorry.'

The man drove away; there were no other parking spaces. Back briefly in my reverie, I saw Anthony's mother come out of the house, with Teo carrying his football and Gewza in the pram ... and Peter, with a parcel of goodies smuggled from the camp, approaching from the Gardens. Anthony's mother sees the parcel, smiles and ushers Peter into the house: the courtship has begun.

I got into the car and drove off, passing on my way out the driver who had wanted my parking space. I smiled at him, and he glowered back. Across the road Ta Pawlu was busy; there were three cars lined up waiting for petrol and a fourth just pulling in. I wondered if

Anthony had spoken to his son. I doubted it, not if he wasn't ready to tell his wife. I turned right, down the road that would eventually lead me back, past the cemetery, to Mellieha. On my right were shuttered houses, in front of them a red phone box and, a little further along, the red pillar box that I had noticed before. I remembered I had a card to post, a card to Beth that I'd written a couple of days ago. I would post it here. It was the nearest letter box to Anthony's house. Perhaps Peter had posted a letter here. Oh come on, Jane, stop this. Not everything here is significant. There was, amazingly, a space by the letter box. I pulled in, got out and popped the card into the slit. Back in the car, I was just about to move off when I saw Anthony, letter in hand, walking along the pavement. Hardly a great coincidence, considering where we were.

Torn between wanting to speak to Anthony – surely this was a heaven-sent opportunity – and not wanting to complicate any negotiations with his mother already in hand, I made my decision, then pulled away from the kerb without looking. A lorry going fast up the hill clipped my offside front mirror and brought me rocking to a halt. The impact turned the mirror on its swivel in towards the passenger window. Both the mirror and the window glass shattered. People stopped and looked my way. Including Anthony. Suddenly he was there. He leant in at my window.

'Jane. Are you all right?'

'Anthony. Er … yes, I'm all right. Just a bit shaken. It was my own fault, I wasn't looking.' I was looking at you, but you don't know that, thank God. The damage aside – it wouldn't be a major repair job; I'd had this happen once before – was this serendipity, throwing me almost literally into Anthony's path? Of course he might decide not to be helpful, but somehow I didn't think he was that kind of man. Besides which, cars had been his business. And Ta Pawlu – did Pawlu do repairs? – was just up the road.

'What a nuisance. I shall have to get it repaired … I suppose. I'm not sure what you do about damage to a hire car.' It was a temptation to play the helpless, appealing female, but I resisted it; it wasn't me, and I didn't want to put Anthony under any obligation. 'Oh well, I'd better get back to the hotel and let the care hire man know.'

'No, no. You cannot drive the car back like that …'

'It's only a window, and it isn't as if I need to shut it.'

'I will not let you drive it like that.' Oh. Possessive. Will not let me. This is serendipity, make the most of it.

'I don't see what else I can do.'

'Pawlu will repair it, and lend you another car to drive back to Mellieha.'

'Oh. Are you sure? I mean, I don't want to infringe any agreement with the car hire people.' But I do want to stay in Rabat and talk to you.

'No, it is okay. Pawlu does repairs for them.'

'Oh. Well, in that case … I would be most grateful.'

I turned the car round and drove slowly back up the hill to the garage. Anthony walked, getting there at almost the same moment. He explained the situation to his son, while I sat in the car. Pawlu came over, grinning. 'Hi!' Oh yes, you find it very amusing, don't you, that you can career around like a maniac and nothing happens to you, while I drive sedately and …

'Maltese drivers, they are always in a hurry.'

I picked up my bag, got out of the car and gave Pawlu the keys.

'Half an hour and I will have another car for you. Okay?'

Yes, okay. Fine. But what do I do meanwhile? Do I wait here, or what? And is that a Maltese half-hour or an English one?

There was a rapid exchange in Maltese between Anthony and Pawlu.

'I would like you to come to my house, while you are waiting. My wife would like to meet you.' Then, loud enough for anyone around to hear: 'I have told her about you ...' You've told her! '... that your father and my father served together in the war and that you are doing research for a novel.' Very wise; wife, mother and all the local busybodies get the same story.

'Thank you. If you're sure I'd be no trouble?'

'No trouble at all.' His look said: if you are, that's the last bit of help you get from me.

'You're very kind.'

We left Ta Pawlu and waited for a break in the traffic to cross the road. I smiled up at him.

'Why are you smiling?' he asked.

'Oh, what a tangled web we weave.'

'We have to. I will not have any of my family hurt by this ... revelation.'

'No, of course not.' A van slowed, signalling to turn into the garage; we crossed the road. 'But at the same time I do want to find out everything I can about my father. To know who I am.' I felt on the verge of tears. 'I need you to help me, Anthony.'

He looked away, just as he had done yesterday in the hotel lounge.

The little square was deserted, parched in the afternoon sun. I stood, waiting. What I wanted to do was touch him, draw him to me, show him some sisterly affection.

'I will help you.' He was still looking away. Then he turned to me; his look was fierce. 'But on my terms. Understand?'

'Don't worry. I made a hash of it last time I know, but I promise you it won't happen again. I shall be totally professional; I shall simply interview your mother as if there was no connection between us whatsoever. Does that satisfy you?'

He nodded. 'Yes. All right. Now come and meet my wife.'

We had been standing only two doors away from Anthony's house. He opened one side of the double front door and stood aside for me to enter before him. The house was similar to his mother's, the same dark, shuttered room on the ground floor, the staircase, on the right this time, hugging the wall all the way to the floor above.

'Upstairs?' I said.

'Yes. Please go up.'

I put my hand on the curving handrail, my right foot on the bottom step.

'Anthony?' A woman's voice from above, speaking in Maltese. To which he replied. Then she spoke again.

'Come,' he said. 'it will be all right.'

'What did you say?'

'I said you had had an accident and you needed to rest. All right?'

Yes, that was all right. I followed Anthony up the stairs. He led the way, past open doorways through which I glimpsed beds and cupboards, into a large airy kitchen-cum-breakfast room. The furniture looked as if it had been there since the Sixties: formica-topped table and bright plastic seated chairs, a bit like my mother's kitchen in Enfield.

A small, grey-haired, homely-looking rounded woman in a flowered dress and flat shoes was standing by the stove, stirring something in a large pot. Anthony's wife. No wonder she and his mother didn't get along; it was hard to imagine two women less alike. At first sight anyway.

'Maria ...' The woman turned from the stove. '... this is Mrs. Thornfield.'

The woman wiped her hands on her apron.

'How do you do?' I said, and we shook hands. This woman was my sister-in-law, the only one I had, yet I must greet her as a stranger.

'This is my wife, Maria.' I smiled, she smiled. We were both waiting for Anthony to make the next move. He spoke to his wife in Maltese. Did she speak no English? Yes, she did.

'Please, do sit down. You will have some tea, yes?'

'Oh. Well, yes. Thank you. It is very kind of you.'

And so I had tea and biscuits – custard creams; again I might have been in England – in the kitchen with Anthony and his wife. She had wanted Anthony to take me into the lounge, but I had said, 'Oh no, please, let's have tea in here; I love kitchens,' and then wondered if I had once again said the wrong thing, but Maria looked relieved and Anthony took off his jacket and hung it over the back of a chair. He seemed more relaxed than he had been in his mother's house.

How could I keep this relaxed feeling, draw them close to me and make myself part of their family, yet stay within the boundaries that Anthony had laid down for me.

I would ask about their children. Maria's eyes lit up at my question: 'How many children do you have?'

'Five,' she said. 'Would you like to see their photographs?'

'No, Maria ...' Anthony began, his voice sharp.

'I would love to see them, I really would.' They're only photographs, Anthony. Don't worry, I'm not getting too close to your family, even if they are also mine. His face was dark, brooding. Ah, yes; nothing to do with his family: he was recalling my strange behaviour when I saw his mother's photos.'

'I will bring them,' said Maria, and she left the room. Anthony and I sat, not speaking.

I drank the last of my tea, looking down into my cup.

Maria returned with an armful of silver-framed pictures. I looked and listened eagerly, as one at a time she handed them to me. First there was Joseph, the eldest, who had emigrated to Australia, with his Australian wife and their daughter, Geena; then Pawlu, with a car in the background; next Anna and Rosina, qualified nurses, in their uniforms. They were both married and living, as far as I could make out, in Mosta and somewhere called Pieta, near Valletta. The youngest son, Dominic, was at university, doing business studies. He had a girlfriend who was studying to be a doctor, I think. There was so much to take in, what with all the husbands and girlfriends and grandchildren. It might have been one of the husbands who was studying medicine. Anyway, it didn't matter: the important thing was that I sounded interested and impressed. In turn I got out my picture of Alex.

'Only one? How sad.' I would have liked more, I said, untruthfully. This was not a day for truth.

I looked at my watch. Pawlu's half hour had already stretched to three quarters.

'Don't worry, Pawlu will be here soon,' said Anthony. 'He will have taken the car to Mosta.'

'To Mosta?'

'We have another garage there. That is where we do the breakdowns, and the re-sprays and that sort of thing. He will bring back another car for you from there.'

'It is very good of you to do this for me.' Perhaps I sounded weary because Maria then said, 'Would you like to rest?' and feeling that our conversation had run its course, I said I would. She led me into one of the rooms I had passed on the way in, closed the curtains against the fierce afternoon sun, gestured to the bed, with its blue candlewick cover – 'Please, you make yourself comfortable.' – and left. I felt she was glad, too, not to

go on talking. Beyond admiring her children and the
house I was at a loss to know what to talk to her about. I
couldn't ask her what I really wanted to know: why she
didn't get on with her mother-in-law.

I slept: the heat of the day and the forced conversation
had made me more tired that I had realised. I was roused
by a knock, quite loud, and then the door handle turned
and Maria appeared.

'Your car, it is ready.' she said. 'Anthony has just
phoned from the garage.'

I jumped up. 'Goodness! What time is it?'

'Half past four.' I had slept for hours.

'Would you like to wash?' Oh, how I would. There
was a clean guest towel in the bathroom and a fresh
tablet of soap. And then, in the kitchen, another cup of
tea. I warmed to Maria; she was caring and thoughtful.

'You have been so kind to me,' I said as I left, then
impulsively kissed her on the cheek.

'I hope your book goes well.'

'Thank you. I … um … I need to talk to more people
… people who remember the war years.'

'There is a man in Mosta, an Englishman, who was
here then. He could help you; he talked to Carmela,
when she did the radio programme in May.' Yes, well,
thank you, Maria, but it's really my father I want to hear
about and the only person who can help me there is your
mother-in-law, and I don't think you will take kindly to
my suggesting that you take me to see her.

'I'm really trying to picture things from a woman's
point of view,' I said hopefully, 'You know … how the
wives of servicemen felt about that time, coping with the
shortages … and getting on with life after their husbands
had been killed.' I might as well plunge in; she didn't
have to rescue me. 'As your mother-in-law had to.'

'Oh, she will talk to you,' she said. Her voice had
gone hard. 'She never stops talking about the war. To

hear her talk you would think Anthony's father had won the war single-handed. My father too, was killed in the war. He was digging out a building that had been bombed, and it collapsed upon him, and they did not get him out for two days, and by then he was dead.'

'Oh, Maria, I am so sorry.' I put my hand on her arm.

'Anthony thinks I am cruel to his mother. I am not, it is just that she is not the only one who has suffered. But I cannot say that to her. Do you understand? I can say it to you, but not to her.'

'Of course I understand.' Oh, how I do. 'Does Anthony know ... how you feel?'

'No, it would hurt him. He loves his mother very much and he ... what is the word ... he admires his father. No, it is not admires ...'

'Reveres?'

'Yes, that is the word. Reveres. He thinks well of his memory. Yes?'

Of course he does; he has had no reason not too. Until now, when I have come along and dented that image. Poor Maria, it is hard to compete with a dead hero. I would love to tell you that your husband's father was just an ordinary man, easily tempted, unfaithful to his wife ... but I can't. One day maybe, but not today.

'Thank you again,' I said, and kissed her again. Anthony was waiting for me at the garage; Pawlu was nowhere in sight. My hire car, complete with new wing mirror and window was parked at the side of the kiosk.

'But ...? It's been repaired,' I said unnecessarily.

'Yes,' said Anthony. 'Pawlu thought while he was in Mosta he might as well do it. It is better this way, that you drive only the car you have hired.' In other words, he doesn't want me bashing up one of his. 'Did you have a good rest?'

'I did. I'm so sorry, I had no intention of going to sleep.'

'It will have done you good.' Anthony was all solicitous and brotherly. Was this the moment to ask him when I could talk to his mother?

'I think it has. I've also had a lovely chat with Maria.'

'Oh.' A pause. 'What about?'

'Oh, this and that. Women's talk. You know.' We smiled warily. 'Now … what about this car? Do I get an invoice, or what? I am insured.'

'No invoice. Forget it.'

'But …?'

He looked away, then back. 'Family,' he said.

I could have hugged him. Instead I just said, 'Thank you,' as warmly as I could. Then, because what I really wanted to say was: Thank you dear, kind brother such as I have never had before, I said, '*Grazzi*, Anthony.' and put my hand on his arm. Enough, Jane. Don't get sentimental, don't overdo it, you're not there yet. I took my hand away quickly. 'Well … I'd best be getting back to Mellieha.' I hope I sounded brisk. 'I've taken up enough of your time. Please thank Pawlu for me, I do so appreciate it.' Oh Anthony, say something. Suggest a time for me to see your mother. Come on, I'm going. Damn it, I don't want to do this but I can't waste this opportunity. Hand on the car door, about to get in: 'Anthony …'

'Yes?'

'When can I see your mother?'

'Ah. Yes, I almost forgot. Would tomorrow be convenient?' Of course tomorrow would be convenient, any time would be convenient and if it wasn't I would make it so.

'Tomorrow?' Not too eager. 'Yes, that would be fine. Any particular time?'

'She suggests four o'clock. She will give you an English tea.'

'How lovely. I shall look forward to that.' A smile,

that I hoped was charming. He didn't respond. 'I will behave, I promise you.' Still no smile. 'Oh dear, I can see you don't really want me to meet her, do you?'

'You will respect her, won't you?'

'Of course I'll respect her! Oh come on, Anthony, I'm not a fool, I'm not going to do anything stupid. You forget, this is important to me and I know I won't get another chance. Are you going to be there?'

'I feel that I should be.'

'You mean you don't trust me?'

'No, it's …'

'If you want to be there while we talk, that's okay by me. Whatever you say.'

'Let's say I'll be there to begin with.'

'And if you decide she's safe with me you'll leave us alone?'

'She has to be safe with you.'

'Oh, Anthony I'm teasing you. I'm sorry, that was quite wrong of me. This is not a joking matter.'

'No, it is not.' Indeed it is not.

'Till tomorrow then, at four.' I started the engine, waved goodbye and drove off.

Down the hill to the Mtarfa crossroads – should I stop at the cemetery, see if the flowers needed renewing? Not today; tomorrow perhaps when I had spoken to his widow. His widow. How strange that sounded. My mother was a widow; had she mourned the loss of Tom? I had no idea. Some day I must ask her. At this distance I can't recall how I felt about Tom's death. Shamefully untouched I fancy.

On to Mellieha – I had the route off pat by now: through the village, past the church and down the steep winding road that led to the coast, past the beach and the promenade, both now deserted, up the hill on the other side and into the drive of the hotel. I pulled up behind a coach and watched as a procession of weary-looking passengers alighted, all of them clutching bags and coats and umbrellas: the forecast had been rain. Among them was Ken, looking every bit as tired: it must have been an exhausting trip to the Three Cities.

Should I call to him, ask him what sort of day he'd had, tell him what I had been doing? No, if I was going to do that I should have done it spontaneously. It was too late now; he was almost at the hotel door. I would see him at seven in the bar. It was his last night. A cliché came to mind: I would see that he had 'a good time'. Well, I would. He had been a good companion, and more, all this week. He deserved my consideration.

I showered and towelled myself. At home I rarely saw myself naked, but here, as in so many hotel rooms, a large mirror over the basin faced the bath and as I stepped out I couldn't help but look at myself. As objectively as possible, starting at the top, I took an inventory. Hair: still bright and glossy, thanks not to any fancy shampoos, but to the use of an old-fashioned recipe which had come from Beth's mother: I strained camomile tea as a final rinse. Skin: still tight and supple. Boobs: firm, almost no droop, with a presentable cleavage. Stomach: could be flatter, if I exercised more. Navel: perfect for holding a jewel. (I had once thought of inserting one, but wasn't sure how you kept it in place.) Fortunately the mirror cut off at this point. I didn't have to look at my thighs to know they needed to lose some of their folds. 'They're your centre of gravity,' Neville used to say, 'Safer than being top-heavy.' My legs had always been shapely, my best feature, which I had happily flaunted in Sixties miniskirts.

Taken altogether, not bad for the mid-fifties. Check list over, I finished drying myself, slipped on my bathrobe and laid out a choice of clothes on the bed.

Cream silk trousers and a black top, or a long black

skirt and a striped blouse? Or the black skirt and the black top? What does it say about me that I can never decide what to wear when it matters. Did it matter, tonight? No. Not at all. Ken wouldn't be judging me, whatever I wore. In the end I wore black trousers and a white silk top.

Completely the wrong things; I had forgotten that this was the night of the formal dance, when the floor of the lounge bar was cleared of tables and chairs and quicksteps and foxtrots to the music of a three-piece band were the order of the evening.

'Very elegant,' said Ken.

'But inappropriate. Let me just go and change,' I said after dinner.

'This is where I came in.'

'What do you mean?'

'When we met, the first evening, you were wearing the wrong clothes.'

'And when I changed them we went for a walk. And that's what I'd really like to do now. Walk down to Mellieha beach, and splash my feet in the water! How about it?'

'Beats dancing any time.'

There were two old men smoking, and a young couple, entwined, on the promenade benches, but apart from a man and his dog we were the only people actually on the beach. We took off our shoes and stood side by side at the water's edge. The moonlight rippled on the bay and all was still, the only sound the gentle lap-lap of the water as it touched the shore. I felt at peace, as if I could stay there for ever.

Then Ken skimmed a stone and my moment of tranquillity was gone. The moon's reflection, agitated, broke into a thousand splinters. Gradually it settled back into shape, and then Ken shattered it again.

'Are you doing that on purpose?' I said.

'Does it bother you?'

'I find it disturbing, like a kind of vandalism.'

'I won't do it any more.' He let the stone that was in his hand fall on to the sand. 'Let's go back.' Slowly we walked up to the promenade, sat down on a bench and put on our shoes.

CHAPTER TWELVE

Ken had left before I came down for breakfast. Although his plane didn't take off until late afternoon he had caught an early bus into Valletta, intending to visit the War Museum which somehow he had missed. 'Can't come to Malta and not see the George Cross,' he had said. There were other things he wanted to see there, too: the Italian E-boat and the tank camouflaged to represent a rubble wall.

I might have driven over there and joined him – it would have helped to pass the hours before I was due to see Anthony's mother – but something quite unforeseen intervened, banishing both Ken and my forthcoming interview from my mind.

At half past eight, just as I about to leave my room, the phone rang.

'Is that you, Jane?' The voice was distressed, female and unmistakably Australian. Col was being held by the police in St. Paul's Bay, and she needed someone to vouch for him, and possibly pay a fine, before they would release him. 'Gee, I know it's a terrible cheek, but we don't know anyone here, and you did say we could call you …'

Call yes, not call on. But of course I went, to the police station in St. Paul's Bay. I wasn't sure that I wanted to vouch for Col, but Ronnie sounded so miserable I felt I had no choice. I didn't wait to find out what he had done, what crime he had committed, in case it was so heinous I might prefer to let him sweat it out. One drink too many no doubt. I remembered bailing Alex out in similar circumstances. Neville was abroad somewhere and I got a call to go to Canterbury where Alex and three of his mates, having imbibed too much real ale, had committed some impropriety – that was the phrase used – in the Cathedral precincts, and been arrested. Shamefacedly, a now sober Alex confessed to having peed in one of the porches and then, catching his foot on a loose paving stone, had fallen over, straight into the path of a church official, who might have been lenient, considering Alex's youth – he wasn't more than eighteen at the time – but this sort of thing had happened once too often and it was time someone was made an example.

It took me some time to find the police station where a tearful, bedraggled Ronnie awaited me.

'Oh, Jane, I'm so glad you're here.' She practically threw herself at me. I put a comforting arm around her shoulders. She looked as if she hadn't slept a wink, nor had a wash.

'Well, now that I am here, what is it you want me to do?'

She looked taken aback. 'Help me get him out, stand surety for him, or whatever it is you have to do.' Stand surety? A tall order to ask of a stranger.

'What has he done?' I asked.

'Nothing!'

'He must have done something, Ronnie, otherwise he

wouldn't be locked up and you wouldn't be in this state.'

'D'you have a tissue?' I found a small pack in my bag and passed it to her. 'Thanks.' She spat on a tissue and rubbed it over her cheeks.

'Here, let me do it. You're just making things worse.' I took some cologne from my bag, sprinkled it on the tissue and gently wiped her face.

'So, tell me ... what has Col done?'

'He hit a guy.'

'I see.'

'No, you don't. He was right to hit him. We were in this bar ... And before you ask, no, Col was not drunk. He never gets drunk, he doesn't like alcohol.' An Aussie who doesn't drink? 'They don't all live on Fosters, you know. Anyway, this guy, I don't know, he was English, I think ... pig ignorant, starts talking about Jews, you know, the usual stuff: gas chambers were too good for them, that sort of thing, and so Col just goes up to him and punches him, right on the nose, knocks him off the bar stool. The guy hits his head on the bar and next thing you know there's a pool of blood and someone's grabbing Col and carting him off here. Must have been about midnight.'

'Good for Col.' A bit like Beth, by the sound of it. She, being Jewish, could mock her race as much as she liked, but just let anyone else say even one derogatory word and the fur would start to fly. 'Come on, let's get him out.'

I did what was necessary and Col was bound over to keep the peace. 'Very commendable,' I said, when we were safely outside the police station, 'but please don't do it again.' It's what I would have said to Alex; I shouldn't have said it to Col. Before he could remonstrate I quickly said, 'Unless you have to, in which case you have my blessing.'

He smiled; it was the first time I had seen him smile –

a lovely, boyish lop-sided grin – and the tension was diffused.

Smile apart, they were a sad-looking pair – grimy, sweat-stained, weary, and probably hungry.

'Where are you staying?'

'Well, we're not right now.' Ronnie answered.

As I thought. 'Well, you'd best come back to my hotel, have a wash and I'll see if I can find you some breakfast.'

After they had cleaned themselves up – used my shower and my clean towels – I bought them breakfast in the foyer café. Coffee and croissants and as much fruit juice as I would drink in a week. To save any embarrassment and also to save myself being annoyed if they didn't offer to pay, I had already made it clear that this was my treat. It was readily accepted, without any protestations, in that easy way that antipodeans have of taking you at your word.

I'd had enough of playing Mother Hen; it was time to set these two chicks on the road again. But not without asking where they were going next. And that was a mistake.

'We thought we'd have a look at Mosta,' Ronnie said.

'Oh, the church, with the unexploded bomb?'

'No,' said Col. 'The market. They've got cheap CDs.'

So, of course, I ended up taking them, as I knew I would, after we had walked along the headland by the hotel and they'd had a swim from the hotel beach and eaten a sandwich in the hotel bar – which they paid for – and sunned themselves in the garden while I got dressed for my interview. It was an agreeable way of filling the day. More to the point, it had prevented my getting in a panic at the thought of meeting Anthony's mother again.

Today she was dressed in a sage green silk shirt, pleated skirt and matching jacket. Three strings of pearls, pearl earrings; grey court shoes, grey tights. She had greeted me at the front door – there was no sign of Anthony – and taken me upstairs. I was invited to sit on the sofa, where I'd sat on my previous visit. There were tea things on a trolley nearby: silver teapot (it might have been plated), strainer, floral patterned bone china cups and saucers and matching milk jug, linen napkins, dainty sandwiches and fairy cakes, all very English, as Anthony had said.

My hostess – that's how it felt, rather formal, I hoped I wouldn't spill my tea or drop crumbs on the rug – asked politely about my holiday: where had I been, what had I seen? Had I been to her shop? Her shop? In the main square in Mdina, a smart clothes shop. Rosaria's it was called, after her.

'What a beautiful name.'

'Thank you.'

Of course she didn't work there now, but she still looked in occasionally to make sure everything was being run properly. She had bought the business in the Sixties, when Malta began opening up to tourists. It had been just a small shop then, selling Maltese lace and a few souvenirs. Then in the Seventies she began to employ workers, women who knitted at home during the winter months and needed an outlet for their goods in the tourist season. Just jumpers and cardigans at first, then one of her knitters offered her a silk two-piece in dusty pink and it sold the day it was put on show. It wasn't long before Rosaria's shop became a boutique, specialising in hand-knitted silk garments. Demand couldn't keep up with supply and she had had to bring in imported goods, always of the best quality.

Rosaria showed no inclination to talk about the war. Perhaps she was waiting for me to broach the subject. Having eaten two cakes and refused a third I judged it was time for the interview proper to begin. I wiped my fingers on the napkin, folded it and put it beside the plate. I took my notebook and my cassette recorder from my bag, smiled at my hostess and said, in what I hoped were encouraging, friendly tones, 'Would you be willing to talk to me about the war now?'

'Certainly,' she said, 'but not here.'

'Oh.' Not here?

'We will talk downstairs. This room belongs to the present, as you can see. The room downstairs belongs to the past.' Then, as if she felt an explanation was required: 'It is a long time since my husband died and though I wish to remember him I do not think about him all the time now. He is not part of the life I now live. He does not fit in this room, among this furniture. Downstairs, among the old furniture and the old pictures I can relive those faraway times more easily. It is as if, by talking about him there, he is alive again, but in his own time. Downstairs he is still as he was, a young man. And I am a young woman. Up here, he is... out of place.' She smiled, 'With an old woman. Do you understand?'

Yes, I did understand. Although it wasn't really comparable, Neville had no place in my new home; I could be free of him there, but if I went to a restaurant or a hotel we had visited together the memory of that other time would intrude upon the present. I refrained from mouthing a platitude about a time and place for everything and simply nodded. I now understood why Anthony had been so concerned when Rosaria asked him to bring the photo albums upstairs.

She led the way to the ground floor room and indicated that I should sit down at the large centre table. An impressive foliage plant, in a brown lustre pot on a lace mat, stood in the middle. To one side there was a pile of photograph albums.

'I think we will move this,' she said. She picked up the plant and the mat and placed them carefully on the sideboard among the silver-framed family pictures. Then she sat down, opposite me.

'Now,' she said, sitting upright, clasping her hands in front of her – she had beautiful nails – and resting them on the edge of the table, 'what is it you want to know?'

Everything. Absolutely everything, every last detail.

'Well ...' I began, 'there's so much, isn't there?' Don't waste time, get to the heart of it. She knows about your book, your proposed novel about war-time Malta. 'Anthony says his father was a hero. Will you tell me why?'

I asked if I might switch on my cassette recorder and Rosaria agreed, if a little reluctantly. 'It is only for reference,' I said, 'I shan't quote you directly.' That seemed to reassure her. She was a good storyteller. Graphically she took me back to 1941, to the airfield at Ta' Qali.

'My young brother Wenzu ... he's the one who now lives in America ... well, he used to help at the airfield; all the young boys did. There was so much to do and the soldiers and the airmen got so tired ... and they didn't have the time to see to everything. And sometimes when they needed help to fill the aeroplanes with petrol, the Spitfires and the Hurricanes ... You must understand that this was a very bad time for Malta, for everyone, the people, the servicemen, for those in authority ... every day there were air raids and it was most important that the fighter planes should be kept in the air as much as possible. It was very dangerous for them to be on the ground, because there they became targets for the German bombers. And it was because of this, this urgency, that the boys were there, because normally they would not have been allowed on the airfield. You understand?'

'Yes, I understand.'

'All the rules, they were broken.' Her silver bangles

clicked, as with her fingers spread she waved her hands to emphasise the point. 'The rules did not matter, it was survival that was important.'

Carefully she had prepared the ground, now came the story. As she spoke I pictured it in my mind, almost like a film …

The ceaseless buzz of fighter planes taking off and landing, plumes of smoke dotting the airfield, piles of debris, great cavernous holes in the tarmac, make-shift pens to give temporary shelter to incoming planes, personnel rushing hither and thither, shouted commands, the mingled smells of petrol, oil, smoke and sweat. Above all, the sense of urgency.

An RAF sergeant is hustling a young lad towards one of the Nissan huts, holding him up by the collar so that his feet barely touch the ground. The lad is protesting in Maltese. Roughly, the sergeant pushes the boy into the hut. A tall, fair-haired Royal Artillery bombardier is running at full pelt in the direction of the hut. Reaching it, he flings open the door, almost falls into the room. Behind the desk is an RAF officer, in front of the desk is the sergeant, still holding on to the boy. The gunner is livid. 'What the hell are you doing with that boy?'

The officer, rising to his feet: 'How dare you barge in here!'

The gunner, momentarily checked: 'Sir. I beg your pardon, sir.'

'That's better. Now what do you want?'

'The lad, sir. He's … he's my brother-in-law. Sir.'

'This boy?'

'Yes sir. I'm married to his sister.'

'Well, I'm sorry about that, bombardier, but you know the rules.'

'Rules? What rules? What's he supposed to have done?'

'Oh come on, you know what he's done.'

'No sir, I don't. I just saw him being hauled off like a piece of meat.'

'Instead of putting petrol into the Spit he was putting in oil.'

The boy looks imploringly at the bombardier.

'Is this true?'

'No. Well, yes, but …'

'But what? Come on, Wenzu, what happened?'

'On the drum it say petrol … it does not say oil … but when I have filled the Spit and I take out the pipe … I see it is oil. I not mean to do it, Pete.'

'Okay, Wenzu. You leave this with me, mate.' He turns to the officer. 'It was a mistake. He can siphon out the oil …'

'I'm sorry, bombardier, brother-in-law or not, this has nothing whatever to do with you. This lad has committed an act of sabotage … and he must pay the penalty.'

'Sabotage! Christ almighty! Are you telling me you're going to shoot him? Over *my* dead body.'

'Sergeant, put this man on a charge.'

'Oh no, you don't. And you are not going to take this boy either. You shoot him, you shoot me.'

'Pete, don't let them shoot me.'

'Of course I won't let them shoot you, you little idiot. Come here.' The boy wriggles out of the sergeant's, by now, loose hold and throws himself at the gunner and hides his face in his tunic. There is a long pause. The officer eyes the sergeant and the bombardier. The sergeant looks straight ahead not showing any emotion; the bombardier is stroking the boy's head, whispering to him in Maltese.

The officer speaks: 'Very well. I'll look into it.' The bombardier's shoulders relax; the boy stays where he is, closely pressed against his protector; the sergeant remains immobile. 'But I'm afraid I can't allow your conduct to pass, bombardier.'

'No sir. Thank you, sir.'

'All right. Now take him away.'

'Yes sir, thank you, sir.'

'And I don't want to see him on this airfield again.'

'No sir. You won't. Sir.'

The bombardier disentangles himself from the boy, draws himself to attention, salutes smartly, puts a hand on the boy's shoulder ... and leaves the hut.

'Do you not agree that that was heroic?' I don't know how long I had been sitting there, still in the past. Rosaria had finished her story and she was looking at me anxiously.

'Oh yes.' It was easy to respond to her obvious need. I stretched out my hand and put it over hers. I could feel tears pricking my eyelids. And why not? You didn't need to be personally involved to be moved by that story, anybody would have been; it had all the right ingredients: a hero, a victim, authority to be flouted, a risk to be taken, a happy ending.

'God, to think a boy's life could depend upon something like that. What if your husband hadn't been there? Did he ... was he punished?'

'Yes. I think he had to stay in the barracks for a few days. That part I don't remember so well. A few days, not long. Anthony was a baby. I think I went and asked if my husband could come home.'

'And they let him?'

'I think so. There is a blank, do you know what I mean? I am not sure. I remember so clearly the story of Wenzu because everybody tells it so many times. You know?'

I nodded and smiled at her. 'The other story I also remember. He was a hero that time, too.'

'May I ...' I pointed to my cassette recorder. 'May I tape this one, too?'

'Yes. Of course.' She smiled. 'I don't think this one,

though, is quite the sort of story you will want in your book. It is ... what is the word ... soppy.'

'Heroes can be soppy.'

'Oh no, Peter was not soppy. Maybe that is the wrong word. I think the word I want is tender. Soft, you know, not ... not tough.'

'Gentle?'

'Yes, gentle.' I waited, while she looked back. 'He was a very gentle man, Pietru. Very clever, too.'

'In what way?' I spoke softly; I didn't want to disturb her concentration.

'He was ... he was a poet.'

'A poet?' In my head my voice sounded loud. Damn, why had I spoken at all. Rosaria was embarrassed. I felt I had stumbled on something deeply personal.

'Yes, he wrote poems. Now, the story. It is about a cat.'

'A cat. Oh.' I don't want to hear about a cat, I want to hear about my father's poetry. 'Please, tell me.'

'You know we have many air raids ...'

'Yes, I do.'

'Well, one day a bomb drops on a house near to my home. Pietru is at Ta' Qali, and he hears there is a bomb in Rabat and so he comes home, to make sure that we are all right ... that I am all right, because at that time I am expecting Carmela. Well, when he arrives he hears a child crying and he thinks it is Anthony, and that he has been hurt. But it is not Anthony, it is Stella, the little girl in the house that has been hit. Her mother is cross with her and tells her to stop crying. Peter wants to know why she is crying and Stella's mother tells him it is because the bomb has killed her cat. Pietru says, "You mean the cat is still in the house?" and Stella's mother says, "It was in the house when the bomb fell, so it must be dead." So what does my Pietru do? He goes into the ruins of the house to see if he can find it. It is not safe, it is still burning, stones and wood they are still falling down, but he goes in. I stand there watching and I am so frightened, for Pietru. Stella's mother says "You should not have let him go in there." I say to her, "How can I stop him? He is a British soldier." while in my head I am thinking, I am going to be a widow, my baby will have no father. Then I start to scream. I want to go in there, to be with him. Stella's mother has to hold me back. She is yelling now, "Pietru, come out of there!" There is a big crash, more wood and stones are falling. I cannot look, I hide my face. And then I hear Pietru's voice. "Here you are, Stella, here is your cat." For a cat he risks his life!'

Tears were pouring down Rosaria's cheeks; the retelling of this tiny incident had affected her deeply. The sophisticated businesswoman was gone; in her place was the young widow, angry, hurt, grieving. She wiped away the tears, smoothed her hair, offered me a brave smile. 'I am sorry, I do apologize.' Her voice was back to normal, controlled. 'It's just that … well, that's what war was like for us. Bombs every day, never knowing when or where the next one would fall. I was so angry with him! It was enough that he was under fire at the airfield all the time; he shouldn't have put his life at risk for a cat! But then that was Pietru. You have that saying about fools rushing in …'

'Where angels fear to tread.'

'That was Pietru.'

'Brave.'

'Foolish. He never gave a thought to the consequences of anything he did.' A bitter note had crept into her voice. 'I think perhaps he was too young to have the responsibility of a family. If you have a family you must take care … of yourself. And he did not.' I sat very still, willing her to go on. 'He did what he wanted … and that is why he died. If he had not gone to Mosta that night …'

'Mosta? What happened at Mosta?' She looked up at me, sighed, then looked down at her hands, twisted the rings on her left hand with the fingers of her right hand, almost as if she were performing some kind of sacred ritual. At last she spoke.

'There was an air raid, and he was rescuing wounded civilians; a wall collapsed and he was badly wounded. He was not supposed to have been there; he should have been in Rabat.' The memory was very painful; I didn't want to press her. 'The war did strange things to people. It made my husband a hero.'

'And you were very proud of him?'

'Oh yes. Of course I was. I still am proud of him. The cat was ... nothing, but Wenzu ... Pietru saved Wenzu's life.' She reached across the table and patted my hand. 'Come, we will go upstairs. I will show you the poem he wrote, for me ... about the cat. I really should keep this downstairs... but I like to look at it now and then,' Rosaria said, apologetically.

Back upstairs, seated again on the sofa, a fresh cup of tea on the low table in front of me, I read Peter's poem. It was called simply, Cat.

Blackened fur, scrabbling claws, pathetic meows
She looks at me with frightened eyes
Puss, puss I say, reach out a hand
Frozen with fear she hisses back.

The flames encroach, the air is hot
If she will not come to me I must go back.
Puss, puss I say, reach out my hand.
Grab her fur and hold on hard.

She spits and growls, she bites my hand
The pain is sharp, the air is hot
I hold on still and lift her down
Her fur is singed, her eyes are sore.

They call me a hero, say I was brave.
I was not brave, I was a fool she said,
To venture in among the flames
And all for what? A little cat.

Sorry, wife, it is my way
What more then can I say?
I do not try to give you pain
I love you dear with all my heart.

Tiger, tiger, burning bright ...
That could have been your fate
That would have been the terrible sight
If I had come too late.

All the time, as I read, I was aware of Rosaria's eyes upon me. Was she expecting me to praise it, comment on it? It wasn't the best poem I had ever read; it wasn't the worst either. It was heartfelt, and for her.

'As poetry goes, it's ... well, it is not very good. I know that,' she said, 'but I treasure it.'

'Of course you do.' So would I. 'Could I make a copy of it?' I asked, quite suddenly, surprising myself.

'Yes, if you wish, but ...'

'You can't see the relevance to my project, my book?'

'Not really, no.' Time to flannel.

'It's a very poignant reminder of ... of the war and the effect it had on people's lives. I'm sure that lots of small incidents, like this one, made up the fabric of ... of life here at that time.'

She seemed satisfied. 'You are right, because life did go on, somehow, even though we were starving, and afraid. There was even time for ...'

'Laughter?'

'I was going to say, love.'

Oh yes, plenty of time for that. Had Peter been faithful to Rosaria? It was not an avenue I wanted to explore. 'And poems,' I said, and we both laughed. It was time for me to leave, even though I hadn't yet looked at the war-time photograph albums. I handed back the poem and stood up. 'Thank you. I am most touched that you showed me that.'

She took the sheet of paper from me. 'What sort of man was your father?' she asked. The question took me unawares.

'My father?'

'Yes. You said my Pietru knew him.'

'Oh.' I hoped I hadn't looked startled. 'Oh, he was ... well, he didn't write poems, he ... he liked tinkering with engines, motorbikes, that sort of thing. He was a very practical man, very down-to-earth.' Don't go on, you've made the point.

'Would you not want to make him the model for the hero in your book?'

The thought had never crossed my mind. 'Er ... no.' Invention came to my rescue. 'It would be difficult to base him on someone I actually knew, someone I was close to. Besides,' – back on firm ground – 'he didn't marry a Maltese woman.'

'Ah, I had forgotten that. Perhaps you should talk to some of the men who did marry Maltese girls, those who stayed on after the war.'

'I would like that, very much. But how do I find them?'

'Oh, that's simple: you talk to Carmela.'

'Yes, of course. She did those interviews.'

'I don't think there is anyone living in Rabat, but there is certainly someone in Mosta. Oh dear, I can't remember his name and I have no idea where he lives, but he would be very helpful: he was in the Royal Artillery, and he knew Pietru, not well, but he did know him, so he might have known your father. If you let me have the telephone number of your hotel I will ask my daughter to call you, and she can put you in contact with him.'

I left feeling exhilarated: at last I was making some progress. At the same time I was vaguely troubled by something Rosaria had said about Peter, about the night he died. 'He should have been in Rabat.' She had said it so remorsefully. Had he gone out, seeking glory, when he should have been with her? Or had he been with another woman?

CHAPTER THIRTEEN

In the hotel foyer I was stopped by a call from the desk.

'Mrs. Thornfield.'

'Yes?'

'I have an urgent message for you.' The girl handed over a folded note. Oh dear, not Col and Ronnie in trouble again.

'Thank you,' I said, taking the note and walking on towards the lifts. If it was Col and Ronnie they could wait. No, better look; it might be to do with my mother, or … I stood stock still, the unfolded note in my hand. 'Please telephone me immediately, Carmela Farrugia.' And a number. Carmela? Already? Rosaria must have phoned her the moment I left. Things were moving fast; this was wonderful. Or was it? Why the hurry? Well, that was easy. Rosaria knew I was here for only another few days and if Carmela had lots of information to give me it was sensible for us to get together as soon as possible. Even so … Immediately? It was almost a summons. In my room I dialled Carmela's number. After only three rings it was answered. In Maltese.

'Hello,' I said. 'May I speak to Carmela Farrugia.'

'Speaking.'

'Oh. Hello. It's Jane Thornfield. You left a message for me to call you.'

'Yes I did.' No emotion, no warmth. The pause lengthened, and just when I was about to break it, she said, in a now very emotional voice, 'Go home, Mrs. Thornfield. Go home and stop making your enquiries. Please, I beg you. It can only lead to trouble.'

'But ...' She had gone; there was only the dialling tone. 'Hello. Hello,' I said, jiggling the phone rest up and down. 'Carmela? Mrs. Farrugia? Are you there?'

Go home. It can only lead to trouble. What the hell was going on? And more to the point, what do I do now? Phone Anthony? Try Carmela again? Or Rosaria? No, not Rosaria. Anthony, he was the one. Anthony – of course, that was it. Anthony had, after all, told Carmela about me and she was upset and anxious for her mother. Perfectly understandable, even if the reaction was a bit dramatic. Still, perhaps that was the Maltese way, fiery, explosive. If Rosaria had phoned Carmela and Carmela had spoken to Anthony and said 'What's all this about?' and Anthony had said, 'Ah well, this woman is your half-sister ...' No wonder Carmela was disconcerted. No, dammit, disconcerted or not, that was no way to speak to someone. 'Go home.' It's nothing to do with you, Carmela Farrugia; I'll go home when I like!

As I reached for my handbag to find Anthony's number the phone rang. I snatched it up.

'Hello?'

'Mrs. Thornfield?'

'Yes.'

'It's Carmela Farrugia.'

'Oh.'

'I'm very sorry, I shouldn't have said that. It was very rude of me.'

'Then why did you say it?' I hope I sounded affronted: I had no reason to be polite to her.

'Because …' A deep sigh. 'I was upset. I don't like people troubling my mother; she's an old lady and …'

'Oh come on, your mother's an intelligent woman, don't put her down like that. It's Anthony, isn't it. He's told you who I am.'

'Yes, he has.' She didn't sound pleased; I would have to tread carefully.

'How do you feel about it?'

'Well, I'm not delighted.'

'Oh.'

'Did you think I would be?'

'Well, no … it's a difficult thing to take in.'

'Difficult …? There's nothing difficult about it.' She sounded really angry now. 'It's quite simple: you're writing a book and you want to base the hero on my father.' She didn't know; Anthony hadn't told her. She was this upset because I was writing a novel? 'Well, I don't want you to do that,' she went on. 'And I don't want you to ask my mother any more questions, particularly not about my father's death.'

'I didn't ask her about his death; she told me.'

'She told you?' Was it alarm I detected in Carmela's voice, or annoyance.

'She said he was killed in an air raid.'

'Oh. Right.'

'That's not the truth though, is it?'

'Well … in a way it is.'

'Look, I'm sorry, Mrs. Farrugia, I don't know what this is all about. My interest in your father is that he was a British serviceman who lived here during the war. Why should I want to know how he died?'

'Forget it, please.'

'No, I can't. How did he die?' No response. 'Is it important?' There was a long sigh from Carmela.

'I think we'd better meet. I don't think we can continue this discussion on the phone.'

Good, I had played it right; I would get to meet Carmela. 'I agree. When do you suggest? I don't have a lot of time left.'

'Tomorrow?'

'Yes. Fine.'

'I'll come to your hotel. Will one o'clock suit you?'

'One o'clock's fine. Come and have some lunch with me.'

'Thank you. That's very kind.'

'Not at all. It will give me a chance to repay some of the hospitality I've already had from your family.'

'Oh. Tea with my mother you mean.' She sounded amused.

'And with your sister-in-law.'

'Maria? You've met Maria? I didn't know that.' And you don't like it, do you.

'I found her charming and helpful.'

'Yes, well, she would be. Right … I'll see you tomorrow then.'

'Yes. Tomorrow. Goodbye.'

Before she could say any more I put the phone down. My hand was shaking. It had cost me dear to appear so detached. I might not have cared before about the manner of Peter Andersen's death, but I bloody well did now.

He obviously wasn't just killed in an air raid. He had been in Mosta illegally, that much I had gleaned from Rosaria. Carmela knew this, too, and wanted it hushed up. It had not been a hero's death by the sound of it, although that was the story that had been put about, the legend that Anthony and Carmela had grown up with. And now Carmela, through research for her programme, had learnt the truth of what had really happened that night in Mosta. From the ex-serviceman who still lived there, presumably. Well, if Peter had had a mistress in Mosta it wasn't going to bother me, but I could see how distressed Rosaria would be. Carmela was right to keep it from her mother, and Anthony too. No good could come of raking up the past. If I really thought that, what the hell was I doing here? In my case it was different; I wasn't going to be hurt by any revelations about my father. I knew him for what he was: a lovable rogue, a bit of a dare-devil, charming, irresponsible. He would have made a lousy father, but I would have loved him as a man. The thought brought me up sharply. Was that what I was doing: falling in love with my own father? What if I was; there was no harm in it. He hadn't been there when I was growing up, so it didn't feel as if he was my father in that sense.

I would meet Carmela, and if she couldn't give me any help – come to think of it, how could she? She wasn't alive when all this was happening – if she couldn't help I would go straight to the man she interviewed. It was one of the basic rules of journalism: go direct to the primary source. Feeling very buoyed up I was looking forward to the next day. But first I had to get through the rest of this one, on my own, without Ken. Dinner by myself. Not a pleasing prospect. As it happened it didn't arise. The lady from the plane, Joan Ling, approached me in the foyer, as I was on the way to the dining-room. She was with two of her usual group.

'I see your friend has left, so I wondered if you would like to join us.' It was a well-prepared, though nonetheless sincere, speech.

'Thank you. I would.' We were shown to a table in the centre of the dining room. Better than being tucked away by myself in a corner. If conversation dragged I could always tell them about Col and Ronnie and we could have a moan about the irresponsibility of the younger generation. As it turned out I didn't even mention the Australians. I hardly spoke at all; they did the talking, right through the starters, to which we helped ourselves from the buffet, and the main course served at the table: I had the Maltese dish – there was one every evening – a gorgeous pie stuffed with fish and spinach. Thankfully, they didn't seem at all interested in what I had been doing, content to chatter on about their day out, the postcards they had sent, the bargains they had found, their plans for tomorrow. Joan was a relative newcomer to Malta but Olive and Barbara, I learnt, had been here many times before. Barbara, a sturdy Lancashire woman now in her seventies, had been a nurse here during the war. That could be useful. By the time we got to the dessert – fruit salad for me – I managed to get a word in. I wondered if Barbara knew about the tin coffins.

'Oh yes, I know all about them. Terrible things, gave you the creeps. Aye, I've helped lift more than one poor lad into one of them. The other thing they used was a coffin with a hinged bottom, so you could re-use it. You had the service, you know, pall-bearers and all that, then when they got to the grave they opened up the bottom and slipped the body out. It was wrapped in a sheet of course.'

'Barbara, please! I know you and Olive like to reminisce, but really; we are having dinner. Besides, I doubt whether Jane wants to hear all this.'

'Oh, but I do. It's fascinating.'

'It was Jane mentioned coffins, not me,' said Barbara. 'I'll tell you something else interesting. I was here when they had the polio outbreak in '42.' Blank expressions greeted her. 'Did you not know about this? Olive, you knew?'

'No. I wasn't out here till after the war, remember.'

'Of course. I'd forgotten that. Anyway, it's fully documented. Now. At the time it was very hush-hush.

We didn't want the Germans to find out. Things were bad enough here without them knowing we had polio. Infantile paralysis they called it then. We had an iron lung at the hospital and we had a soldier in there and it stopped functioning. Well, we had to get the sappers in. I can't remember the exact details but I know there was something wrong with the bellows, the rubber had perished I think. Anyway, this REME fitter, nice young chap he was, I quite fancied him! Well, he did something clever with an inner tube from a car tyre, and within a couple of hours we were back in business. I tell you, there was lot of mend and make do. Had to be, we had no supplies coming in, you see, none at all.'

'These funerals ...' I said, tentatively.

'Oh, can't we talk about something else,' said Joan.

'I'm sorry. Another time perhaps.'

Fortunately Barbara was not easily deflected.

'No, no. If you want to know.'

'It's not gruesome, I assure you.' I smiled hopefully at Joan and Olive.

'Go on,' said Barbara. 'Don't take any notice of them.'

'More wine, Olive?' said Joan, loudly.

'I'll say.' Olive held up her glass.

'Jane?'

'Thank you.' I let my glass be re-filled. I smiled at Joan.

'Go on,' she said. 'Ask her.'

'It won't take long, I promise.' I turned to Barbara.

'What I wanted to know was ... were they all military funerals? What I mean is, all those soldiers and airmen who're buried, in the Imtarfa cemetery, for instance ... were they all killed in action?'

Barbara laughed. 'It depends what you mean by action! The actual phrase was 'on active service' and I can tell you some of the service those boys saw was very active, too active some of it, down by the waterfront in Valletta.'

'So …' I wanted her to be more specific. 'If a soldier, say, was killed, or badly injured, in an air raid, and then died later, and at the time of the raid he had been in … in …'

'In bed with someone?'

'Er … yes.'

'As I said, active service. He was in a war zone. Any serviceman killed in a war zone is a casualty of war. Whatever he's doing at the time.'

'Mm … that's very interesting. So, if …' Joan groaned, and I took the hint. 'Sorry, I won't go on. Thank you, Barbara, you've answered my question.'

'Good. Now can we talk about something else. Is anybody going to see the film tonight?'

'Depends what it is.' From Olive.

Barbara knew. 'It's *Witness*, with Harrison Ford. A brilliant film. I've seen it at least twice, but I'll happily see it again. It begins with a murder.'

That was enough to put off Joan, and Olive. 'No thank you,' they said, and no amount of persuasion by Barbara, including a graphic description of a wonderful scene in which a whole Amish community builds a barn, could make them change their minds.

'I'll come,' I said. The movie was well worth seeing a second time. And I was grateful to Barbara. I was all but convinced now that Peter had been up to no good the night he died. And that Carmela knew this.

CHAPTER FOURTEEN

It was with a sense of *déjà vu* that I waited in the hotel lounge for Carmela. Would our meeting be a replay of my conversation with Anthony? Hardly; I had no intention of disclosing our blood relationship. The less she knew about me personally the more I would learn about Peter. I was unconcerned with my dress this morning; I wasn't out to impress, as I had been with Anthony and his mother. I flung on a pair of beige slacks and a red and brown over-shirt: I was simply a novelist doing research, meeting another media person.

She was on time. I recognised her immediately. She had Anthony's build and the same blue-grey eyes and sharp nose. Her hair, though, was dark and pulled back from her face. She wore court shoes, a black suit and a cream shirt, very business-like. I wished I hadn't dressed so sloppily. I got up from my seat and walked towards her.

'Mrs. Farrugia?'

'Mrs. Thornfield.' A statement, but at the same time a question: who are you and why are you here? If it had been a man looking at me as she did I would have said he was mentally undressing me. As it was I felt she was taking me apart and putting me together again, trying to make the pieces fit. It was a very uncomfortable feeling, one I had never experienced before, with a woman. But then, when I met a woman at a business meeting I was always the one in charge. Not this time. By her gaze and her dress and the way she said my name it was clear that Carmela was the one in control. Well, all right, I could go along with that, probably turn it to my advantage.

I held out my hand. 'Thank you for coming.' She shook my hand firmly, but briefly. Not a woman who would waste time on trifles. There would be no polite foreplay with her. No waiting till the dessert course to get down to the reason for our meeting.

I was wrong. Through the parma ham and melon we exchanged pleasantries – holidays, the weather, air travel: I might have been at the hairdresser's. Then, with our main course in front of us – a local fish, *lampuki,* served with rice and *kapunata*, the Maltese version of ratatouille – she suddenly said: 'So ... you want to know about my father.' It wasn't a question, and therefore didn't require an answer. I waited. I knew how to play this game; I had done it often enough with nervous job applicants. The good ones waited, the hopeless ones began to gabble. It seemed to put Carmela off her stride slightly. I felt she had been expecting an answer that would give her a chance to slap me down. I sensed that she didn't like me, that she'd made up her mind about me and nothing was going to change it.

'I should have thought you knew all there was to know, for the purposes of your book,' she said. 'What sort of novel is it anyway?'

'I'm not sure yet.'

'Oh.' She raised her eyebrows.

I decided I didn't like her either. Half-sister? No thank

you. Not on the present showing anyway.

'It might be a romance, an Ellen Field.' She looked blank. 'I write in two genres: romances as Ellen Field; mysteries, that is, crime … as Jane Gaunt. I think you'll find some of my books on sale at the airport.' Well, one: the latest, slightly erotic, Ellen Field, that had gone into paperback.

'I can't see how this is either.'

'Can't you? It is certainly a romance: war-torn Malta, young, handsome British soldier, Maltese …'

'Yes, yes, I know all that. I should have thought you had enough data for that already.' So why was she here? She knew something she didn't want me to know, and she wanted to find out if I already knew. Something to do with Peter's death, something shameful that she wouldn't want me to use in the book.

'Tell me about your job,' I said suddenly. Maybe I would get to it this way. Carmela began to talk about her work. She was not only a producer for Radio Malta, she was also their Head of Outside Broadcasts.

'Sounds fascinating,' I said. 'Do you get to broadcast from outside Malta at all?'

She laughed. 'Only Gozo,' she said, helping herself to more *kapunata*. 'And once from Sicily. To complain on behalf of tourists from Malta about the appalling rip-off of some recent day trips to the island.'

'So your special end-of-the war programme would come under the heading of an O.B.?'

'Yes, it did.'

'It always amazes me how clear old people's memories can be for events far in the past. Not that they always want to talk about them. My mother shuts up like a clam when it comes to the war; she doesn't want to think about it, won't discuss it at all. I think she must have some very painful memories, probably to do with the Blitz.' Now why had I said that; it could have no relevance to Carmela. I could use it, though. 'Did you find that people wanted to talk, or did they want to bury the past?'

'A few did, but I think for most of them it was very cathartic.'

'Talking to someone who was really interested, instead of family who'd heard it all before.'

'Yes.'

'Did you uncover any new facts as a result of your research?'

'What do you mean, new facts?' It was a question she didn't like.

'Oh, you know … things that might have been hush-hush at the time, but couldn't possibly affect anything now? Military secrets, that sort of thing.'

'Oh no.' Her laugh was one of relief.

'Or maybe personal ones. I presume you use a tape recorder?' Carmela nodded. 'I don't know about you but I usually find that once they've got used to the machine people just go on talking almost without realising what they're saying, as if they're not talking to a person and they don't need to be discreet any more.'

'If that does occur you have to edit it out.' Her tone was frosty. So she had learned something detrimental about her father. If I don't ask she won't tell me.

'Was your father with another woman the night he died? Is that what you're afraid I'll find out?' As soon as I'd said it I wished I hadn't. To suggest that her beloved father, her hero, had been … 'I'm sorry, that was a terrible thing to say. It wasn't meant to hurt you, it was …' She wasn't hurt, she was relieved. I'd guessed wrong; that wasn't the secret. Now what? Keep on apologising for a start.

'Oh God, I'm so sorry. It was … I just felt you were hiding something from me and I couldn't see why. I don't want to pry into your family history, Carmela, I …

I just want background stuff. Look, can we start again?'

'Of course.' She was in control again. 'What do you want to know?'

'Well ... anything you can tell me. Perhaps I could have a cassette of your programme. Or, better still, could I speak to some of the people you met? I think your mother mentioned somebody in Mosta.'

'No!' Like a shot from a rifle, then a pause and a faint smile. 'That would not be a good idea.'

'Why not?' I could feel anger welling up.

'Oh ... he's ... he's unreliable. And he's deaf.' You don't want me to meet him.

'All right, someone else then.' Her relief was palpable.

'Yes, if you wish. There's an old man in Naxxar, a lovely old man, an engineer, married a local girl, settled there, very nice man, he was on my programme; he'd be just right for you to talk to. I'll arrange it if you like. Oh, and there's another one in Sliema, he was in the Royal Army Medical Corps; you could see him.' Too enthusiastic by half.

'Well, thank you.' No point in antagonising her. On the other hand I didn't have the time to gallivant around seeing old men in Naxxar or Sliema. Relaxed now, she helped herself to more rice.

'Lovely meal,' she said.

'Yes, the food's very good. So important when you're on holiday, good food.' The waiter cleared our plates, brought our dessert: we both had fresh fruit.

'We have good wine, too.' she said, nodding to the bottle on the table.

'Oh yes, very good, it's up there with the best.'

'It is now, used not to be. We've just won some awards, quite prestigious ones, competing against wines from all over the world.'

'Really? How interesting.'

I refilled her glass, put the bottle down. It was time to stop dissembling. 'This man ... the one in Mosta ...'

'What about him?' Her hand was frozen in the act of moving towards her glass.

'I'd rather like to talk to him.' A warming smile. 'Even if he is deaf. You see ... the thing is, if he knew your father ...'

'I never said he did.'

'I'm sorry, I got the impression that he did. Oh well, anyway, the point is ... What's this man's name?'

'Joe Crowther.' She hadn't meant to tell me his real name, but I'd not given her enough time to invent one.

'Okay, well whether or not Joe Crowther knew your father, there's always a chance that he knew my father, Tom Harper. Same age, about, both in the Royal Artillery. It would be very interesting for me to meet him. I really would appreciate it if ...'

'No, I'm sorry, I cannot let you talk to Joe Crowther.'

'Why not?'

'I've told you why.'

'That he's unreliable and deaf. Oh come on, that's no reason. He knows something about your father that you don't want me to find out, that's what it is, isn't it? Listen, Carmela, I don't care what your father did. I know you're thinking of your mother, naturally. I won't do anything to hurt her, I promise you.'

Elbows on the table, hands clasped together against her mouth, Carmela raised her shoulders and let out a deep shuddering sigh. 'Oh God, this is so difficult.' A long pause, while she looked, not seeing, at the plate in front of her. Then she lifted her head and looked at me. There was real pain in her eyes. 'Please, don't ask this of me, Jane.'

She reached out a hand and placed it over one of mine. 'It really is best if you go home and ... and stop asking questions.' She pushed her plate away, reached down to pick up her bag, stood up. 'I have to go. Thank you for lunch.'

I wanted to grab her arm and say, 'Wait, sit down, there's something you ought to know.' But no, if she were to learn who I really was, it must come from Anthony, not me. If I told her I should lose all contact with her and probably with her mother as well.

'My pleasure,' I said, standing up. We shook hands.

'I'm sorry I couldn't be more help.'

I watched her go, trim and efficient, but not with the same degree of control that she had shown at the beginning of our interview. As Jane Gaunt I would end the chapter: 'Carmela Farrugia was a woman with a secret.' Secret was perhaps too strong a word, but certainly there was something troubling her. Whatever it was she wasn't prepared to tell me. I had a gut feeling that it was important and I couldn't leave Malta without finding out what it was. Obviously Anthony did not know, nor Rosaria, so who did? Besides Carmela. The answer was Joe Crowther. I would have to see him, whether Carmela liked it or not.

Tomorrow was Sunday; I could go to Mosta, make enquiries: there couldn't be that many British ex-servicemen living there. If only I had something to go on. Perhaps Anthony would know. From my room I phoned him.

'Anthony. Hello there. It's Jane Thornfield.' I explained that I had met Carmela – no, of course I hadn't told her who I was – and she had promised me a recording of her radio programme and I'd like to get hold of it as soon as possible, and could Anthony give me her home phone number as it was now the weekend and presumably she wouldn't be at work until Monday. Oh, and by the way – casually, just about to ring off, having got the number – Carmela had also told me about a man who lived in Mosta who might be able to help me.

Did Anthony know him? No, he didn't. Thanks anyway, nice to chat; I'll see you before I leave. When? Oh, next Friday, plenty of time. I'd like it if you and Maria could have dinner with me one evening. I'll ring you. Goodbye. Well, I'd got Carmela's number, which was something: I really did want to hear the recording. That at least was honest.

I went out on to the balcony and looked out over the bay. Not seeing anything, my mind elsewhere.

Oh, why is it so hard to talk about the things that matter, to say what we really think and feel, especially to those who are, or should be, closest to us. I never said what I really meant to Neville, never explained fully that although I loved him I couldn't live with him, not if I was to work as I wanted. Should I have given up my work, my writing, for him? To make him happy. What then of me? Was his happiness of more importance than mine? How do you measure these things? Right now I wasn't rating my career very highly. So often the drama of my books had been more real to me than real life. Now it seemed that the drama in my own life was superseding anything I had dreamed up on my computer. Drama in fiction, in my fiction, was fine: I was in control, I could make my characters act at will, my will. Not now, not here. I felt like a character in someone else's novel, involved in a plot whose outcome I couldn't foresee. And I was lonely. Lonely for Neville? Yes, lonely for Neville; for his arms around me, for his good counsel, for his ability to put things into perspective. Well, it was a bit late to start appreciating him. I know what he would say about all this. 'Janey,' he'd say, 'You are you, whoever your father was. You are not a different person just because you've discovered a different parent.' But I think I am. And so we would have argued and I would have gone my own way, as usual.

I turned away from the view I wasn't seeing, caught a glimpse of Michael in the garden below, waved to him but he didn't see me. What should I do for the rest of the day? First I must phone Carmela. I dreaded making the call, being rebuffed. Put it off till later. No, get it out of the way and then go out and see a bit of Malta. If I was going to write a novel set in wartime Malta I ought to see as much of the island as I could. Yes, that was a positive thought; I felt cheered by it.

Carmela's number was engaged. I changed my shoes, checked my bag – made sure I had my notebook and tape recorder – then redialled. Still engaged. Was Carmela talking to Anthony, about me? Oh come on, Jane, be sensible, she's probably not home yet. Go out and call her later.

Olive and Joan were in the foyer. They had just come in from a shopping trip to Valletta; they were going to have a quick cup of tea and then a soak in the bath and a good rest before dinner. Valletta, that's where I would go.

'Surely you're not setting off now? It's dark in a couple of hours; and you'll catch the rush hour. Why don't you leave it till tomorrow, then you can have the whole day there, and go to the market as well.' Oh how practical some people are. Joan didn't have my sense of frustration though, my need to be continually pursuing my goal. I couldn't just stay in the hotel, drink tea and chat. I hadn't that much time left; I couldn't waste it. If Valletta was out, and it was, where could I go? To Mosta, track down Joe Crowther. Not see him, not do anything to upset Carmela. Just a recce, that was all. The important thing was, it would give me a feeling of doing something, of being in control. Carmela didn't want me to meet Joe Crowther. Too bad: this was my story, not hers; he wasn't her property and if I wanted to talk him, then I damn well would. I drove fast all the way to Mosta.

CHAPTER FIFTEEN

Nobody in Mosta had heard of Joe Crowther, certainly not anyone I spoke to. 'Where does he live?' I didn't know. 'What was his wife's maiden name?' I didn't know that either. 'Look him up in the phone book.' How stupid of me not to think of that. But when I did, at the Post Office, he wasn't listed. He probably lived with his in-laws, or one of his children. I had come on a fool's errand. I sat dejectedly in a car park near the Cathedral and wondered what to do next. It was four o'clock; there was just over an hour of daylight left. I could drive back to the hotel, have some tea, have a bath ... or ... I could drive to Rabat. If Anthony didn't know Joe Crowther, perhaps Maria did, or Pawlu; and if Carmela found out I was still asking questions ... well, tough. It had become a matter of supreme importance to me to discover exactly what Peter Andersen had been doing the night he died. And why Carmela did not want me to know.

I parked the car and rang Anthony and Maria's front door bell. Would they be at home, and if so, was it the done thing in Malta just to turn up on someone's doorstep? The door was opened almost instantly, by Anthony, who looked as if he was dressed to go out.

'Jane.' His tone was wary, questioning. Then: 'How nice to see you,' determined to sound as if he meant it. Perhaps he did. 'Come in. Maria ...' He called up the stairs, in Maltese. 'She will be pleased to see you. Please go up. I am sorry, but I was just on my way out.'

'Oh, that's all right; I expect Maria can help me.'

'Oh?' Don't worry, I'll tell you why. And I did.

'Jane.' Maria had come down the stairs. 'This is nice. You will have some tea with me?' Her welcome was really warm, and sincere.

'Well, yes. Thank you. I'd love that. Actually I wanted some information. I've asked Anthony but he can't help.' I smiled at Anthony; he was looking anxious. 'It's about a British ex-serviceman who lives in Mosta, Joe Crowther. I really do want to get in touch with him.'

'Joe Crowther? I know him,' Maria said.

'Oh, that's wonderful. Do you know where he lives?'

'Of course. Anthony, you do know him; his wife was Concetta Zammit. He lives with his daughter Teresa. You know, Teresa Mifsud.'

'Oh yes. Yes, I think I know her.'

'Oh!' Maria raised her eyes in disgust. 'He knows nothing. Jane, you come with me I tell you all you want to know.'

Anthony looked relieved to be let off the hook. He also looked innocent: Carmela had not spoken to him and he really did not know Joe Crowther. I must not become suspicious of everything and everyone. We said goodbye, he closed the door behind him and I followed Maria upstairs.

'What do you like to eat?' She sounded genuinely pleased to see me.

'I don't mind. I'm not very hungry. Anything.'

'A sandwich, yes? I make you a sandwich and then you have some cake.'

'Thank you, that sounds good.'

'You sit in here.' She led me towards her lounge, 'You can make yourself comfortable and I will bring in the tea.'

'Couldn't we have it in the kitchen, like we did before? Then I could talk to you while you're preparing it.'

'Oh yes. Yes, that would be nice. You don't mind?'

'I like kitchens, they're friendly, relaxed, you know?'

'I know. I too like to talk in the kitchen. In Anthony's mother's house I am not allowed in the kitchen.'

'Oh?'

'So I do not allow her into mine. If she did come in she would only criticise.'

'Yes. I know what mothers-in-law can be like.' Hardly a fair comment, as Neville's mother never criticised and she loved my kitchen, but it served. I perched on a stool by the table. Maria filled the kettle, took a sliced white loaf out of a stainless steel breadbin on the work top, butter, cheese, ham and salad from the fridge, knives from the table drawer.

'So,' I said, when she'd got everything ready, 'you know Joe Crowther.'

Maria turned round from the counter. 'No, I do not know him.'

'Oh I thought you …'

'I know who he is, because Concetta Zammit was my mother's second cousin by marriage. My mother was a Micallef and she married Joseph Caruana, that was my father, and his brother Spiro married a … But you do not want to know all this.'

I didn't, but I might learn something else that was useful to me. 'No, please go on.'

She smiled, apologetically.

'Families here, they are very … um … very mixed up, what is the word?'

'Intertwined? Connected?'

'Yes, connected. Everyone is related to everyone else. The police dare not arrest anyone for fear the man's relatives will come after them.'

'Really?'

'Well, no. It is a joke, but it is … also true.'

The sandwiches were made and the kettle had boiled. 'Come, we will eat. This is why I am fat. Every time someone comes I eat with them.'

Even if I got nothing more than food from Maria I was glad I had come: there was a definite rapport between us.

I took a bite from my sandwich – it was chunky and well-filled, not the sort of thing that Mrs. Andersen would have served.

'Okay then,' I said, 'so you don't know Joe Crowther, but you know about him. Did you know that Anthony's sister had interviewed him for her programme?'

'Oh, please do not talk to me about that programme.' Maria threw up her hands in disgust. 'I am so tired of hearing about it.'

'Oh. Why?'

'Why? Because it is just another example of how very clever Carmela Farrugia is. And how stupid I am.'

'Oh, I'm sure …'

'No, it is true, Jane. Whatever Carmela does it is good, whatever I do it is wrong.'

'I don't understand … Who says so?' As if I didn't know.

'Anthony's mother, who else. I do not go to work, I am not clever, I am not good enough for her son. I give her grandsons, I am polite to her, but no, all the time when I am with her she is making me feel … inferior. I am so sorry, I should not say these things to a stranger.'

'No, you go ahead. If, as you say, everyone here is related to everyone else, then a stranger is probably the only person you can say these things to.'

'That is very true.' Laughter relaxed us both. 'Even so, I should not have said it. She is a good woman, it is just that … it is her husband, you see. He was, well you know, she has told you … he was a hero in the war and … how can I say this? … we all have to reach … no, measure, that is the word, we have to measure up to him. You know what I am saying?'

'Oh yes.'

'It is … it is as if she has made a god of him. You know? He is not an ordinary man any more, he has become like … like Superman. She says he was very clever and that is why Carmela is so clever. She says Carmela has got the gift of writing from her father. I would not mind that so much but she also makes out that he was from some important family.'

'Oh?' This was a new angle.

'She did not tell you? Huh. I am amazed. Oh yes, his mother was from Denmark.'

'Yes, she told me that.'

'But not that she belonged to an important family there?'

'No, I don't think so, unless I missed it.'

'Oh, you would not miss it. If Anthony's mother wanted you to know she would have told you, more than once.'

'She said Peter had been brought up in an orphanage and also that he was …'

'That his mother was not married?'

'Yes, she told me that.'

'But not that Peter's father was a married man who had, she says, "taken advantage of a lovely girl from a good home" and so her father had thrown her out of the house because she had disgraced the family name?'

'No, she said nothing about his mother's family being important.'

'This is, I think, something she has added, because it sounds, you know, better, maybe more respectable. She would not tell you because your father knew Anthony's father and perhaps you would know she was not telling the truth.'

'Maybe it is the truth.'

'I do not think so.' She shook her head; she sounded very certain.

'Why?'

'Because ... I will tell you. About four years ago, I think it was, no five years ... Anthony went to England on business and he said that while he was there he would try to find the place where his father had been as a child, you know, the orphanage. And then if he could, he would go to Denmark and try to trace his family there.'

'So what was the problem?'

'Anthony's mother would not hear of it. This is when she said that her husband's father was an important man and she did not want the family in Denmark to be upset, you know, by bringing up the story of the disgrace. She begged Anthony not to do this. She said Anthony's father would not have liked it, that Peter's mother had suffered enough in her lifetime and Anthony should leave things as they were.'

'And did he?'

'Of course. Anthony would not go against his mother.'

'So who do you think Anthony's grandmother was, really?'

'Who knows? Some poor girl who got herself into trouble.'

'And was she Danish?'

'I don't know. Does it matter?'

'Well, no, not to you perhaps, but it might to Anthony

and Carmela. They would want to know where their father came from.' I paused. 'I know that I would.'

'I cannot see how it matters. It is not as if they do not know who their father was. Now that, that is something you would want to know, yes?' Oh Maria, if you only knew. 'No, it is just Mrs. Andersen …' – she said it with scorn – 'she is so proud of her name and she wants people to think she is somebody because she has a Danish name.'

'You don't like her, do you?'

'No, I do not.' She got up suddenly. 'I am sorry, all this talking and I forget to give you tea. It must be horrible by now, I will make some fresh.' She picked up the teapot.

'Maria, it will be fine. Put the teapot down. I like it well-brewed.'

'You are very kind.' Maria put the teapot back on the table.

'Well, go on, pour it.'

'I am sorry.' She poured the tea. 'Do you have milk? I forget.'

'Please.' She put in milk. I lifted the cup and drank, under Maria's worried gaze. 'Mm. Just the way I like it.' I held out my cup for a re-fill. 'Maria …?' I judged this was a good moment to get back to Joe Crowther.

'The cake! I forgot the cake. And you were too polite to ask.'

'I had forgotten it too.' But I had to eat some – it was no hardship; the cake had a delicious filling of dates and some kind of alcohol – before I could get back to my question.

'It wasn't the cake. I want to know about Joe Crowther; where can I find him?'

'I give you his daughter's address; he will like to talk to you. Teresa says he never stops talking. Mostly about the war, how brave they all were.'

'So … he must have had a lot to say to Carmela when she made her programme?'

'No. No, I don't think so. I don't remember much of him on the recording, but then I didn't listen to it very carefully. You want to listen to it?'

'Yes, please!' This was a bit of luck, bypassing Carmela.

'Okay, I lend it to you. I cannot give it, although I would like to, in case Anthony's mother asks for it. Although I don't expect she will, it is only a copy; she gave copies to everyone.' She began to root around in a drawer. 'You have a machine?' she said, turning round, the tape in her hand.

'Yes, I have it with me,' I said, reaching for my bag.

'No, please Jane, you take it with you. I do not want to hear it again.'

I took the tape from her and put it into my bag.

'Maria,' I said, 'what sort of man do you think Peter Andersen was?'

Slowly she walked to the table, sat down in the chair. I felt she was framing her answer, carefully.

'You don't need to be polite,' I said. 'He's nothing to me.'

'I am glad you said that. I do not wish to give offence … I would not say this in front of Anthony, but … how can I say this?' She paused. 'I think he was … There is an expression you have, not a dare-devil, that is not the word. Oh, I wish I could think.'

'Jack-the-lad. Is that the word you want?'

'Yes! That is exactly it. Jack-the-lad. And also … devil-may-care. Yes, that is a word?'

'Yes, devil-may-care. Impulsive, easy-going, fearless.' Maria nodded. He was a young man, and there was a war going on. What else is there to say? He behaved like so many young men in time of war. 'Do you think he was faithful to Rosaria?'

A daring question, but I felt the need to risk it.

'I do not know. If he had wanted to … to be unfaithful it would have been very easy. There were lots of girls, you know, girls who would go with anyone. Why do you ask this? I do not think he was a bad man, Anthony's father.'

'No, of course not. I wasn't suggesting anything, I am just trying to develop a character, that's all, for my novel, trying to get a picture of a young soldier here in war-time.' It had been a mistake, asking that question; Maria was looking worried. 'Well, I'd better go.' I smiled, hoping to reassure her. 'Thank you for your help, Maria, and for the sandwich.' I got up from the table and extended my hand.

'No, wait. Sit down, Jane. There is something. I don't know if I should tell you this, but … well, Concetta Zammit, who married Joe Crowther. You remember, I tell you about her?'

'Yes.' Now what?

'Her sister, Antonia – she was younger than Concetta. – she was seeing a soldier during the war; he used to come to the bar … you know, Bernie's Bar? In Mosta?'

'No, I don't know anything about Bernie's Bar. Tell me.'

'Oh, well, Bernie's Bar was owned by Concetta's father; he was Bernado Zammit, and it was in his bar that all the soldiers and the airmen from Ta' Qali used to meet. It is not good to say this but … well, Bernardo, he could get alcohol when other people could not. Do not ask me where he got it from, but he did. And so his bar was a popular place, you know? Bernardo had three daughters and when the bar became crowded he let them serve the drinks. Concetta, who married Joe Crowther, she was the oldest one; and the youngest girl Rosa, she had a Maltese boyfriend. But the middle one, Antonia, she was … she was a flirt, no, more than a flirt. I don't like to say it but she would go with anybody.'

'And you think …?'

'If I tell you this, you must not tell anyone.'

'No, of course I won't.'

'Well, one day Concetta … Concetta is dead, God rest her soul,' Maria crossed herself fervently, 'so this cannot hurt her. One day she say to me … she was telling me about something Rosaria had said to her, I don't know what it was, but it had annoyed her. Concetta said, "If Rosaria knew what her husband was really like she would not put her nose in the air like that." And I said, "What do you mean?" and she said "If you want to know, ask Antonia." It may not mean anything, but you know the saying about smoke …'

'No smoke without fire.'

She nodded. 'Please, you will not say anything?'

'Of course I won't.'

'It is probably nonsense.'

'Don't worry, it won't end up in my book.'

I thanked Maria again and took my leave of her. She had given me a lot to think about. If Peter had gone with Antonia … It didn't bother me, but it would upset Carmela. Oh yes, Carmela would be most upset. And she certainly wouldn't want Anthony or Rosaria to know.

CHAPTER SIXTEEN

The drive back to Mellieha Bay was frightening. It was dark by now and car headlights and hooters came at me from all directions; only by keeping well to the left did I avoid a collision. It was without doubt the most terrifying drive of my life. I would not again drive in the dark on Malta, no matter what. I needed a stiff G and T to revive me before I went to my room to change for dinner.

Joan and her cronies were in the bar, and I was really glad to see them.

'You know what they say about the motorists here, don't you?' said Olive.

'That they're all mad?'

'No. That they drive on the left … mostly.'

I managed a feeble laugh.

'Have dinner with us,' Olive said, 'and we'll tell you our horror stories. We went to the winery, and we got lost. Down by the docks.'

'We bought some marvellous wine,' said Joan.

'And drank some!' added Barbara.

'That's probably why you got lost,' I said, standing up, wanting to get away.

'Oh no, we got lost on the way there. Coming back was no problem,' and she went into gales of laughter.

'I'll see you later,' I said and escaped to the lift. The drink, or possibly the conversation, had steadied me. Now all I wanted to do was listen to that tape.

In my room I switched on the overhead light, then the lamps by the bed. I closed the curtains, took off my clothes and put on my dressing gown. I slotted Maria's tape into my cassette recorder, and lay down on the bed. I took a deep breath and pressed the play button.

Hell and damnation! The whole bloody thing was in Maltese. Christ, how stupid of me not to have thought of that. I felt so frustrated I wanted to scream. Sod it, sod it, sod it. I took a sherry from the mini-bar and drank it in one go. If I got drunk, well so be it. A pity Ken had gone, I needed him tonight. I ran a bath, and was about to step in: the tape Carmela was sending me, would that be in English? Like hell it would. Oh yes, what a brilliant bit of stalling that was! By the time I had the tape from Carmela – no doubt she wouldn't send it straight away, certainly not till after the weekend – and I had discovered I couldn't understand a blessed word of it and had got in touch with her and asked her for a translation – always assuming I could contact her – it would be time for me to get the plane home. Okay, Carmela, I can play dirty too. Tomorrow I go and see Joe Crowther.

After my bath I slept … and missed dinner. It was gone ten when I awoke, with a dry, furry mouth and a headache. There were two empty sherry miniatures on the dressing-table: I didn't remember drinking the second one. My dinner companions had obviously given up on me; well, who could blame them. I would make restitution tomorrow, not now. Now I wanted a sandwich

– which reminded me that I hadn't eaten a proper meal all day – and a cup of coffee. I rang room service. Then I rang Reception and left a message of apology for Joan: it would save a possible anxious knock on the door later. They were nice people; I didn't want to offend them, but neither did I want to speak to them tonight.

Consciousness returned with an awareness of the stale smell of tuna from the remains of my sandwich. Sunday morning. My resolution to see Joe Crowther had weakened overnight. Perhaps I should explore another avenue first. But what? Who else was there to approach? Anthony seemed to have brushed our relationship aside; he had told no one who I was: perhaps he didn't totally believe me. Carmela had effectively given me the cold shoulder; Rosaria, I felt, had said all she was going to say; Maria knew nothing, and anything she might say would be fuelled by her dislike of both Rosaria and Carmela. So who else was there?

If only Ken had not left; if only Neville were here. Or Beth. I had to talk to somebody. I couldn't even begin to talk to the women I had met. Nor to Michael the gardener. That left Ronnie and Col. A lot of good they would be! On the other hand they might be just the people I needed: young, brash, and with a fresh outlook on life. Somewhere I had their address, or what they hoped would be their address: a student hostel, I think they said. I got out the piece of paper on which they had scribbled it down; I hadn't actually looked at it, hoping, when they gave it to me, to have seen the last of them. I unfolded it, peered at the scrawl: it looked like Hibernia House. I couldn't make out the name of the road, but the town was Sliema. Well, I wasn't going to trek all the way over there: they could come to me; they owed me that much.

At the reception desk I asked for the phone number of the hostel and put through a call from the box in the foyer. I looked again at the paper the Aussies had given me. No surnames, just Col and Ronnie. It would probably be enough. It was. Yes, Col and Ronnie were staying there. Right now – the accent was American – those guys were out, but she would be sure and give them a message to call me the moment they came in. 'It's urgent,' I said, and rang off. I gave the hotel number and asked the desk to page me. Not at all a satisfactory situation. I should have arranged to ring again in half an hour; well, I could still do that, and I would. Or I could forget about Col and Ronnie and go straight to Mosta and knock on Joe Crowther's door. It wasn't like me to prevaricate: perhaps I was afraid of what Joe Crowther would reveal about my father, something Carmela had discovered and didn't want me to know. If I took Col and Ronnie with me it would break the ice, appear more casual. Ronnie's Gramps had been here in the war; she would love to talk to Joe. That was it, that was my intro. Joe would warm to this young woman, and I could then make a second appointment with him, on my own.

It was half-past ten. The chances were that Col and Ronnie were out for the day and wouldn't call me until the evening. I couldn't wait that long. To hell with it, it was a crazy idea; they might not want to come with me. I would go to Mosta now and seek out Joe. I gathered my things together – cassette recorder, notebook, camera. I was about to leave my room when the phone rang. It was Maria, inviting me – 'If you are not doing anything else; I know I do not give you much time' – to have lunch with her and Anthony and Pawlu.

'I'd love to,' I said.

Good, that gave me something positive to do, and fortuitously, an opportunity to talk to Maria again. After a walk along the headland to clear my head, I had a shower and changed my clothes. I left a message at reception asking anyone who called to ring me at

Maria's, and if I wasn't there, to phone again in an hour's time.

At Xemxija I bought a pineapple and some black grapes from a stall and hoped the smell from the bay had not permeated the fruit. It was nearly one o'clock when I reached Rabat.

Pawlu answered the door. 'Hi. Come on up. You got the full works today,' he said, as he led me upstairs. 'Mama doesn't often get the chance to do this; it's usually my grandmother who does the entertaining, but she's at Carmela's today.'

Anthony met me at the top of the stairs. 'Thank you for coming,' he said, formally. He shook my hand, then as an after-thought, smiled. Maria came flying out of the kitchen, her hair dishevelled, her face red, from standing over the cooker I presumed.

'Jane!' She kissed me on both cheeks. 'You are early.'

'Oh, I am sorry. Is that wrong?'

'No, no. It is good. It is just that in Malta people do not always arrive on time, and …' She looked embarrassed.

'And you're not quite ready for me. Don't worry about it. Is there anything I can do to help?'

'No! Oh no, you are my guest, you must not work. Please, go into the dining-room and Anthony will bring you a drink.' No kitchen for me today, no cosy informality; Maria was entertaining à la her mother-in-law and I must support her and play my part. I had a feeling that a report of this occasion would get back, via Anthony or Pawlu, to Rosaria, and it was important that Maria came out of it well.

'Oh, do take these,' I said, handing over the fruit. 'Just a little contribution.' How ungracious, how patronising that sounded; it was not at all what I meant to say.

Maria took the pineapple and the grapes. 'Oh, you are

very kind. There was no need.' It was not a reprimand.

'I know that,' I said. I felt that Maria and I instinctively understood one another. 'I just wanted to buy them for you.'

'Thank you,' she said. 'I am very fond of pineapple, but Anthony does not like it.'

'Too acid,' he said, sharply.

'Yes, well …' I said, 'some fruits are.' A silly thing to say, but I felt distinctly ill-at-ease. I sensed what my mother used to call an 'atmosphere', between Maria and Anthony.

'Excuse me,' Maria said. Then: 'Oh Jane, I am so pleased you could come.'

'So am I.'

She turned and went into the kitchen. There was defiance in her shoulders. I was right: there was an atmosphere.

Without words, with just an outstretched hand to show me the direction, Anthony ushered me across the narrow hallway and into the dining-room. The furniture was dark walnut; the table with heavy legs and claw feet, the chairs with carved backs; there was a huge matching sideboard. I wondered where the suite had come from. Was it Anthony and Maria's choice, or was the suite one of Rosaria's cast-offs, out of keeping with her modern businesswoman image. It overwhelmed the small room.

'Do sit down,' said Anthony. Where? At the table? There were four chairs around it, one at each end, one on either side. Four other dining chairs were lined up in a row against one wall, like seats in a doctor's waiting-room. I half expected to see a table with a pile of magazines at one end. There was a small table, covered with a lace cloth; on it was a large foliage plant in an ornate red and gold jardinière. Anthony made no move to pull out one of the chairs at the table, so I perched myself on the chair next to the plant and the window.

'Oh,' I said, for something to say, looking out of the window, 'You have a good view of the old city from here.'

'Yes,' said Anthony, 'we do.' I wished Pawlu would join us; he had disappeared through the kitchen. To the floor above, presumably, judging by the music thudding through the ceiling.

'What would you like to drink?'

'Oh, anything.'

'It would be simpler if you chose something,' he said. 'We have most things.' His manner was stiff and uncomfortable. The invitation must have been Maria's idea, not his, but if he had protested she would have wanted to know why. It had been easier to agree and hope I would behave myself.

'I'd like some wine, actually. I see you've got some Maltese wine there; I'd like *that*,' I said, in what I hoped was a warm, reassuring way, friendly but not presuming on our undisclosed relationship. Silently he poured the wine and handed me the glass. 'Thank you.' He might have a waiter in a restaurant, and I a client.

'Excuse me,' he said, and left the room. Hurriedly. This was not going to be a very jolly party. Unless I got drunk, which I had no intention of doing. What was I supposed to do now? Sit here and wait until he came back or someone else came in? Get up, with my drink in my hand, as I would in England, wander over to the kitchen and lean against the door frame? The table with its lace cloth was laid with good quality, old fashioned silver and we were beginning the meal with soup. For want of something to do, I stood, and picked up one of the soup spoons and turned it over: it was heavy plate with a rat-tail back.

'My mother-in-law's.' Anthony spoke from the doorway, as if afraid to enter. I put the spoon down.

'Sorry,' I said. 'My husband liked silver, he knew

quite a bit about it, and I just, you know, got in the habit of looking at things. The table and chairs, are they …?' Relieved to be onto a safe subject Anthony advanced a step into the room. Delicious aromas were floating in from the kitchen opposite: chicken? I hoped it wasn't rabbit. I'd been told that fried rabbit was a popular Sunday dish. Whatever it was, I prayed that it wouldn't be long coming.

'They were my mother-in-law's, too. They're Italian.'

'Oh, really,' I said, with cocktail party over-enthusiasm. 'How interesting. Are they very old?'

'I'm not sure. I think so. Excuse me, I'll ask Maria.' Poor Anthony, he was hating this.

'It doesn't matter, I'll ask her myself when she comes in. Food smells good. What are we eating, d'you know?' I didn't want him to leave again.

'Um … Chicken, I think.'

'Oh, lovely. And home-made soup?'

'Yes. Maria makes … she makes very good soups.'

'Anthony, stop worrying. I'm not going to say anything to upset you, or Maria. Just relax, okay? Let's just enjoy lunch together. Ah!' Maria was entering with a steaming tureen; she looked flustered. 'I've put you out, haven't I?' I said.

'No, it is okay. I am ready,' Maria said, placing the tureen on a cork mat at the far end of the table. 'I will get the bowls,' she added, rushing back to the kitchen, calling to Pawlu on her way. Anthony and I stood, smiling weakly at one another.

'Where would you like me to sit?' I asked.

'Wherever you like.'

'Then I'll sit here.' I pulled out a chair at the side of the table.

'Who serves the soup, you or Maria?'

'I do,' he said, and took his place in front of the tureen. What on earth were we going to talk about for the duration of the meal. If only I could hit on some neutral topic. Thankfully Pawlu entered at that moment, took his seat opposite me, and shook out his table napkin. Alex would have ignored his, I thought, even if I had guests.

'So,' said Pawlu, crumbling a bread roll, 'how do you like our roads?' Contentious maybe, but not personal: I could deal with this subject.

'Well ...' I began, 'they're ...'

'They're horrendous,' said Pawlu.

We talked about cars and roads and drivers and potholes and near-accidents right through the soup – clear chicken soup, with lots of chunky vegetables; very good – and into the next course, which was baked macaroni, *timpana* Maria called it. By the time we reached the main course – chicken roasted with potatoes and onions – we were discussing the sights of Malta, the ones I had already seen and others that Pawlu said 'you absolutely must not miss, Jane'. Throughout the meal Maria quietly came and went, putting food on the table and clearing plates, while Anthony filled the glasses. I was careful not to drink too much. Gradually we worked our way to the end; that's how it felt, like work. Maria, who had been so voluble on her own with me, hardly said a word. When Pawlu and his father got into a bit of an argument about who should be responsible for repairs to hire cars, I tried to engage Maria in a separate conversation, using the lace table-cloth as a starting point. Was it Maltese lace? Was it old? Had she ever done lacemaking? Where was the best place in Malta to buy lace? Her answers were hesitant and monosyllabic, and she kept on looking at Anthony as if she shouldn't be talking to me when he was speaking. I gave up and concentrated on my food. Food. We could talk about food. Why hadn't I done that before?

'This is delicious,' I said, taking a spoonful of my

pudding, a cheese *torta*. 'Now tell me, is this your own recipe?'

Maria gave a quick glance at Anthony. 'No,' she said, 'it's … it's my mother-in-law's. It is one of Anthony's favourites.' Oh dear, better not ask about anything else we had eaten. I was searching my brain for something else to talk about – clothes, family, TV programmes – when the phone rang.

'That'll be for me,' said Pawlu, scraping back his chair and dashing out.

'Pawlu!' his father called, angrily, but Pawlu had gone. 'I do apologise for my son.' he said.

'Mine's just the same. Always in a hurry, can't wait.'

'It's for you, Jane,' said Pawlu, from the hallway. 'Someone called Ronnie. A girl.'

'Oh, thank you,' I said and got up. 'I'm sorry, I should have said I'd given your number. I do hope you don't mind.'

'No, not at all,' said Anthony, but he looked worried.

'She's an Australian I met. I just want to see her again, before I leave. Excuse me.' I went into the hall and picked up the receiver. 'Hello,' I said.

'Hi, Jane, how're you doing?'

'Fine.'

'So what's up?'

'Nothing.' There was no sound from the dining-room. Oh God, they were all listening. Had I committed a bad breach of Maltese etiquette? 'Well no, not nothing. I just wanted to see you, that's all. Before I leave.'

'That would be great. Tell us when and where and we'll be there. Hey, I like that: when and where, we'll be there.'

'How about this evening?' I tried to make it sound casual, not urgent, which it was. 'Dinner, seven-thirty, at my hotel? Can you manage that?'

'That would be terrific. Gee, thanks Jane. You want

us to look, sort of … nice, huh?'

'It doesn't matter, but yes if you like. It's nice to dress up a bit, isn't it.' Still there was silence from the dining-room. 'Well, I'll say goodbye. See you tonight.'

I rang off quickly, set my face into a smile, and went back to my place at the table. I looked from Anthony to Pawlu to Maria. 'Thank you,' I said. 'That was very helpful. I'm seeing my friend this evening.' As you know. Somehow we got to the end of the meal; it had not been a success. I felt sorry for Maria, whose idea it had been. I must have a private word with her before I left, see if I could find out why it had all been so stiff. I took the plunge. 'Maria,' I said, brightly, 'I need your help.' I felt Anthony tense. I beamed at him. 'Clothes,' I said. 'I want Maria's advice.'

'My mother's the one to advise you about clothes,' he said.

'Yes, but Maria's here and she's not.' To hell with it; if you're offended that easily, too bad. If you won't stick up for your wife, I will. 'And I need this advice now. Come on, Maria, let's go into the kitchen.' I stood up, waited for Maria to stand, grabbed hold of her arm and almost dragged her out of the room and into the kitchen. 'Now,' I said, shutting the door, 'what's going on?'

'I don't know what you mean,' she said, not looking at me.

'Oh come on, Maria. I've seen the looks Anthony's been giving you. He didn't want me to come here, did he?' She didn't answer. 'I see. Well no, I don't. So tell me.' Again no answer. 'Is this anything to do with Carmela?'

'Well …'

'She didn't want me here either, is that it?' Did Carmela know I had talked to Maria? Was she worried that through her I would get to Joe Crowther?

'No, it wasn't that. Oh Jane, it is so hard.' She put a

finger in her mouth and began to bite the nail furiously. I took her hand away and held it.

'What … happened?'

'Carmela invited us to go to lunch.'

'Today?'

'Yes, today. But I had already invited you.'

'You didn't invite me till this morning.'

'I know, but I had already decided to invite you and I had planned the meal.'

'And Anthony had agreed?'

'Yes.'

'So, if Anthony agreed, what is the problem?'

'This morning after I had spoken to you, Carmela phoned Anthony …'

'And he discovered that she had invited him to lunch, and you had said no!'

'Yes.'

'Maria! How very brave. Good for you.'

'No, it is not good for me, Jane. I have made Anthony angry and I will have made his mother angry, too, because she would be at Carmela's house and she will think I did not accept the invitation because I did not want to see her. And that is not why I did it.'

'So why did you?' She was in tears now and I sat her down at the table.

'Because I wanted to see you. Because you were … because you treated me like a … like a friend. You did not tell me what to do, as Carmela does.'

'It's different; Carmela is your sister-in-law.' And so am I, Maria. But the way things are going, that is something you may never know. 'I'm glad you told me. I knew something was wrong. Don't worry, it'll blow over.' I opened the kitchen door, then shut it again. 'Did Carmela know it was me coming to lunch?'

'I don't know. I don't know if Anthony said.'

'You hadn't told her?'

'No, it was not her business.'

But being Carmela she would have asked and Anthony would have told her. And she would have been angry.

'Thank you,' I said loudly, opening the door again. 'That's a very good idea, I'll do that. Gosh, I never thought of that.' Pawlu and Anthony were still at the table. 'Your wife is marvellous,' I said. 'And she's a wonderful cook. That was a super meal, Maria.' Perhaps I was laying it on a bit thick, but at that moment I felt Anthony deserved it.

I said goodbye to Anthony and Maria upstairs and promised to phone Maria, and hopefully see her, before I went back to England. Pawlu took me to the door.

'Thank you for coming,' he said. 'You are good for Mama.'

CHAPTER SEVENTEEN

'So …' I said, 'you think I should see this old man?'

'Of course you must see him, Jane, he's the key to the whole thing. Jeez, this is exciting.' Ronnie beamed at me, and at Col.

'Yeah. Sure thing,' he said.

They had arrived at the hotel looking quite presentable, clean and with no obvious holes in their clothes. I didn't reveal my true reason for wanting to meet Joe Crowther. I simply said that I wanted to talk to him because he had probably known my father, Tom Harper, but that someone here in Malta – I couldn't, daren't say who – didn't want me to meet him; why I didn't know, but it wasn't going to put me off. However, as I couldn't just blaze in and ask if he had known Tom, maybe they, Ronnie and Col, could come along as … well, a sort of *entrée* to Joe was what I wanted. Between us, over dinner, we concocted a story about Ronnie's Gramps: how she was sure Joe would have known him, because Gramps had talked about a Joe, a gunner he had known in Malta in '41 or '42. She really did, or said she

did anyway, think Joe might have known her Gramps …
'and that would be just magic, if he had.' And Col, as I
had anticipated, liked the idea of having a poke at
whoever it was who was trying to prevent my meeting
Joe.

'We're not having some guy in a suit telling you what
you can and can't do, Jane,' he said.

We arranged to meet next morning, in Mosta, on the
steps of the Cathedral, where Ken and I had talked. It
was the sort of place where people, tourists, would meet,
casually.

'Yeah,' said Col, 'we can be asking you if you know
the times of buses, or if maybe you know a good place to
eat.'

'I think if we just meet, that will be enough,' I said.

'You can't be too careful. These sort of guys, they're
smart, they're one step ahead all the time.'

My God, he's entering into it; he'd be talking about
the Mafia next. Well, it did no harm, and if it got him
fired up, all to the good. I could see Ronnie was pleased;
she shot me a look of thanks, almost as if I had made the
whole thing up just to bring Col out of his grumpy shell.

'I don't think we should set off together,' he said. 'We
should split up and go to Joe's house separately, by
different routes.'

'No, Col, we are not on the run from the law,' I said.
'We shall go together; I shall knock on the door, explain
to whoever answers why we are there, and then,
hopefully, we shall go in … and talk to Joe.' Col looked
crestfallen. 'And if anyone doesn't like it, too bad.'

'Too bloody right,' Col said.

They were late arriving and I began to have second
thoughts. Serious ones. What the hell was I playing at,
involving a couple of young Aussie back-packers in my
affairs? On the other hand, I didn't know what dark
powers might be behind Carmela's obfuscation; maybe

something really horrendous had gone on, something illegal, dangerous; perhaps Peter Andersen had been a spy, a Quisling – no, that was Norway, not Denmark. Oh, for God's sake, Jane!

After performing our charade on the Cathedral steps, we walked, together – I had insisted – to the side street where Joe Crowther lived. The house was dilapidated, with peeling paint and broken shutters; double doors opened directly onto the street. On each door was a dull brass knocker in the shape of a dolphin; I lifted one of them. The sound as it fell back against the door echoed eerily through the house. A bad omen? Too late if it was. I had not come this far to retreat now. The street was narrow and filled with noisy, hooting traffic pressing close to the houses; we were in danger of getting run over. I was about to knock again when the door was opened. A woman, middle-aged, buxom, in black with a flowered apron, stood in the doorway.

'Good morning,' I said, hoping – assuming – she spoke English, 'I'm a friend of Mrs. Andersen, Maria Andersen.'

'Oh. Yes.' She looked me up and down, uncertain, holding on to the door. 'I know her.' But you're not friends. Start again, Jane, try another tack; maybe this woman is not family.

'My young friends here ...'

'Hi, I'm Ronnie. My grandfather was here in the war and he loved Malta so much he said I just had to come and see it for myself, and, he said, while I was here I was to be sure and look up his old mate Joe. Mr. Crowther. So that's why we're here, but if it's not convenient maybe we could come back some other time.' I could have hugged her; her apparent sincerity and warmth won the woman over. By the time Ronnie had finished her speech the door was wide open and the woman was standing back to let us in.

'Please, you wait here. I tell Joe. He will like to see you.'

The woman disappeared behind a curtain hung across the hallway. A half-moon table stood against one wall; to its side hats and coats on stout wooden pegs bulged out into the narrow space. We stood, waiting, exchanging glances, not quite daring to speak. We could hear a muffled conversation, in Maltese we presumed, going on in the back of the house. Then silence. Still we stood. The house smelt of damp and paraffin and cabbage. I had a definite feeling we should not be there, but Col and Ronnie seemed relaxed, so I decided to take my cue from them. I took a deep breath, let it out slowly, Ronnie put a hand on my arm. 'Don't worry, Jane, it's going to be okay, I know.'

'Silly bitch, you don't know. I think we should go.' Col began to move towards the door.

'Good morning.'

While my attention had been diverted to Col a woman, a younger one this time – in her mid twenties at a guess, dark-haired, smart in jeans and silky top, appeared in the hallway; she must have come from behind the curtain because no doors had opened. Although she was looking at me, it was Ronnie who answered.

'Oh, hi there,' she said, 'I'm Ronnie, and my grandfather …'

Without looking at Ronnie the woman said, 'Yes, I've been told about your grandfather.' To me she said, 'Maria said you might visit. You're writing a book, she says.' I got the feeling she was not going to be co-operative.

'That's right, I am, and …' I was determined to hang on to our story: it might be needed … 'there's also Ronnie's grandfather. Of course Maria didn't know about him, so she …'

'I can't guarantee my grandfather will talk to either of you,' the young woman cut in.

'Oh, you're his ...?'

'Yes. Do you have a problem with that?'

'No. No, of course not. I ...'

'He's had his fill of journalists.'

'Oh, but I'm not a ...'

'You're writing a book, it's the same thing. You want to pick his brains, you all do. Poor old man, it's time he was left alone.'

I was nonplussed: I had not expected such a hostile reception. Oh, to go back and start again. I was also beginning to feel claustrophobic in the narrow hallway.

'If it's not convenient, I could come another day,' I said, 'only ... well, I'm not here for long and Maria thought he might like to talk to me ...' I rushed on, not giving the young woman a chance to interrupt. '... because I think he knew my father; he was a gunner too, stationed at Ta' Qali.'

'First a grandfather, now a father; what is this? I told you, my grandfather has talked to enough of you people. Okay?'

'I'm sorry, I ...'

'Oh, come on, Jane, we can do without this.' Col was making for the door.

'Yeah, let's go,' said Ronnie, following him.

'Okay, you go, I'm staying.' Without another word to the girl they let themselves out. I smiled at the young woman; it was time to turn on the charm. 'I am very sorry to have troubled you, I really am, and I do apologise for my young friends, but I should be most grateful if I could speak to Mr Crowther. For maybe just five minutes?' She was still reluctant. 'I promise you. Five minutes, no more. Time me if you like.'

A piping male voice called from somewhere behind the curtain. 'Antonia'. The girl answered, in Maltese, then turned to me. 'Excuse me,' she said, and disappeared behind the curtain. Antonia ... After her aunt, no doubt. Her great-aunt, the one who, allegedly, according to Maria, might have slept with Peter. So much guesswork, so little fact. I should never have done this, just appeared at the front door without an appointment, offering no credentials, almost demanding an interview. I called out, 'I shouldn't have come, I do apologise.' I was about to say, I'll let myself out, when the girl reappeared. It was as well that I hadn't; that would have been equally impolite.

'I am sorry, I have been very rude,' she said. 'It's just ... he is an old man and I feel I must protect him.'

'No, you were quite right. It was very thoughtless of me just to turn up like this.'

'Will you come through?' I needn't have bothered with Ronnie and Col after all. I hoped they'd wait for me; I didn't want to upset them, but I felt that if I didn't follow the girl right now her mood might change again and I would be shown the door. Antonia held the curtain back for me. 'He feels the draughts,' she said. She opened a door to the right and ... well, it was like being in a time warp, in one of those rooms in a museum that is meant to epitomise a particular period. This was pure 1940s, even down to the radio – wooden, rounded top, needle dial, fretted design over the loudspeaker grill. The posters on the walls – ship and aircraft recognition, British and German at a quick glance – enhanced the feeling of not being in a real room. But the man was real; old and bent over, sitting in a red moquette armchair by an electric fire, a fire so unsafe it that would be illegal in Britain; it probably was in Malta.

'Grandfather.' She spoke very loudly. 'This lady has come from England to see you.'

'Eh?' He cupped his right ear with his hand and turned to look at me. He was unbelievably wizened, his skin rutted by years of exposure to the Mediterranean sun, his eyes cloudy.

'Mr. Crowther.' I stretched out my hand to him. He didn't take it, just nodded. 'Jane Thornfield.'

'What? Tha must speak up, lass.'

'I think you might have known my father.'

'What does she say?' His eyes appealed to Antonia.

'I told you,' she said. Then, close to him and enunciating very carefully: 'Grandfather, this lady's father was here in the war.' To me, 'That's right, isn't it?' I nodded.

'They were all here in the war, all of them.' A pause. 'They've all gone now, there's not one of them left. It was all wrong, all of it, shouldn't have happened, none of it. If I could have done owt I would've, but there was nowt you could do. I told her, I said ...'

'I'm sorry,' the girl said. 'Some days he is very lucid, other days he's ... well, you can see for yourself.'

'Could I just ... I know it's an imposition, but could I just try one question?'

'You can try.'

I leant close to him. 'Mr. Crowther. My father was Tom Harper.' Then louder. 'Tom Har-per.'

'Tom?'

'Yes, *Tom Harper.*'

'No!' Pushing down on his stick, lifting himself from the chair, the old man yelled at me, waved me away with his free hand. 'I'll not go through that again. Go ... go away.' He collapsed back into his chair, breathing hard.

'I'm sorry, Mr. Crowther, I really am ...' I leant forward again, wanting to be of some use.

'Just leave him.' The girl's voice was sharp. I drew back. 'Wait in the hall. I'll be with you in a minute.'

Through the open doorway I watched her tenderly soothe her grandfather's brow, then stroke his hands and finally plant a kiss on his withered cheek, all the time murmuring to him. Poor old man: there was no way he could help me. Yet he must have said something to Carmela for her to be adamant I should not see him. And why should Tom's name disturb him so much?

When Antonia had satisfied herself that her grandfather was calm again she joined me, softly pulling the door to behind her.

'It's not fair, is it, to an old man?' she said.

'No. No, it's not.' I should have left then, gracefully. But there were so many things that niggled ...

'Just ... just tell me something, would you,' I said. 'When Carmela Farrugia ... you know, from Radio Malta ... when she talked to him, to your grandfather, was he ... was he like ...' I nodded towards the room.

'Of course he wasn't,' the girl said. 'I told you, he has his bad days and ...' She was finding it hard to remain polite.

'Did you hear what he said, that day?'

'Not directly. I wasn't here, but I heard him on the radio.'

'Was that all he said, do you know, the bit that was broadcast?' I hoped I sounded naive.

'I shouldn't think so; she was here with him for well over an hour.'

'How do you know, if you weren't here?'

'He told me, afterwards, that's how I know!' She was becoming exasperated; no wonder, I would have been the same. 'Anyway, my mother was here; she told me, too. Are you satisfied now?'

'Thank you, yes.' But of course I wasn't. One more try. 'You don't happen to know, do you, whether he talked to her about his old comrades ...'

'No, I don't! And I'm not going to ask him. I do know this, though,' – she was getting very angry – 'that whatever it was he did talk about, it upset him, very much. He was in a terrible state when that woman had gone. And now I'd like you to go as well. I should never have let you come in.'

'You're right ... I am sorry.'

'And don't come again.'

'No. I won't.' I felt as meek as I sounded. By behaving as I had, I had abused Maria's kindness, and that worried me. This would no doubt get back to her and she would feel betrayed. I began backing to the door; Antonia followed me, all the time talking, her temper rising with every word. Her voice brought the older woman – I never did discover who she was – into the hall.

'That war has been over for fifty years. Why can't you let it go? It has nothing to do with us any more; we're a new country, a different people. We're not British any more, or hadn't you noticed? The Germans and the Italians are no longer our enemies. Why don't you old people just leave it alone!'

By now I was at the front door. I felt for the catch and got the door open. I heard Joe's voice, calling piteously. I looked for the older woman, to acknowledge her, but she had gone. To attend to Joe, no doubt.

'I'm sorry. Good-bye.' I almost fell into the road.

'Goodbye!' The door was slammed so hard that the dolphins bounced.

'Jeez, Jane! Are you okay?' Ronnie took my arm, helped me down the step.

'I think so,' I said. I didn't quite know how I felt. What had I said or done to make that young woman so angry? Was she part of this conspiracy, too? Of course she wasn't; she was just upset for her grandfather. And now I must somehow make it right with Maria.

As for Joe Crowther ... well, that was the end of that.

Despondently I walked with Col and Ronnie to the car ... and found a parking ticket waiting for me, under the wipers.

'Oh no,' said Ronnie, putting an arm round my drooping shoulders, 'That is such bad luck.'

'Ah, forget it,' said Col. 'You'll be gone in a couple of days.'

'I can't forget it. I'll have to pay it.' I looked at the form; I was instructed to report to the nearest police station.

'Besides,' Col went on, 'where's the notice that says you can't park?'

I looked, but couldn't see one. 'You're right, there isn't one. Wait a minute, I parked here a few days ago and nobody gave me a ticket then. I'm not having this.' I marched off to the police station – it was quite close – my dismay over Joe Crowther temporarily set aside. I flung the form down on the counter. I was in no mood for pleasantries.

The policeman picked up the form, slowly, looked at it.

'It doesn't say you can't park there,' I said.

'It does say.'

'Where?' asked Col, who had followed me in.

'Up on the wall.'

'I didn't see it,' I said.

'It *is* there.'

'Okay,' said Col, 'so there's a sign, but why did she get a ticket today and not the other time she parked there?'

The policeman grinned. 'Because,' he said, 'today there was an officer on duty.' He shrugged his shoulders. 'The other day ... there was not.'

'Oh, great,' I said. Argument seemed futile, although Col was all for it. I paid the fine and we left.

'So, what now, Jane?'

'I don't know, Ronnie.'

'Hey, you're not giving up, are you?' Col was looking really concerned. For me? No. It was more likely he was disappointed that the 'fun' was over. Because it was. What else could I do? I hadn't the heart to go chasing hither and thither, hoping to unearth some … some what? Information? Gossip? Facts? Rumours? … about my father. Or Tom for that matter. Definitely not Tom: what he had done in Malta was of no interest. Or was it? Why had Joe Crowther reacted so violently to his name? Maybe Tom had been after his girl, Concetta.

'Yes, Col, I think I am. Giving up. Anyway, what does it really matter, any of it? As the girl said to me, it's all a long time ago; it's time we moved on. Come on, let's go and have a meal or a drink somewhere.'

'Oh, Jane, I hate to see you looking so miserable.'

'Don't worry, Ronnie, I'll get over it.'

We drove to St. Pauls's Bay and ate in a restaurant there. I couldn't tell you what I ate; fish of some kind, I think. Col and Ronnie tucked in as if it was the last meal they were going to get. Col cleared my plate as well as his I seem to recall. We came out of the restaurant and stood on the pavement.

'Look, I'm no use to anybody at the moment,' I said. 'Why don't you two go off, and … and I'll … I'll give you a call.'

'Are you going to be all right? Col, we can't just leave Jane like this.'

'Please, I'd really rather you did. I'm suddenly very tired, believe it or not.'

'Sure you are; that kind of thing takes it out of you.'

'Yeah.' I smiled wanly. I didn't want any more sympathy; I just wanted to be on my own.

'Okay, but you call us now. Anything you want, we'll be there, won't we, Col?'

'You bet.'

I had to get away; I was beginning to feel I had got trapped in an episode of *Neighbours*. Ronnie hugged me and Col shook hands and we all said 'Bye', at least three times each. Finally we parted; I presume they got a bus to Valletta. I drove back to Mellieha; I suppose I must have driven safely because I arrived there in one piece.

There was a parking space close to the hotel entrance; I beat another car to it by inches, smiled 'Sorry' at the other driver, and dragged myself wearily into the foyer. I collected my key and went straight up to my room. The curtains were closed against the sun. I dropped the key and my bag onto the dressing table, kicked off my shoes and subsided onto the bed. I shut my eyes, exhausted, longing for sleep. Which didn't come. Only tears came, hot and stinging, trickling down my cheeks.

If only I could have gone home then; if only I had not gone to see Joe Crowther; if only I had taken Carmela's advice; if only I had not stopped at Pawlu's garage for petrol ... If only I had not come to Malta at all!

There was no way I was going to sleep; I got up, opened the curtains and helped myself to a cold drink from the minibar. I felt wrung out, unsure of anything. The can of drink was synthetically sweet; I poured it down the loo. It was the middle of the afternoon. What, for God's sake, was I going to do with the rest of the day, feeling like this? Well, I could have a bath at any rate; maybe then I would sleep. What I didn't want to do was think. Sleep, drink, sex or work: they were my normal antidotes to thought, but not one of them could I call upon at this moment.

I lay in the bath, trying to make my mind a blank. I would not think about Peter Andersen, or Neville or Ken or Tom or my mother or Carmela or Maria. I would think about Alex. Yes, I could think about him. What would he be doing at this moment? Let's see, what time would it be in Canada? Was it nine hours on or nine hours back? It was nine hours back. Oh God, I wished I were nine hours back: seven in the morning, and not going to see Joe Crowther. Unconsciously I had been scrubbing my forearms with my bath mitt, one of those things that was soft on one side, like a loofah on the other. I never used the rough side ... but I had now. I looked down at the red stripes running up and down from wrist to elbow. What was I trying to do? Inflict pain on myself to assuage the feeling of ... yes, self-loathing wasn't too strong a word. I had messed-up, cocked-up ... Fucked-up. I said it aloud. Fucked-up, that's what I had done. Again. Repeated the pattern: every project, every relationship, seemed to end in ruins. Look what I'd done to Neville: he never deserved that. I was fifty-five: when was I going to learn? Would I ever learn? The marks on my arms began to fade. I set the mitt aside and let myself sink under the water, now almost cold, for a second, then pulled myself up and out of the bath. Dripping, a towel round my shoulders, I cleared the steam from the mirror. My reflection looked back at me.

'So what *do* you do now?' I said to it. 'Go home? You can't. Get drunk? No sense in that. Look for a man? No thank you. Phone Carmela? Absolutely not. Visit Maria? Don't think so. Send flowers to Antonia and Joe Crowther? Yes. Maybe. No. Yes, yes, I will. Won't do any harm. Or will it? If I send flowers that might be interpreted as a bid for a second interview. Which I do not want. Definitely do not want. In fact ... Yes! ... I suddenly felt more cheerful ... I would not pursue my enquiries any further. No more, I said to the mirror, not one more question, to anybody. I had done what I came here to do: I had seen where Peter Andersen was buried, I had placed flowers on his grave, I had wept. Nothing else really mattered; nothing else had anything to do with me, or my mother. It was as if a burden had suddenly been lifted from my shoulders. I smiled into the mirror, finished drying myself, walked into the bedroom. I had three more days here: I would enjoy myself. To hell with research; the idea of writing a novel set in Malta had lost its appeal. Antonia was right. It's a new country, she had said, we're different people. I would get out and see that new country, those new people. Maybe I could write a short, romantic story set in modern Malta, something to defray the cost of the holiday. No, not even that.

I dressed, went out on to the balcony. The sea, sparkling in the afternoon sun, looked inviting. Gentle waves lapped the tiny beach. I knew exactly what I wanted to do: I wanted to swim, in the sea. So what if I had just had a bath. Recklessly, laughing aloud, I tore off my clothes, flung them anywhere, stepped into my swimsuit, pulled on jogging bottoms and top, grabbed a towel and my room key and headed for the door. As I pulled it to behind me the phone rang. I stood stock still, the door handle in my hand. Sod it; whoever it was would ring again if they really wanted me. It was probably Ronnie, in which case I definitely wouldn't answer. Maria would call again, Carmela had no reason to ring. Unless … unless Joe Crowther, or his granddaughter, had contacted her and complained. No, please, not that. I turned the door handle, walked back into the room; the phone stopped ringing.

The water of the bay was cold and strands of seaweed tangled themselves around my feet. I swam briefly, no more than ten strokes, telling myself that the experience was invigorating, that I was enjoying it, that this was what I really wanted to do. But all the time my mind was on that call. Would the desk know who had phoned? Maybe there was a message.

There was: please call Carmela Farrugia at Radio Malta immediately. And the number.

'The moment you come in,' the desk clerk said. 'She sounded very angry,' she added.

'She would be,' I said. 'Thank you. I'll call her from

my room,' – and hope that you are not listening in. I had no way of knowing if she would, but in similar circumstances I would have been very tempted.

My hair was damp, my body, still in the swimsuit under the jogging clothes, felt clammy and uncomfortable. Carmela would have to wait until I got dried. I stripped, towelled and powdered myself – I should have showered but I couldn't face any more water for the moment. Wrapped in a bath sheet, I picked up the receiver, put it down again. There could be only one reason for her call: to tick me off for seeing Joe Crowther. Well, I could live without that for a few more minutes, I could live without it till tomorrow, or even the next day. I could leave Malta, go home, without ever answering her call. The case was closed.

I walked into the bathroom, stripped off the bath sheet, bent over to turn on the shower tap – I had to wash my hair, it smelled of seaweed – and saw again Joe Crowther rising from his chair, the look of consternation on his face at the mention of the name Tom Harper.

'Oh hell. You win.' I wrapped the sheet around me, returned to the bedroom, asked for an outside line, dialled the number, got put through to Carmela's office.

'It's Jane Thornfield; you called me.' Silence. 'Carmela, are you there?'

'Yes, I'm here.' Very held-in, giving nothing away. I hoped to God the old man hadn't had a stroke or something.

'Is it … is it?' No, dammit, let her say, she was the one who wanted to talk.

'I asked you not – to – contact – Joe – Crowther.' Like a snake, spitting venom.

'I know, but … Is he all right?'

'What do you mean … all right?'

'He's not ill, or anything?'

'It would be no thanks to you, if he was.'

'Carmela, tell me … is he all right? He hasn't had a stroke or …'

'He's all right.' My concern for Joe had put her off her stride, diluted her anger. Momentarily. Now it came back. 'I want you here, in my office, tomorrow morning, ten o'clock.' This was the second time she'd given me an order.

'You what?'

'I think you heard.'

'Oh, I heard. Ten o'clock, in your office. Who do you think I am? Some little secretary you can boss around?' I wouldn't have spoken to the lowest of my juniors like that; she must be riled. Get off your high horse, Jane. You'll get nowhere if you yell at one another. So, in, I hoped, my most honeyed tones: 'Carmela … please tell me what is wrong?'

A pause, a sigh. 'I can't. Not on the phone. I think … think you should come and see me.' That's better, why couldn't you have said that in the first place.

'I will, but … can't you give me some idea?'

'No. Tomorrow.' Accept it, Jane. Ring off, see her tomorrow. 'It's what I asked him, isn't it, about my father? If he knew him? If he knew Tom Harper? Oh, for God's sake, Carmela!'

'Don't push me, Jane.'

'Why do I have to wait till tomorrow? Why do we have to meet in your office? What is it you have to say to me?'

'I … I know who you are.' Is that it? Can't be.

'I'm glad you know.'

'Are you?' Genuine surprise.

'Well, of course I am. It wasn't my idea to keep it a secret you know. Anyway, it's out now, and yes, I am glad. I wanted to tell you, but Anthony asked me not to, so …'

'Anthony? Does he know?'

'Of course he knows. Well, surely … wasn't it Anthony who told you?'

'No, it wasn't.'

'Well, who then?'

'No one. I just know … I put two and two … Look, we can't go on talking on the phone. You must come and see me.'

'Well, can't you come here? Tonight.'

'No, Jane. I can't.'

If she can't she can't. No point in asking why, even if can't really means doesn't want to. 'All right, I'll see you tomorrow.'

'Thank you. Goodbye.'

'Goodbye.'

Slowly I put the receiver back on the cradle. I sat looking at the phone, trying to sort out my thoughts. If Carmela knew who I was and Anthony hadn't told her, then … then Joe Crowther must have said something … In the interview, that was it! Not today; today Carmela would have spoken to Antonia, to whom the name Tom Harper meant nothing. This had nothing to do with Peter Andersen; this was to do with Tom Harper. When Carmela said she knew who I was she meant I was Tom Harper's daughter. But she knew that, didn't she? I had made no secret of it; I had told Rosaria and Maria and Anthony; and Carmela, surely, when we had lunch together? Oh, it was all so confusing. My seeing Joe Crowther had sparked off something, something that … worried her? frightened her?

I looked down at myself, and realised with a shock that I was still draped in a bath sheet. It had been only minutes but it felt as if I had been sitting there, on the bed, for hours. With the sheet around me I wandered into the bathroom. I had been going to do something, and instead I had made the call to Carmela. Dress? Bath? I looked in the mirror. Of course: wash my hair. Although it had started to dry by itself it hung lank and smelly round my face. I turned on the shower, poured shampoo into the palm of my hand and stepped under the jet.

Dry, clean and dressed I stood once again on the balcony.

Why had the name Tom Harper upset Joe so much? Had Tom done something to Joe, hurt him in some way? Oh no … No, please no. Had Tom made a pass at, more than made a pass at … raped, maybe? … Joe's woman, Concetta? Would Tom do that? Who knew what men would do in war. Sex-starved Tom who, as even my mother knew, made use of prostitutes. Not rape, no. Perhaps she was willing; perhaps Tom had fathered a child, and Joe knew and then married her, knowing. That had to be the reason, or something like it. Carmela knew, because Joe had told her, in the famous interview. And now she was going to tell me, so that I would stop asking questions and go home, shamed because of what Tom had done. If he had, I was sorry, but it was hardly my fault. I could see why, though, Joe Crowther would be upset. To have a stranger wanting to dig up the dirt after all these years, especially if he had 'told all' to Carmela just months before, would be extremely distressing. No wonder Antonia had got on to Carmela. Oh God, what a mess. I would definitely send flowers, to her: it was the least I could do. And then? Eat, find those jolly Englishwomen, hear what they had been up to, maybe watch a film, anything rather than think about what Carmela might – or might not – reveal tomorrow.

At the reception desk I ordered flowers to be sent to Antonia. Damn, I hadn't thought to ask Carmela where her office was. In Valletta, presumably. If I was to be in the office by ten o'clock I would have to leave early. I asked for an alarm call at quarter past seven, and directions to the headquarters of Radio Malta. An animated discussion behind the desk … 'Radio Malta?

Not television?' – it was apparently an unusual request from a tourist – eventually resulted in one of the girls, Marcella, drawing me a map. I had to go, not to Valletta, but to Gwardamanga, which was on the way there, but I must be careful to take the right lane at Msida ... 'past the park with swings' ... or I would end up in Valletta.

I would need that early call.

CHAPTER EIGHTEEN

I had dinner with Joan and Olive and Barbara, then went with them – 'It'll be a laugh!' they said – to the karaoke session in the hotel's nightclub, all lovely velvet and sparkling lights; and it was a laugh, especially Barbara singing, rather drunkenly after a good two-thirds of a bottle of wine at dinner, *On Ilkley Moor Bar T'at*. It was what I needed; and the half-bottle I had drunk ensured I had a good night's sleep as well.

And so to Tuesday morning. A dull sky and choppy waves in the bay. Not cold, just … gloomy. Not a good portent. As if the weather could make any difference to what I was about to learn. And whatever it was, it had happened so far back in the past as to make no matter. That's what I told myself, as I drove, in rain now, getting heavier by the minute, the wipers going at full speed, through Mosta and Balzan and the ugly, industrial fringes of Birkirkara, to Msida. And now I was on Marcella's little map, which I had taped to the steering wheel. There was Msida Church, on my left; twin towers surmounted by spires, and the ubiquitous red-tiled dome,

Malta's most common landmark it seemed to me. Anyway, it stood out here; there was no mistaking it. Keep in the right lane, Marcella had said. To the left the road was signposted to Sliema, on the right was an area of open ground, and yes, there were the swings. Traffic lights showing red halted me, giving me time to search for the sign to Gwardamanga – there it was, I was in the right place – and glance, through the driving rain and the other lanes of vehicles, at the marina to my left: who owned all those glorious boats; who could afford them? The lights changed – Marcella had been right to stress the importance of getting in the correct lane; the traffic surged like a river in spate and I was carried with it, round to the right, right again, then left into Ta' Gwardamanga. It couldn't be far now. Out of the melée at last I slowed down. My next landmark was St. Luke's Hospital. On my right was a small square with a taxi rank and leading from it was St. Luke's Road. Long, straight … and awash. Peering through the windscreen as best I could – the wipers were having no effect now and the inside of the car was steamed up – I searched for the Radio Malta building. There was no sign of it anywhere, and I mean that literally: no sign, no identification, nothing to indicate in which of the many blocks of offices I might find Carmela.

At the risk of getting soaked – I would anyway, when I got out – I wound down the window and asked help of a passer-by. He didn't know: the television tower, yes, but radio? No, sorry. I closed the window, started up the car; opened the window again, called out: 'Excuse me.' The man, hurrying away, didn't hear me. Maybe he didn't want to. Rain poured into the car, soaking me and the upholstery. I shut the window again. I would just sit here till the rain eased. I switched on the car radio. Ironic: a broadcast in Maltese, but I couldn't find its place of origin. The rain was even heavier now, banging

ᴊf and bouncing up from the pavements,
down the gutters. This couldn't last; this sort of
ᴨever did. Short and sharp, then the sun would come
ᴊt and the pavements would steam. I just had to sit tight
and wait. At last it stopped; the sun came out and people
emerged from their places of shelter. There was a group
approaching me now, three adults and two children, the
adults avoiding the puddles, the children jumping in
them. I opened the car door.

'Excuse me,' I said. 'I'm looking for Radio Malta.'

'Radio Malta? You're there,' a man said.

'Where?' I asked, looking round. All I could see were
nameless office blocks.

'Here,' the man said, pointing to the building on his
left. White stone, set back from the road, a circular
flowerbed, a forecourt with plenty of space for parking
… but still no sign.

'Yes,' said the man. 'See the sign there,' and he
pointed towards the doorway.

'What, that tiny plate?' How was anyone expected to
read that? It was like the no parking signs in Mosta. The
man nodded.

'There's a big sign on the television tower, if you
wanted that.' If I had wanted that I would have asked for
it. I wound up the window, started the engine. It wasn't
the man's fault I was cold and uncomfortable. I wound
down the window.

'It was good of you to stop,' I said. 'Thank you,' and I
stretched out my hand. The man took it, smiled.

'The sign, it is very small,' he said, and we both
laughed.

'*Sahha*,' I said. It was the first time I had used the
word, Maltese for goodbye. It felt right, offering it as a
sort of apology.

'*Sahha*,' the man said, grinning, and the women and
children waved. I waved back, then turned the car into

the forecourt of the Radio Malta building. I parked in the shade – the sun was now beating down – close to the steps that led up to the entrance. To the right of the door was the plate that had been pointed out to me. Not only was it was small, it gave no mention of Radio Malta; if I had seen it I wouldn't have known I was in the right place. The initials on the plate, P.B.S., meant nothing to me. Had I merely been fobbed off by someone anxious to go home and get dry? The door was open; I would go in and ask. Up four wide marble steps, through a cream-painted wrought-iron opening, up another four steps and I was in the foyer, for want of a better name. On my left was a counter, behind it a small glass fronted room dominated by two burly men in uniform; Security, their badges read.

I leant on the counter; I felt tired and bedraggled. A glass panel was slid open.

'Radio Malta?' I enquired, uncertainly.

'Yes.' The shorter of the two men.

'Ah, good. I have an appointment with Carmela Farrugia.'

'Who?'

'Mrs. Farrugia. Perhaps I haven't said it properly. Farru-ja ... is that right?'

'She's not here.' It was the taller one this time.

'Oh, but ... she's expecting me. Could I go up to her office?'

'You got a pass?'

'Er ... no.'

'You can't go without a pass.' He folded his arms, stared me out.

'Then would you call her for me, please.' My patience was running out.

'Told you, she's not in.' The big guy again.

'Sorry, lady; without a pass, or a letter, we can't let you upstairs.' The shorter one this time, apologetic.

'Oh, this is ridiculous! I have an appointment at ten o'clock and it's …' I looked at my watch, '… it's almost half past.'

The big guy shrugged his shoulders, turned to his companion, said something in Maltese. To me he said, 'That could be why she's not here.'

'I'll wait,' I said, and sat down on a bench seat. I folded my arms and crossed my legs; my lips pressed tight, my eyes narrowed, I stared at the security men. The big guy looked at me and laughed; the phone rang, he picked it up, talked amiably, at least it sounded so. Maybe it was me, tense, overwrought, anxious about why Carmela had demanded I come to see her. I let my shoulders drop, put my hands in my lap, uncrossed my legs, tried a smile. The shorter officer smiled back, slid open the window.

'Mrs. Farrugia says she'll be with you in five minutes.'

'Is that her on the …?'

'Yeah. Sorry about that.'

'You can't be too careful, I suppose.' But you could have been more polite.

A car drew up outside and seconds later Carmela was with me. She offered no explanation for her absence, I asked for none; too much time had already been spent on trivialities. I followed her up a wide flight of marble stairs, our heels tip-tapping in unison; down a long corridor, vinyl-floored, our footsteps now muted; past half a dozen wooden doors, all with peep-hole windows and name plates. Neither of us spoke a word. We stopped outside a door which bore Carmela's name; she pulled it open. 'Go in,' she said, holding the door to let me go past.

'Thank you.'

'Sit down, I'll get us some coffee,' she said, and the door swung to behind her.

There were four chairs in the room, all upright, uninviting; I preferred to stand. It was a spartan room: three windows with Venetian blinds, all of them down; three desks, wooden, knee-hole type, a bookcase, a filing cabinet, two ancient-looking typewriters, on one wall a framed picture of a girl – a reproduction of a famous painting, but I couldn't say which, a Velásquez perhaps – a row of coat pegs, piles of papers. Not a computer or fax machine in sight, and only one phone. It reminded me of my office at *DAMES* back in the Seventies, before our lives were dominated by computers and our floors continually littered with curled-up fax paper, spewing and clunking from the machine.

'Do sit down.' Carmela was carrying a plastic tray; on it were two mugs, bone china with a design of strawberries, a spoon and several sachets of sugar. 'I hope you take milk,' she said.

'Yes. Thank you.'

She put the tray down on the desk in the corner, under the picture. She seated herself in the upholstered chair behind the desk; my chair, on the other side, was plastic and hard.

'Oh, do sit here,' Carmela said, getting up.

'No, I'm fine here.'

She passed me a mug of coffee. 'Sugar?'

'No thanks.'

We sipped our coffee, neither of us, I felt, wanting to make the first move.

'Pretty mugs,' I said.

'Yes. I bought them in England.'

'Oh. Where?' I didn't really care where she had bought them, but I had the feeling that while I was drinking my coffee some kind of small talk was expected of me.

'On a market stall. In Skipton; it's in the ...'

'Oh, I know Skipton. My husband came from near

there.' If I ask how you come to be in Yorkshire and you tell me you have a cousin living there, or a friend, we'll soon be deep into a cosy chat ... and I don't want that. I put my mug down on the tray. 'Tell me why you asked me to come here,' I said.

Carmela clasped her mug tightly between her hands.

'Oh Jane,' she said. 'I wish I didn't have to do this.'

I could see the pain in her eyes. Not just pain, regret ... and some compassion, too.

'Well, whatever it is you must think it's important, or you wouldn't have brought me here, so ... so let's get on with it, shall we. I have to tell you, though, that anything you are about to reveal concerning Tom Harper is not going to upset me. He and my mother did not have a good marriage, and I know that while he was out here he went with various women, prostitutes and so on, so you're not going to shock me, don't worry.' I reached across the desk, touched her hand.

'It's not that simple, Jane.' Her voice was surprisingly gentle. 'I wish it were. It's obvious that you misunderstood me when I said I know who you are.' Our eyes locked; my heart began to race. 'I wasn't talking about Tom Harper.' She squeezed my hand, blinked away her tears. 'You're ... you're Peter's child. Oh, Jane ...'

She withdrew her hand from mine, lifted both hands to her face, shook with sobs.

'Carmela ...'

I reached out to her again, touched her cheek. She lowered her hands, then raised them again to wipe away the tears. She took a hankie from her jacket pocket and blew her nose.

'I ... I don't understand. In fact, I'm ...' I ran my fingers through my hair. 'I'm totally confused. I thought you were angry with me ... and now this. I just don't ...' I wafted my hands in front of me, vague, uncomprehending. 'If Anthony didn't tell you, then … then who?'

Her eyes were dry now, the handkerchief tucked away. 'I've known for a long time,' she said. 'Since March. And I am angry. Very. But not with you, not now. You weren't to know.'

'Oh, for Christ's sake, Carmela! Whatever it is you know, that you've been keeping from me, for heaven's sake, tell me!' The fact that she had acknowledged our sisterhood paled into insignificance beside my impatience to know what it was that so distressed her. She sighed deeply, as if she was relieved to be talking openly at last.

'Yes, I'll tell you. Well, I shan't; Joe Crowther will.'

'Joe Crowther? He's coming here?'

'No,' she gave a faint smile, 'he's here already. On tape.' She reached down into the corner by her chair. With both hands she lifted up a case with a shoulder strap; it was a Uher, a reel-to-reel machine used by professional broadcasters. Instinctively I cleared a space on the desk – those machines were heavy. 'Thank you,' Carmela said.

She opened the case, unwound the lead, plugged it into a socket in the wall, unlocked the drawer of her desk, took out a tape reel, put it on the machine … and switched it on. She leant forward, elbows on the desk, head in her hands. I sat upright, consciously trying to relax my tense shoulders. I wished to God I could take something to slow the pounding of my heart.

Carmela's voice came from the built-in loudspeaker: *'Interview with Joe Crowther. Thursday, the second of March, nineteen ninety five.'* A pause. *'Mr. Crowther. Joe … it's good of you to see me. Thank you.'*

'Nay, it's good to see you, lass. What do you want to know?'

'Well, as I said in my letter, I'm doing this broadcast

for V.E. Day, you know, the fiftieth anniversary, and I was hoping you had some interesting memories – in fact I'm sure you have – that you'd like to contribute to the programme. As you know, I'm going all over the island, talking to people who remember those years, the Siege and ... and everything.'

'Oh aye, I've got memories ... not all of them good. It was a bad time; some terrible things happened. Terrible things. I wish I didn't remember some of them.'

A longish pause, Carmela obviously hoping Joe would begin to retell his war experiences. He needed prompting.

'You were stationed at Ta' Qali, I believe.'

'Aye.'

'In the Royal Artillery, yes?'

Carmela took her hands from her face and pressed the pause button. 'I'm sorry about this,' she said, 'I could run it on, but I thought you should hear it all, you know, see how reluctant he was ...'

'No, it's fine,' I said. My heart had steadied. I smiled at her. She released the pause button.

'Aye, that's right.'

'Did you see much action?'

'Oh aye, there was plenty of that. And not all of it on the airfield.'

'Carmela, can you stop it a minute,' I said. She pressed Pause. 'I've just thought of something. Two things actually. Does Joe Crowther know who you are?'

'What do you mean?'

'Does he, did he ... when you interviewed him, know who your father was?'

'No. And I didn't tell him. I was simply there as an interviewer from Radio Malta. I'd never met him before.'

'Okay. Just wanted to know. The other thing was ... was this all in English?'

'Yes.'

'But … when I listened to the tape …'

'Did you get it? I only posted it yester …'

'Maria lent me a copy.'

'Oh.'

'It was in Maltese.'

'No, not all of it. The intro was, and some of the interviews. Not Joe's though; Joe's was in English.'

We looked at one another; we knew only too well what the other was thinking: if I had persevered with the tape, or waited till I received Carmela's copy – she had been stalling, I was right – and persevered with that, I wouldn't have contacted Joe and I wouldn't be sitting here.

'Put it on again. Please.' Carmela released Pause.

'So … do you have any stories of … well … that time, any event you particularly remember, someone's bravery perhaps? Maybe even something funny that happened.'

'Funny? There was nowt funny. Not that I recall. Unless you count the time I had to go to Naxxar… to get, I don't know, some kind of supplies; can't remember now. Had to take a donkey cart, I remember that; there was no petrol.'

'I'll run this on,' Carmela said, doing so as she spoke, 'it's not relevant, it's just a story about smuggling a girl into camp hidden among the supplies. I used it in the broadcast; he said I could. Then I asked him if he had any other stories, about his army friends. I was hoping … I knew he'd known my father … well, I was hoping there might be another story of … I don't know … bravery, something he'd done, something that would be a pleasant surprise for my mother.' She stopped fast-forwarding. 'It's not nice, Jane, what you're going to hear.' She pressed Play.

'Aye well, pals. Trouble with pals, lass, was … you

*lost them. Lost a lot of pals ... Johnny, lost him ... Stan
... Good bloke was Stan, do anything for you would
Stan. Then there was Henry Cox. Been a boxer, big
strapping chap. Went to Valletta ... never came back. A
bomb dropped on the ... where he was, and ... Worst
one of all was young Pete. Pete – oh, can't remember
his other name. Faces, I remember faces ... see them
now, all of them. Married a Maltese girl. Should never
have happened; all he was doing was having a good
time, not hurting anyone. He shouldn't have drunk that
amount; he could never hold his liquor. But it was a
party, see; one of the lads was having a birthday ... Any
road, we'd gone to this bar, Bernie's Bar ... we often
went there; Bernie could get beer when ... you know,
when no one else could. Well ... this night news had got
round ... that Bernie'd got a shipment ... well, it
wouldn't be a shipment, but you know what I mean ...
there was plenty of booze. Beer. Looked all right, didn't
taste too bad; it was only after you'd had a few that you
began to realise it was ... it was awful stuff ... rot your
guts in no time, but ... well, you're all there, you know,
together ... and you don't care. If it helps you forget for
a few hours, and ... well, he'd had too much, had Pete.
If he'd been sober he'd never have said ... He was a
nice chap. Loved a bit of fun, but he was, you know,
quiet, sort of ... well, a bit of a softie really, liked poems
and that. He had a kid. Aye. Great shame, great shame.'*

'What was it ...'   I could hear the tremble in
Carmela's voice. *'What was it ... that he said?'*

'He said ... The thing was, he was a nice lad,
wouldn't ever go with ... well, you know, down by the
harbour ... he wasn't like that ... but when the other lads
started joshing him ... they'd no respect. Didn't care
that he had a wife ... thought the women here were just
... just so they could have a good time ... They had girls
back home, wives, some of them ... but he was the only*

*one who'd wed a local lass ... They said things like ...
Didn't he have a girl in England? Could he not wait?
Well, you know the sort of things men say. I'll not repeat
them, they're not for a lassie's ears. He said it wasn't
like that and anyway he* had *been with an English girl ...
They said, go on, tell us her name. He didn't want to,
but ... well ... they didn't believe him, so in the end he
told them ... he said her name was Alice.'*

'Oh no.'

'I'm so sorry,' Carmela said, in a whisper. Joe
Crowther's voice rambled on, above hers.

'I remember 'cause the lads started singing Sweet
Little Alice Blue Gown *... and he joined in. Leant up
against the bar, singing. I can see it now, like it was
yesterday. Bloody fool, begging your pardon. "She had
a kid," he said, "mine, my kid." I've never told anyone
this; don't know if I should be telling it now ...'* A long,
long pause. *'Then ... then an older bloke, bit of a misery
he was; he didn't take his drink too well neither, he'd
been sitting in the corner, this bloke, saying nowt, but ...
well, now he came up to the bar ... picked up a bottle ...
there was lots of them on the counter ... he smashed it
down on the edge ... grabbed hold of young Pete with
one hand, pulled his head back and ... and held the
broken bottle in front of his face. He was that angry, this
chap, and young Pete ... he was that scared. He'd not
known Tom was there, you see.'*

'Tom?' Yes, Carmela, it had to be Tom. Tom, hearing
that his wife had been unfaithful, that the child he
thought was his was ...

'Aye. Tom Harper.'

'I don't want to hear any more,' I said. 'If you don't
mind.' Carmela switched off the machine. For a moment
I just sat there, trying to take it in. I could see what was
coming; well I thought I could. 'I see now why you
didn't want me to talk to Joe. Poor Tom: so he knew I

wasn't his daughter ... all that time he knew. It wasn't until I read my ... Peter's letters to my mother ... that I ...'

'He wrote ... my father wrote, to your mother? From Malta?'

'Yes.'

'Love letters?'

'I suppose you could call them that. He wasn't married to your mother ...' I wanted to reassure her '... not then, not when he wrote.'

Carmela got up from her chair, peered through the slats of the Venetian blind. 'I think it's going to rain again,' she said. The slats snapped as she let them go. She turned from the window. 'Jane ...' Her face was drawn, her eyes full of pain. 'I think you should ... I think you should listen to the rest of the tape.'

I knew that I had to. 'Put it on,' I said. Carmela sat down, switched on the machine. Innocently, on the tape, she was asking *'Who was Tom Harper?'*

'He was just one of the lads, like I said, a bit older than most of us. Seems young Pete had been sweet on his missus; he'd taken Pete home before the war and while Tom's back was turned – I think he had a sick mother – they had a ... I could have stopped it, Bernie could, any one of us could. But we didn't.' There was another long pause. Then Carmela – I could tell she was trying her utmost to remain detached, professional: *'What ... what happened then?'*

'He ... Harper ... he raked the broken bottle over the lad's face. Not just once. Twice. Three times. From side to side, like he was slapping him. It was ...' Joe Crowther was crying now, *'it was ... horrible. His eyes, his mouth, his throat.'*

'Why didn't you stop him?' All professionalism had gone. *'How could you have let it happen?'* It was almost a whisper.

'What d'you say? You'll have to speak up. I'm a bit deaf.'

'I said, why did you let it happen?'

'We were drunk, lass. All of us. You don't react, like you should, when you're... I wasn't even sure, afterwards, later, you know ... if ... if what I'd seen was real. It was like it had all been a bad dream.'

If this had been a normal interview Carmela would no doubt have stopped now, moved on to another topic, drawn the old man's mind away from his gruesome memories; maybe even switched the tape off, said thank you, and left. But this had ceased to be a normal interview by any standards.

'Did no one help him?'

'No. No one. That's why ... that's why we could never point the finger ... at Tom Harper. If we'd done summat then ... pulled them apart ... They were down on the floor, wrestling. The bottle had gone, but Harper was laying into him with his fists and then he got up and started kicking him. There was blood everywhere. And then ... and then the bomb fell. We'd not noticed the siren ... there might not have been one ... we were all so ... It must have been very close ... the windows came in and part of a wall collapsed ... there was dust and smoke and ... somehow we got out ... crawled ... ran ... I don't know; there was a lot of shouting and confusion. Our truck had been blown up as well ... we weren't supposed to have one; we'd pinched it.'

'Did ... Pete, the young man ... did he get out?'

'No. No, he ... he was ... When we went back in ... when the raid was over ... he was ... There was nothing ... anyone could have done for him by then; he'd lost so much blood and ...'

'And the other one, Harper? What happened to him?'

'Oh, he got out ... when the rest of us did.'

'You mean he left ... he left the young man ... to die?'

'Aye.'

The room had darkened; the rain had returned. I felt numb and cold; my mouth was dry and my chest was tight.

'Oh, Carmela.' I reached out my hands to her. 'I don't know what …'

Joe Crowther's voice cut across mine.

'He didn't mean to … to kill him. Just wanted to spoil his pretty … Lost his rag … Drink and … He'd been humiliated and … a man doesn't like that. We all knew, all of us standing there that … if it had been us … we'd have done the same. You couldn't let a chap get away with … insulting your wife.'

Abruptly, Carmela switched off the tape. 'There is more,' she said – her tone was abrupt, too – 'but you don't need to hear it from him. Briefly, what happened was: my father, and a soldier who had a broken collar bone – he was beside Peter when the wall collapsed, but he managed to crawl out – they were taken to the Military Hospital.'

'Mtarfa?'

'Yes. And … Joe says they tried to revive him, but it was too late. That's all there is. Except that … Joe made me promise not to use that story. And never to tell anyone. He said he wished he'd not told me.'

We sat, silent. What was there to say? Tom Harper had killed my father, our father. Nothing either of us could say would alter that, make it better, erase it.

The silence grew, lengthened. I went on sitting there, elbows on the desk, hands clasped together against my forehead, eyes shut … seeing Peter's face, slashed, and Tom's face, suffused with anger, hearing my mother's voice denying there'd ever been anyone other than Tom, seeing Rosaria's family photograph with the proud young soldier standing behind his wife, seeing again the inscription on the grave: 23 years old.

After I don't know how long – it was probably only minutes, but it seemed like eternity – Carmela spoke.

'By the time they got him to the hospital it was after midnight, so, officially, he died on the twenty-second.'

I looked up at her. As if it mattered.

'It was a Sunday.'

Injured during an air raid, died in hospital on a Sunday: that was acceptable. Dying as the result of a Saturday night brawl in a bar was not.

Carmela began to lift out the reel.

'Do you have to keep that?' I said. 'Legally.'

'No. No, I can destroy it.' She reached into a drawer, withdrew a pair of scissors, unwound the tape, began to cut. Snip, snip … the tiny pieces fell onto the desk. When she had finished she gathered them all together and brushed them into the waste basket.

For her it was over. Catharsis was complete. She had lived with her dark secret for nine months – nine months, how appropriate; it had come to full term – and now she was rid of it. She had grieved for her father, she had agonised inside, she had told no one. Then I had come, uncovering the past, and released her. The terrible urge to tell someone, to confide, the fear that she might, was gone. Now she was free, and the burden she had carried was mine.

I got up from my chair; my body felt stiff, awkward.

'I'll go now,' I said.

'Will you be all right?'

'No, but I'll manage.'

'Did you drive? You shouldn't drive. Let me get you some tea, something to eat.'

'I'll be fine.' There had been enough talking: what would we say anyway, after that? It would be therapeutic to drive; you can't think and battle with Malta's traffic at the same time.

'Will I see you, before you go?'

Hopeful? Apologetic? Polite? All those.

'I don't think so,' I said. She looked relieved, and a little disappointed. I wanted us to part friends: I walked round to her side of the desk; she stood up. I put my arms around her; she put hers around me, pulled me close. For a moment we held one another.

'Bye,' I said, as we let go.

'Goodbye, Jane,' she said.

I turned, walked out of the room, along the corridor, down the marble stairs, past the security guards, down the four steps, through the doorway, down the other four steps, got out the key, got into the car, started the engine, drove out of the forecourt, went past the hospital, the swings, the church, Birkirkara, Balzan, Mosta ... Mosta; no, keep going, it doesn't matter where Bernie's Bar is, was ... through the outskirts of St. Paul's Bay, through Mellieha, past the beach, up the hill, into the car park of the hotel, switched off the engine, collected my key from the desk, took the lift to my floor, walked to my room, opened the door, shut the door, threw the key on the bed, threw myself on the bed.

Nothing. Absolutely nothing. No feeling, no thoughts, no pain, no tears ... nothing. Not cold, not hot. Not anything.

CHAPTER NINETEEN

I must have slept; the room was dark when I came to, sat bolt upright, remembered. I dragged myself off the bed, used the loo, came back, sat on the bed.

'Could I have an outside line, please.'

I dialled Neville's number. After four rings, Neville's voice, on his answerphone. I put the receiver down. It was him I needed, not a recording. Maybe he was there, maybe he'd left the machine on – so many people did that now, were selective about the calls they answered. I rang again.

'Hello?'

'Neville.'

'Janey! Did you just ring? Where are you?'

'Yes, I did. I'm in Malta.'

'Malta!'

'Can you come?'

'What?'

'Here. I need you.'

'Janey, what's happened? Are you all right?'

'No, no I'm not. Please come. You always said, if I ...'

'Of course I'll come. Where are you?'

'Hotel Melita; it's in Mellieha Bay.'

'Melita?'

'Yes.'

'Darling, sweetheart, are you going to be all right? You're not hurt, are you?'

'No. Just come.'

'Tell me …'

'I can't.'

'I'll see you. Quick as I can.'

He came the next day, Wednesday, landing at Luqa airport mid-afternoon. For nearly twenty-four hours I had been in what I now realise was a state of shock, something I had never experienced before. The women in my books, when they were on the receiving end of terrible news, did wild and crazy things, wept copiously, had hysterics, flung themselves into the arms of unlikely lovers. I just slept, and sat, in my room, drinking occasionally, but not eating, not wanting to. Eventually in the middle of Wednesday morning I roused myself enough to phone Reception and make sure that it would be all right for my husband to stay in the hotel, in my room.

My husband: yes, he was still that. I had suggested a divorce, but he hadn't wanted it. 'What for?' he'd said. 'You might want to marry again.' 'Never,' he said. And so we had just separated; free but not free.

And now he was coming, as he'd always said he would. The situation was so ridiculously like an Ellen Field novel: at the last minute, when all others have abandoned her, the heroine turns to the man she has spurned, the only one who truly loved her. He opens his arms to her; she melts into his embrace. Well, it wouldn't be like that. I had no doubt he would open his arms and I would be comforted, but most of all I needed to talk. Malta had taught me one thing if nothing else: I was not the self-sufficient woman I thought myself to be. Fine when life was going well, when I was deep in a book – then I revelled in my single state, free to live, without distractions, within my fictional world; but come a real-life drama, whose plot lines and denouement, especially the denouement, were not of my making: what did I do? I fell apart, in a way that I would have thought was totally out of character. How little we really know ourselves. The man I knew as my father had killed my natural father ... and my foundations were rocked.

By now, early on Wednesday afternoon, I could let myself think again about the events of that night in 1942. For twenty-four hours I had blanked them out; now I needed to recall them. If Neville was to help me, I wanted to be able to tell him what had happened without breaking down. The fact that the murder, for that was what it was, had taken place over fifty years ago, did not lessen the impact. All the years were suddenly concertinaed together ... and it is the morning after. Sunday morning, March 22nd ... and someone has to tell Rosaria. Rosaria, heavily pregnant with Carmela ... so they simply say: Your husband has been killed in an air raid, and with the addition of a small lie, that he was helping people out of a bombed building, his reputation as a hero is maintained. And the Royal Artillery saves itself the trouble of an inquiry and a possible court-martial. Or perhaps they never knew. As Joe Crowther said, in a sense they were all to blame; if they kept quiet, there would be no harm done. Peter Andersen was dead, a trial would not bring him back; and as for Tom Harper, well, he would probably get a bullet of his own any day now, they all might.

It was four o'clock when Neville got to the hotel. I was sitting on the balcony when they rang from Reception to say he had arrived. For a brief moment I felt I couldn't go down, couldn't meet him. God knows what he thought had happened to me; how would he react when he discovered that I had gone loopy over a piece of fifty-year-old news. A quick look in the mirror, a finger wetted and wiped over an eyebrow, a check to make sure my breath was not sour, a hitch to a bra strap … a quick survey of the room – yes, it was tidy: Neville hated disorder – and I was ready to go.

I didn't give him time to open his arms; I didn't kiss him either.

'Thank you,' was all I could manage. I turned away. The sight of him, tall, still slim, attractively grey, his face creased in a smile of – relief that I was in one piece? – was too much for me. I didn't want him to see my tears, not there, in the foyer, with curious eyes upon us. As I had walked to the desk I had glimpsed Olive and Joan in the lounge. They had seen me and they were now both agog.

'We'll take the lift,' I said, over my shoulder.

Thankfully there were others in the lift; we didn't even stand next to one another.

'This way,' I said, stepping out of the lift, not even looking to see if he was following me. I strode down the corridor as if all the devils of hell were after me.

'Janey, for God's sake …' I was half way across the room before he caught up with me. I turned to him.

'Oh, Nev …'

His arms were round me and I let the tears flow, my face pressed against his jacket. Not just tears, great rending sobs, painful yet healing. And all the time Neville held me. When I could cry no more, I lifted my head, drew back from him. He looked down at his jacket.

'A fine mess you've made of that.'

'Sorry.'

'Now … come on, sit down and tell me what all this is about.'

'I need a drink first.' I went to the mini-bar. 'Oh God, Neville ...' and the tears started again.

'Janey, enough! I can't help you if you go on like this.'

'I'm sorry. Oh, Nev ... it's been so ... Oh God, I am so pleased to see you.'

'Drink!' It was an order. 'I'll have a shandy.' I took two shandies from the bar; we opened the cans and drank. Neville slid open the door to the balcony and stepped out. 'Nice view,' he said. I didn't follow him; I sat on the bed, exhausted. Neville put his can on the balcony table, came inside, sat down beside me, took the can from my hand, put it on the floor.

'Now ... Talk.'

I told Neville everything ... well, not everything: I didn't tell him about Ken; it seemed irrelevant ... and he listened calmly, as I knew he would, prompting me with a judicious question here and there. When I had finished he took both my hands in his, lifted them to his lips.

'I love you,' he said. It was all that really mattered.

We didn't make love that night: I had expended all my energy in tears and trauma. Had I been twenty-five I would have had energy to spare, but at fifty-five all I wanted was to sleep, with Neville beside me in the other bed. We had kissed and held one another; for now it was enough. There would be tomorrow, and the day after, and maybe ... the day after that, too.

On Thursday I took him to Mtarfa, to the cemetery, and we laid flowers; I showed him Mdina and Rabat and we walked in the Buskett Gardens. We sat on the cliffs at Dingli and ate the sandwiches we had bought in Mellieha; we drove on to Hagar Qim, and I felt again the peace and calm of that ancient place.

Friday was our last day. In the morning we walked hand-in-hand – it was a long time since we had done that – down to the beach you could see from the hotel, the beach where Ken and I had walked, barefoot, in the moonlight. We sat on the promenade, on a green wrought-iron seat overlooking the bay. We had let go of one another as we approached the seat; now I took hold of his hand again: the need to touch him was great. The air was warm, the breeze gentle and caressing; I felt I was being nursed back to health after a long illness. We sat, not saying anything, content just to be together. Suddenly it clouded over and the air went cold. I shivered, let go of Neville's hand, pulled my cardigan around me.

'How much will you tell your mother?' Neville asked.

This was the one question I had not yet faced. I had come here so that I could talk to her; to see my father's grave, then go back and talk about him. It had seemed so simple.

'Janey?' His voice was concerned.

At last I answered him. 'I shall tell her ... that I had a nice holiday.'

'Nothing more?'

'No.'

'Will you tell her about me?'

The sun came out again. 'I might ... or again, I might not. I fancy having you all to myself, just for a while anyway.'

He stood up, held out his hand. 'Come on, Janey love,' he said, 'let's go home.'

My mother died in 1997, Rosaria died the same year; Carmela wrote to tell me, and to say that now their mother had gone she had told Anthony the full story. Neville and I now live in Yorkshire and we have a grandson. It was Alex's idea to call him Peter.

Made in the USA
Middletown, DE
06 January 2017